HELL
BENT

D1556951

Tor books by Ken Gross

A Fine Line
Rough Justice

HELL BENT

Ken Gross

TOR

A TOM DOHERTY ASSOCIATES BOOK
NEW YORK

This is a work of fiction. All the people and events portrayed in this book are fictitious, and any resemblance to real people or events is purely coincidental.

HELL BENT

Copyright © 1992 by Kenneth Gross

All rights reserved, including the right to reproduce this book, or portions thereof, in any form.

This book was printed on acid-free paper.

A Tor Book
Published by Tom Doherty Associates, Inc.
175 Fifth Avenue
New York, N.Y. 10010

Tor® is a registered trademark of Tom Doherty Associates, Inc.

Library of Congress Cataloging-in-Publication Data
Gross, Ken.
        Hell bent / Ken Gross.
             p.   cm.
        ISBN 0-312-85304-1
        I. Title.
    PS3557.R583H44   1992
    813'.54—dc20   92-849
                                                                     CIP

First Edition: June 1992

Printed in the United States of America

0 9 8 7 6 5 4 3 2 1

To all my doctors, especially my book doctor, Al Zuckerman.

Prologue

December 1990

He could barely hear his footsteps whisper along the tile floor of the hospital corridor. Moe Berger's rubber soles made only a soft, stammering echo, but it was enough to disturb the deep hush that settled like fog over Cornell Medical Center after visiting hours.

A handful of attendants and guards looked up from day-old tabloids or flickering security consoles, annoyed at the interruption of their private routines. A janitor didn't even bother to glance at him, just shoved aside the pail with an unfriendly foot. The resentment was strangely comforting to a dying man. His passing didn't go completely unnoticed, after all.

When he hit the street, with its stirring gust of car horns and howling distant sirens, the cold air surprised him. He shivered and started to button his coat. He wasn't mentally prepared for the cold weather. The radiation treatments had scorched him like a sunburn. He'd forgotten that it was winter. His last season.

The two detectives from the Internal Affairs Division were

waiting for Moe in an unmarked car on York Avenue. When they saw him fumbling with the bone buttons on his duffle coat, they were jolted by how suddenly he had aged. Overnight he had grown frail. They almost thought that they had the wrong man. But that's how it went with this sort of thing. A few weeks ago, the lymphoma had appeared as a lump under Moe's right arm. Then he'd begun the radiation treatments that ate him up alive. The two detectives hesitated for a split second, then leaped out of both sides of the cruiser.

Detective Sergeant Vincent Manero took up a position on Moe's left and Detective Rocco Valone was on his right. Cops, thought Moe, seeing them coming at him. Too well dressed for street crooks and too shabby for Mafia thugs. Definitely cops. He surrendered before they put a hand on him and without uttering a word of protest.

They flashed badges and muttered "Internal Affairs" and moved him ungently towards the backseat of the cruiser. Two men, one on each side, pressing close to pin his arms. Then they spun Moe around, dominating him, throwing him into confusion. He was surprised at how little stomach he had to resist. Like losing his appetite for food. But they took him like professionals. Textbook stuff. Moe had executed the same moves a hundred times. If there's no chance of resistance, get the target off the street as quickly as possible. Reduce the chance of a fuss.

He collapsed in the backseat beside the smaller of the two detectives, his hands folded passively on his lap. Beside him, Detective Sergeant Vincent Manero—a man Moe would think of as the one without a chin—was poised to go for his own gun if Moe made the slightest aggressive move. Detective Rocco Valone—the one with two chins—was in the front, in the driver's seat, half turned around, and Moe knew that in the hidden hand below Moe's line of sight he clutched a service revolver.

"We're gonna take you downtown," said Sergeant Manero. Moe nodded.

"Where's your piece?"

"In my car," said Moe. "The car's in a lot on Seventy-first Street."

The detectives nodded. "We're gonna hafta pat you down," said Manero, and again Moe nodded. He uttered a little cry when Valone's rough hands went under his right armpit, hitting the sore, swollen and cracked skin where the radiation had burned away his will to resist, if not the tumor.

"Sorry," said Valone, who looked at Manero. The sergeant nodded and said, "That's enough."

It all seemed routine. Expected. He could almost doze off, he thought.

They rode in silence down to the loft building on lower Broadway where the IAD had its headquarters. Moe was a good prisoner, not even curious about the ambush. It could have been anything—a free cup of coffee or some false accusation by a bustout cop trying to buy his way out of a jam. Nothing better for the IAD than to bring in a cop with a swollen reputation for virtue. In spite of his innocence, Detective Moses Berger felt a queasy sense of guilt. After almost thirty years on the job, he had a schoolboy terror of the shoeflies—cops who spied on other cops for Internal Affairs. No one with a shield was immune. If they wanted you, according to the tribal wisdom of precinct house locker rooms, they always got you.

Their bad luck is that they got me at the wrong time, when I don't give a shit, thought Moe.

The guard on duty at the front door of IAD headquarters barely looked up from his security console. It was a kind of shame over their treacherous assignment; they didn't look the prisoners in the eye. They could bring in the police commissioner and the guard wouldn't look up.

They rode up a wheezing elevator, then moved down a corridor of closed doors. Finally, the detectives unlocked one of the doors. Moe knew the room. Over the years he had broken a hundred suspects in a hundred such rooms. Green walls with peeling paint. No window. A blunt metal desk (no drawers) in the center. Three chairs, all defective, all drawn into a tight circle. An ugly, hard, menacing room, wielded like a club. They sat him behind the desk, then left, slamming the door behind them. He could hear the lock engage. He knew all the tricks. He understood the psychological pressure. Yet he felt a slow sinking weakness in his knees anyway.

Moe glanced at his watch. It was 8:45. He was late for his medication. The prescription bottles of antinausea pills and the painkiller, Darvon, were in his coat pocket. But he could stand it for a while. He tried not to look at his watch. He spotted the camera in a corner ceiling fixture. The next time he looked at his watch it was 9:12. Not much of a holdout. He tried to let his mind turn cloudy and sat quietly.

They came in again an hour later. They didn't speak, just banged the chairs in closer and slapped a file down on the desk. They glared at him, as if he were to blame for all this trouble.

"You think I could get a glass of water so I could take my medication?" Moe asked the smaller one, the sergeant, Manero, who was staring at him with some anger.

"In a minute." The sergeant's hands clenched and un-clenched. "You know, Detective Berger, you think that we're dumb, am I right?"

Still, he didn't speak. It was all a trap and he wasn't sure where the pitfalls were. Safest to let them lay the groundwork, see how it developed.

Manero went on. "Which is where you are wrong, my friend. We may not have been to John Jay College, but we know our business. I bring in professional killers who clam up like you."

Yes, Moe thought. He was right. But professional killers know what he knew—you only get in trouble by opening your mouth.

"Let's cut the crap and get down to business, all right? Then you can take your medication, take a piss, and go home."

The chinless sergeant opened the file and Moe tried not to

look at it. Manero put on a pair of glasses and read something, then slammed it shut and looked at Moe and smiled. "How's Jack?" he asked.

Startled, Moe answered before he could think. "How should I know?"

Rocco Valone pulled his chair closer to the desk. "We think you know." He opened his mouth wide and spoke softly. "We know you know."

"Listen, Detective Berger." Manero adopted a tone of official business. "We are not here to hurt anyone." He was the voice of authority. "We just have to get in touch with your guy. No choice." He shook his head. Rocco Valone's double chins waddled as he joined in the assent. "Nobody in this room has a choice," continued Manero. "In fact, you'll be doing your partner a big favor. We want to protect him from some very dangerous people. You know what I mean?"

Moe knew. They wanted the money. They wanted to kill him.

"We can help him. You know that they got an outstanding contract on him. That's not like an outstanding warrant. These people, and I think you know who I mean, do not give a Miranda warning when they execute a contract. The only right you got is a right to die."

Moe understood. These two cops were mob cops. They were paid by the New York City Police Department, but they really worked for the crime family that ran the city. Of course Moe had known that sooner or later the mob would come after the money. After all, it was their money. Or, at least they believed that they had the best claim on it. Never mind about the virtue of their claim. What mattered was that they felt owed. And they would not consider the loss of three million dollars a simple business expense. And the last guy who had it in his possession was Moe's old partner, Jack Mann.

The sergeant spoke slowly. "Look, let me speak plain. If these people are not satisfied, they are going to kill your partner. No question."

"I haven't seen Jack for a couple of years," said Moe.

The sergeant turned away, scooping up the file. He and Rocco Valone left the room, letting Moe stew another fifteen minutes. When they came back, they looked relaxed, as if matters had been settled, and Valone handed Moe a paper cup full of water. "Take your medication," said Manero gently.

Moe's hands shook as he worked the childproof bottles and removed the capsules. He swallowed them, with gulps of water, and waited. Manero smiled. "You know," said the short, chinless sergeant, "you got some problems of your own." He walked away, as if he might head for the door. "Not the money. We know you didn't grab any of that dough. You wouldn't be pulling midnight shifts while taking chemotherapy if you had any money. But you have problems."

"Nothing that can't be handled," chimed in Valone.

"You have a major case of fraud waiting to fall on your head."

Moe didn't look worried.

Sergeant Manero shoved a paper across the desk. It was Moe's resignation from the police department, giving up all claims to pension and medical benefits. *For the good of the department*, it said.

They weren't offering him freedom. He could not live without medical benefits. Moe pushed the paper back across the table.

"No? Okay! We got time."

Sergeant Manero pulled another document from the file. An old trick from an old hat. It was a discharge paper from the Israeli army, issued to Captain Moses Berger. It was dated July 12, 1967, right after the Six-Day War. At the time, Moe was on a leave of absence from the New York City Police Department. He had fought a war in a foreign army while he was technically still a New York City cop. He had served a foreign prince, in the eyes of the law. They had him on a technicality.

"All these years, you have been working under false pretenses," said Manero. "Israel is still a foreign country no matter what Congress says. You claimed on your application for readmission to the department that you hurt your leg in a car accident in Rome."

He pushed a medical report from the Israeli government across the desk, showing that Captain Berger had been wounded in a tank battle on the Golan Heights.

"So, what we have here is a pretty clear case of fraud," said Manero. "All your pay, your rights, and benefits, they were obtained under a false oath. We can make a case. We can force you off the job now, without a pension, without medical benefits, without dink. Immediate suspension without pay. I don't believe that you are in any condition to take that, are you?"

Moe looked up and, for an instant, an old fire rose in his belly. He considered leaping for Manero's throat. He could manage it. The other one would have trouble ripping his fingers free. He might have time to kill him. But he didn't know if he had the strength.

"As far as your savings go, we can put a claim on them in the morning and tie you up in court. Forever."

Moe's face began to twitch.

"What about Chris? What about your wife? What's she gonna do for the rent? She has no money, no resources. What's gonna happen to her?"

They sat quietly in the room, the two detectives staring at Moe, watching him shrink.

"Look, we really have no problem with your friend," said Manero finally. "From what I hear, he's a good guy. Nobody wants to hurt him. That's why we came to you. You're his partner. You'll protect him. All's they want is their property. You can understand that."

The chinless sergeant could see Moe waver.

"Listen, we're not asking you to do anything bad, like finger him."

Moe reached over and took one of Manero's cigarettes. He hadn't smoked in twenty years.

"What do you want?" he asked, exhausted finally. His voice croaked.

Vinnie nodded. They had him. "Not much. Just a little cooperation. Actually, when you get right down to it, we just want you to save your partner's life."

1

December 22, 1990

The locomotive from Gatwick Airport sighed into London's Victoria Station and the passengers exploded out of the coaches. They were wound up tight by the long glide into the berth, as well as the annual high-pitched frenzy of travel during the holiday season. They headed for cabs or buses or the underground or someone's waiting arms. They breathed steam and sweated icicles in the early winter cold, weighed down by heavy suitcases, bright packages, and the unbearable stress of being between destinations. And so they moved quickly, forcefully, as if everything depended on getting someplace friendly fast.

All except for one passenger, an ordinary man of average height and unclear age—he could have been anywhere from thirty-five to fifty—who emerged from the train cautiously, watching to see if he could detect among that great surging mass of people the telltale squint of a stalker or the athletic twist of a tracker. Finally, with an almost dainty grace, he planted himself in the open camouflage of the crowd, slipping between travelers, an elusive dancer darting evasively from cover to cover. Only a professional would notice that he acted as if he were a target.

No matter how many times Jack Mann told himself that he was exaggerating the threat, that time had probably wiped clean the blood debt, he still felt that coiled tingle of something menacing. And over the years, Jack had come to rely on his body's independent sense of danger. The fact that he was utterly innocent of wrongdoing didn't change a thing as far as the hairs on the back of his neck were concerned. When they remained on alert, Jack Mann obeyed.

Not that he was helpless. Jack Mann had natural talents when it came to blending into the environment. A man of plain looks and medium physical appearance, he took pride in his quiet, unremarkable appearance. He might be wearing a Burberry raincoat and a Savile Row suit, but expensive clothing had a way of adjusting to Jack's own rumpled, off-the-rack slouch; it became mere cover. Such was his gift: he deflected attention. It was the thing that had made him valuable when he was a plainclothes policeman in New York City—he was as unremarkable and solid as stone. And he was content in that dim role. He preferred being a bystander in a world jumping and twisting for position in front of a camera. Not that in a pinch he shunned the limelight. He had the old cop's curse of leaping into the middle of someone else's quarrel. He couldn't help himself. At first glance, however, he usually passed for someone's inconspicuous uncle.

In spite of being American, Jack Mann was familiar with Victoria Station and moved with the hunkered determination of a native who knows the prospect and does not have to scan the overhead signs for travel instructions. Neither did Jack pause to admire the nineteenth-century architectural loft and grandeur of old Victoria. A target had to keep moving.

The Red Lion pub near Piccadilly Circus, with its etched glass and polished mahogany wood, smelled of English ale and sour chutney and, above all, the moist aftermath of a chilling rain. It was an old pub weathered by the wind off the Thames and a hundred years of the carbon belch of locomotives coming and going from the nearby train station. Tonight it was thick with customers unwinding from a whole year's worth of office battle. So it had a kind of seasonal coziness. Jack Mann had to fight his way through London's young professionals, all swank and puffed up with themselves and careless in the sweep of their arms as they spread the tales of their back-chamber glory in this darkening first Christmas season of the nineties. To Jack, the self-satisfied trumpets and blare all sounded like the usual high-handed, back-stabbing swindles you could hear in any bar near any commercial warfront. Someone knew that an earnings report was a stiff and sold short to an ignorant colleague who would have done the same to him. Or someone held off on another transaction, knowing that year-end desperation would eventually sweeten the deal. It had the sound of treachery.

No different from the stuff performed by the hounds of Wall Street, he thought as he listened to the lusty growl of the traders. This could be the Bridge bar, down by the piers of South Street in lower Manhattan, where the sharks and fixers howled through the night their victories and defeats.

At the moment, Jack had his own problems, and his hand trembled as he reached for the first glass of whiskey, putting off the meeting upstairs. After the first drink, he called, "One more," and the bartender, who saw only his lips move, understood and nodded. "And one more," he said when the bartender laid down the second drink. Jack noticed the melancholy understanding pass over the bartender's face. It was an occupational thing—bartenders developed a knack for spotting trouble, Jack thought, as he threw back the second drink.

Nevertheless, the effect of the whiskey was welcome. With the third, he felt himself slipping into the warm tub of liquor. And in that momentary calm, as the heat melted the hairs on

the back of his neck, he straightened a bit and took his bear-
ings. He could hear, or maybe just imagine, a subtle, tenuous
undertone of regret around him as the business-types strung
out the year's triumphant moment; they lingered over their
stories—reluctant sons and husbands—before scattering to
ordinary homes and conventional hearths and the inevitable
reproach of waiting families.

"Another round," cried one strapping youth, and the bartender nodded. The strapping youth had that unmistakable
signature of the British upper class—slack, blond corn-silk
hair that had to be brushed out of his eyes like some hereditary
ribbon of office. For some reason the toss of it made Jack mad.
Even the youth's expensive, sun-yellow suspenders stirred
some ancient Irish resentment. They seemed arrogant.

"No, really, have to get home, Mister Hewes," protested the
object of the youth's attention, a bleached young woman who
was attractive, in a gaudy way—all neon blond and too much
makeup. Jack knew the outcome before it began. She would
give in, take him home, and after the groans of passion in the
dark, the youth would look over and see the smeared lip gloss
and ruined eye shadow and experience a wave of regret. But,
at the moment, in the artificial glow of the pub, only Jack could
see that far ahead.

"Mum's cooked dinner, y'see," she said and Jack could hear
some rough dockside sound in her voice.

"Nonsense," replied the strapping youth in his willful pub-
lic-school tone. "I'll back you up. Say you had to stay late."

"But mum will be expecting me . . ."

The corn-silk stag wasn't listening, as if he didn't have to
listen to objections, not from such as her. For an instant Jack
considered plucking her up under the arms and pushing her
out into the street and sending her home. It was a passing
thought, something out of the professional past. Too many
years facing down bullies. Then he decided that it wasn't
worth it. The price was always high. Always disproportionate.

And, besides, the rescued victim was never grateful. She'd turn on him, all claws and teeth, defending the corn-silk lout. Besides, this was no longer Jack's job.

"I am not a cop anymore," Jack muttered to himself. "I am a civilian in a strange land, and there is no call to duty here!"

He contemplated a fourth drink, shuddered at his own weakness, and left the change on the bar for the knowing bartender. It was time. He had to go upstairs and face his old friend. Or else he could just up and leave. He wavered for a moment, trying to decide whether to confront his friend, to look him in the eye and see Moe's opinion, or flee back across the Irish Sea and into the bosom of his new twilight world where he was—in spite of everything—still a stranger. There was one thing that he knew for certain; he was entering some endgame of this long adventure. And he had a bad premonition about the outcome. Not that it mattered much—he had always counted himself one of life's losers anyway. One way or another, he would have to pay for his past sins.

No, he couldn't walk away from the Red Lion without testing himself with Moe. After all, Moe's eyes were the one mirror he had come to count on for a true reflection of the condition of his mortal soul. And Moe had come all this way to see Jack, and Jack understood why. Never mind the urgency of the summons, Moe was lonely for his old partner. And so was Jack. He turned and began to fight his way to the stairs that led to the dining room on the second floor.

"Pardon me," Jack murmured, slicing his way sideways through the thicket of men who formed a circle around the captive young clerks—weary women whose eyes were heavy with the overtime.

He plunged ahead, driving upstairs, feeling the young stag at the bar watching him, as if he had read his mind about the fantasized rescue and the near combat. Jack bit his cheek so as not to turn and fly at him, grab him by the throat, and fling him against one of the glass partitions that had probably been standing there since Waterloo, and whose destruction would have counted more in this land of ancient emblems than any act of chivalry.

He didn't notice the two men watching him from a far booth, just kept plunging upstairs, reminding himself that he was not involved. "I am not a cop," he said aloud, pushing through the door and coming smack against the hostess, one of those sturdy English oaks who guard the dining rooms of bangers-and-mash pubs. She burst out laughing at Jack's utterance.

"Well, then, we won't have to hide the good silver, will we?" said the hostess in that generous way of big women who were comfortable with men.

Jack blushed and nodded.

"Rehearsing a part," he said sheepishly.

"Do the copper," she advised, whispering sideways, moving him towards a table in the corner where the customer—an American—had told her he was waiting for a friend. "A Yank copper. Suits you like a glove."

Then she left, tossing a conspiratorial smile over her shoulder.

Jack fell into the seat across from his old friend, Moe Berger, who was bent over his turkey dinner.

"How d'ya suppose she knew I was a cop?" asked Jack.

" 'Cause," replied Moe, cleaning his lips with the napkin, leaning across the table, taking his friend's face in his hands and kissing him full on the lips. They smiled at each other for a moment, then sat back to enjoy the reunion.

Jack tried to ignore the dramatic change in his partner. Moe was pale and thin. It had only been a little more than a year since they'd seen each other, but Jack knew about the tumor and he saw at once that it was better not to mention it. Still, even in this frail state, it was good to see Moe. There was nothing strange between them; not even the loose flesh and backlight of pain in his old partner's eyes. It could have been yesterday when he last saw him. Time made no difference between these two. When Jack looked at Moe he saw the unspoiled youth fresh out of the Police Academy who had become his midnight partner in long stakeouts and life-and-death encounters with urban desperados. And Moe saw the faithful friend who had engineered an impossible rescue from Israel in 1967. Moe had been wounded and stranded, but Jack had brought him home, shattered leg and all. Jack had defeated all the bureaucracy and gotten his partner admitted into a New York hospital as a car accident victim. He had even gotten him reinstated on the police force after Moe recovered, extracting a few understanding winks from some sympathetic department brass and some cooperation from the medical board. Between these two, there was ancient history and untold affection.

Jack felt suddenly protected. For the moment, he could lay down the burden of guilt and remorse that he had been unable to shake since he'd fled the city almost two years ago. He could relax. Moe was watching his back. It had been a long time since he'd felt safe enough to empty both lungs.

"Seriously. How do they always know we're cops?" asked Jack when he got his breath back.

Moe, ever the philosopher, shrugged. "The way we look around. The way we look at people."

"How do we look at people?"

"Like we wanna pat 'em down."

"Yeah? You think so? I don't know."

"Actually, it's the way we eat."

"How do we eat?"

"On the edge of our chairs. We don't watch the food. We watch the coatrack." Moe shrugged again. "Mostly, I think, it's the eyes. We got presumptive guilt in the eyes. We accuse everybody. They resent it." He shrugged once more. "You can't blame them."

Jack laughed. He'd missed the soft-hearted, world-weary truths of Moe Berger, even if they weren't all true or were only partly true. They carried a sense of approximate truth. "But we're right," Jack replied. "They are usually up to something bad. Hiding something."

"Ah, that's the Catholic in you," said Moe, half laughing. "Original sin. Mortal and venal crimes. Sins of commission and sins of omission. My God! Always mumbling *mea culpa*'s. Always ready to take your place on the cross. Fucking religious fanatic!"

"Me? You Jews are worse! You're more Catholic than Christ."

"Well, why not? After all, we're related. Distant, but blood relations. I had an eighteenth, or maybe it was twenty-eighth cousin, who knew the whole family personally. Had Passover dinner at their stable."

Jack laughed.

"Me?" Moe went on. "I'm not just a Jew. Not strictly. I am a Jew cop, which makes me a rabbi with a gun. I give everybody a Miranda warning, then I issue a summons for not writing home to their mother." Moe smiled. "But you know, in the end, I'm still an orthodox cop."

They were both laughing when the oak lady brought mugs of warm ale. "On the house," she said, winking at Jack, "for the cast party." Moe looked confused, but Jack said it was a private joke, then asked for a Bushmills to go with it, knowing he was raising the eyebrows across the table like a curtain.

"You can't drink," said Moe, and it was a declaration.

"I'm learning," said Jack, avoiding his friend's eyes. "It's like learning French."

"The last time you got drunk I had to hold your head so it wouldn't explode."

Jack didn't reply, just downed the liquor and chased it with the ale, and that was his answer.

At closer examination, Jack shuddered at the sight of his dying friend. Not that they were unaccustomed to death or the shadow of high risk that went with the job. It was just that Jack was not prepared for how far gone Moe looked. Moe was only forty-six, a few years older than Jack, but his once-thick head of hair was melting into patches of gray ice. There were dark pockets under his eyes and loose flesh under his chin. But the tone of his voice was familiar, and he leaned across the table and touched Jack's hand. He had that habit of touching—like stroking a dog. Just now he had a joke. For twenty-seven years, he had been trying to find a joke to which Jack did not know the punch line. So far, he had paid out hundreds of dollars in lost one-dollar bets, but he was determined to win just once. He didn't announce that he was telling a joke, because they didn't need a preamble. There had been too many midnight patrols when the silences were broken by the start of a joke.

"Okay, these three old guys are at the doctor's office in Florida. One of them says, 'I wake up at eight in the morning and I go to the bathroom and I try to pee and all I get is a little tinkle. Nothing.' So the second guy nods and says, 'I wake up at eight and I sit on the toilet and I squeeze and I squeeze and out comes little coffee beans.' So the third guy says, 'Listen, every morning at eight o'clock I pee like a horse and I have a bowel movement like a young bull.' The other two guys are impressed. 'So what are you doing here?' asks one."

" 'Well,' " Jack interrupted, finishing the joke, "the third guy says, 'the trouble is I don't wake up until nine.' "

Moe nodded, handed his friend a dollar and launched into another joke.

"This Texan goes to buy a farm in Israel and he finds a young farmer. The Texan asks the Israeli farmer, 'How big is your farm?' The Israeli says, 'Big. Great big spread. Why, I got a farm so big that it's almost two hundred acres.' The Texan laughs and says, 'You call that big? Lemme tell you something. You know how big my spread is? Why, if I get into my car at sunrise and I drive all day long, by sunset, I still wouldn't reach the end of my ranch.' So the Israeli says—"

Jack broke in again: " 'You know, I had a car like that once.' "

Moe shook his head and handed over another dollar. But he

was thinking that there was something wrong in Jack's voice. His friend knew the jokes and played the old game, but Moe didn't hear the old mirth.

Jack saw Moe's reaction. He swallowed the last of the ale and held up the mug for a refill.

Another young waitress brought it, along with a hot plate of turkey that Moe had ordered for Jack, and he didn't say anything because he was hungry and tired.

"So, how's Christine? How do you like England?" asked Jack, wiping up the gravy with soda bread. He drank the ale in one great swallow.

"Hard drinking," began Moe, and Jack cut him off.

"Well, it's a cold, wet day," said Jack with an unconvincing laugh. "Where's Chris? The only thing your letter said was that you hadda see me, and all this cloak-and-dagger shit about meeting here because it was very urgent. You bring her along?"

"I didn't tell her where I was going. She doesn't know we're in touch. She's shopping at Harrod's," said Moe. "Well, she's window-shopping at Harrod's. Nobody can afford to buy anything; my God, the prices here are insane. She brought five hundred dollars mad money and you can spend that on lunch in this town."

Actually, Chris had been left behind in America. And Moe wouldn't dwell on the cancer. He had only one item on the agenda: to clear up this business of the money or they would both get hurt. He looked at Jack's cashmere jacket and custom-made shirt and said nothing.

Jack knew that Moe was circling the topic, the reason for the urgent summons that had brought Jack out of hiding in Ireland. Jack would let Moe get around to it, in his own time.

Moe leaned back in his chair. He looked around the room. "England," he said. "These people are incredible. You know that? I went on this tour to Stonehenge yesterday, because I wanted to see the rocks and maybe absorb some spiritual enlightenment. Maybe the Druids were right. Who knows?

Great idea for a tour—early morning, long drive, eat and drink in the countryside, come back in the early evening. I figure that I'll get some Old World education about the Tudor Succession and dead kings and ancient dynasties. The tour guy is this very shabby gentleman who delivers what he considers a very sophisticated spiel about the modern lack of morality and sense of duty, contrasted with the devotion and sheer exertion it took to build all these great cathedrals with mile-high spires and how tragic it is, with the whole world coming unglued—ethically speaking."

The sound of Moe was like food to Jack. He missed those clear, elliptical stories which would circle around any topic (informed by those eyes and ears that missed nothing) and always return home to make an unexpected and telling point.

"And this guy, this tour guide with Oxford patches on his jacket, whose face looks like it has been patched on a very cheap medicaid plan, is all the time dropping names and hints about how he was in the foreign service and in India and Africa and your American cities like Las Vegas, you know? Name-dropping, place-dropping, subtle boasting, but in a European style, like a very exotic carnival barker. He raced cars and jumped from planes and screwed Lady Di. It was all connected in loose ways to the scenery. Like, we're passing Buckingham Palace and he mentions that he was there for the Queen's annual picnic, not that it meant much to him, being British and above that sort of thing. Telling us philistines, in his superior manner, that we are being escorted not by some cheap tour guide, but by a world traveler and adventurer who has played the palace."

Jack waved for another refill of the ale. His friend ignored it and went on with his story.

"The last stop, after Stonehenge and Salisbury Cathedral, are the Roman ruins in Bath. It is five in the afternoon and raining, which seems poetic and right—showers in Bath— when we finally get there. We philistines scatter to look at the ruins. We have an hour and a half to eat and see the old hot

baths and get taken for another kind of bath in the gift shops
and then we're all expected back at the bus by six-thirty. Only
some woman gets lost and does not return to the bus at the
appointed time. She's an old woman who walks slow and she's
probably crawling through the crowds of German tourists.
But, get this, this high-minded knight of the Silver Tour
company, this orator decrying the collapse of civilization and
chivalry, this spokesman for righteousness who is passionate
about the moral decline of the West, refuses to wait an extra
twenty minutes for the old lady lost in Bath. Because he could
be in trouble if he gets the bus back late. And he's got an
airtight defense. He whips out the rule book which says that
he doesn't hafta wait more than ten minutes past the rendez-
vous time. And he's right. It's there in the rule book, in case
we wanna check. He's got the old lady on a technicality. The
rest of the people on the bus are all sheep. They sit there while
this creep moves from the defensive and starts to denounce the
old lady for keeping us innocent tourists waiting, claiming she
is inconveniencing us, then tells the driver, to hell with her if
she's so inconsiderate, get going. A very popular decision, by
the way."

Jack and Moe both shook their heads.

"So whadja do?" asks Jack.

"Well, you know me."

"I know you."

"I walk to the front of the bus and I whisper in his ear that
if he moves the fucking bus one inch, that is how far I will
displace his testicles. He can leave, but I'm one of those un-
couth creatures from the New World with no historical
grounding or ethical training and I won't leave without her.
Neither will his balls, I point out, which I plan to hold hostage.
He looks at me and I'm smiling, but he knows I mean business.
He clears his throat and tells the rest of the people on the bus
that he's changed his mind and he's gonna personally ignore
the rules because it's raining and cold and better we should be
a few minutes late than leave some poor old lady to freeze and

catch cold. He sounds like a bugle call. Ten minutes later the old lady shows up all wet and shivering and crying with gratitude that we were still there, waiting for her. So, he takes full credit for defying the rules and doing the right thing."

Jack laughed knowingly. They were street cops. They'd spent many years watching people glue together the slivers of shattered pride.

"Some moral compass," said Jack.

"So that's what I think of England. How's Nora?"

"Ireland agrees with her. She looks like she's blushing all the time, but it's just a kind of Irish bloom."

"Nice woman."

"Nice woman," agreed Jack. "And Seamus is a nice kid."

"I can believe it," said Moe.

The oak lady handed Moe a bill and he whipped out some English notes, reaching over and stopping Jack's hand. "I'm on expenses."

"Oh, really? Somebody got some outstanding warrants in Mayfair?"

"You, buddy. You got on outstanding warrant."

Jack felt something crawl up his back. As if his uncertain voice advanced on thin ice, he asked: "You're not gonna tell me that they sent you?"

Moe looked around, took a swallow of his own ale. Then leaned across the table.

"No one sent me. I'm your friend. Your partner! Don't ask dumb fucking questions. Nobody sent me."

"But you're here for them."

"I'm here for you, you shit! Listen, Jack, I know some guys in the special squads—you know, the anti-anti-anti task force assholes. Murdering bastards. You know how they work, they're tight with the mob guys, they got undercover connections—and they picked up some rumors about this contract that's still in effect. On you."

Jack felt the news sink in. The reflex was right, thought Jack. The hairs on his neck had known it before he did.

"They know that we're partners," said Moe, using the present tense because once you were partners for a long time, you were partners forever. "They thought I might know how to get in touch with you, so they asked me—very discreetly—if I could pass the word. You know, how you could cancel this contract. They said, if I could, as a friend, I should tell you, because it could get extremely ugly, and you know what I mean."

"I know those guys are homicidal maniacs," hissed Jack. "They're not undercover anything, you schmuck. Before they're cops, they're soldiers for the fucking Mafia."

Jack looked around the room. There was no one else there, but that didn't stop his flutter of panic. The waitress, the little girl in the party dress who brought the ale and food to their table, it could be her. She could have an automatic on the tray, and fall into a crouch and take him out. The oak hostess, she could be the one. Anyone. Moe. Anyone.

He shook his head. "You come here for them!"

"For you," insisted Moe, reaching across the table, but Jack was bristling and inching his chair to an angle so that he would have his back to the wall. Moe knew that reaction.

Jack scanned the table, looking for a weapon. Anything to defend himself. The bread knife was small and wouldn't stop a bullet. Moe went on. "They asked me to speak to you. They wanted someone to speak to you so you'd listen. For Christ's sake, who else would you listen to?"

Jack started to get up—the impulse was to avoid being cornered. But Moe laid an iron hand on his friend's arm.

Jack sat down. If Moe is against me, I don't have a chance, he thought. The ale and whiskey and food boiled in his belly.

Moe understood. "If they wanted to kill you, you'd be dead. They don't want to kill you. Not yet, anyway. Look, I didn't tell them anything," said Moe. "I didn't even say I knew where to find you. I wasn't followed and I didn't tell."

"You sent me the fucking letter!"

"I had no choice, buddy. But I made sure the letter couldn't be traced."

It wasn't the long Sicilian grudge that surprised him. He'd expected a tap on the shoulder one day. He'd waited for the ambush. The early-warning hairs on his neck had spoken to him. The surprise was Moe.

Moe leaned across the table. "What do you expect? You thought that they wouldn't come after you? You thought that they'd write off the three fucking million as a business expense? C'mon, Jack, you know these people. They're never gonna stop. You could go to Mongolia and they'd send someone in after you."

"You?"

Moe waved a hand and looked away. "They want their money. Give them the money. It's only money. They don't want blood. They swore."

Jack snorted, shook his head. "I don't have their money."

Moe looked around the empty dining room. "They think you do. You know what kind of people they are."

Jack knew. Crazy thug killers. Rusty codes of false pride. Men who could not tolerate the insult of losing money. Not that he'd stolen their fucking money. He'd just happened to be there when it was stolen. He was the living link to the three million. It had to come back to haunt him.

"Moe, you know I didn't take the money, right?"

"What I know doesn't count. Somebody stole their money. They felt it in their hands. Now they sit there in those storefront social clubs in Little Italy and all they can think about is that somebody is out there enjoying their money. It makes them crazy."

"Where do you think that money is?"

"C'mon, Jack. How do I know?"

"That was mob money. Dirty money out of their filthy gambling rackets, dope dens, whorehouse laundries. If I did steal it, and I didn't, I wouldn't give it back so they could open up another crack den."

"Jack, they want the money."

Now Jack understood: they wanted their money or his ass. And he knew that he wasn't the only one in danger. If they were cunning enough and had their hooks in deep enough to know how to reach him, they could find Nora! Nora was in trouble.

He had to get back to Ireland. Nora had to be warned. He couldn't use the phone. It was too dangerous. If they didn't know where she was already, a phone call might lead them straight to her. This could even be the tactic—locating him and then having him lead them to her. He had to get back immediately without being followed.

"Watch your ass, partner," Moe called after him.

In a far booth on the ground floor of the pub, two men watched Jack run out into the street. One was thin and had a chin that vanished into his neck. The other man had spent too much time at the dinner table and had too many chins. Moe trailed Jack down and went to the back booth and told the two men what had happened.

"He understands," said Moe, taking a cigarette from Manero's pack, which lay on the table. "If he knows how, he's gonna get the money."

"You did good," said Sergeant Vincent Manero. Then he touched Moe's arm. "Listen, it was the only way you could save yourself. And him. Now you don't have to worry about your pension or medical benefits. And your wife will be taken care of. You did the only thing a friend could do."

"He's a good man," said Moe.

"I know, I know." Vinnie reached for his unfamiliar English money. "What's a good tip here?

"Leave a pound," replied Moe. "It's the coin. The thick one."

They paid, left the pub and went to a public phone. While

the double-chinned detective—Rocco Valone—kept watch over Moe, the other placed a transatlantic call to a phone booth in Queens where a man was waiting in the street. "I'm in London with our friend," said the man outside the pub.

It was the signal: Jack Mann was safely out of Ireland, too far away to affect the plan to recover the money.

Then all three Americans got into a car and headed for the airport, where Moe thought that he would head home and die in peace. He was exhausted—worn out by the radiation and the betrayal and the strain of worry. He wanted to sleep.

"He's a good man," he said as the car turned abruptly off the motorway into a deserted street. As he spoke, Rocco Valone, who was in the backseat, moved with surprising speed for a big man. He slipped a wire over Moe's head and tugged, putting both feet against the front seat for leverage.

"Hey! Watch it!" said Vinnie as he was hit with a squirt of Moe's blood. Rocco grew one more chin as he strained until he heard Moe's neck snap and all the struggle went out of Moe. "Now he don't have to worry about pensions or radiation or Jack Mann or nothin'," said Vinnie, who then helped Rocco carry the dead body into an empty house with an AVAILABLE TO LET sign on the front.

They looked like helpful friends assisting a drunk home from an office party. Before they left, Vinnie grabbed Moe's wallet, took the money and flung the wallet in the yard so that it would look as if he had been the victim of a mugging. Then the two New York detectives headed for the airport, where a commuter airline would take them to Ireland.

2

In a windblown street of rugged brick houses on the northern outskirts of Galway, Nora Katherine Burns skated over the frozen puddles of ice, humming some unwritten tune as she made her way to her aunts' cottage for her Saturday dinner. In the bag she had slung over her shoulder she carried two gifts—a brooch for Aunt Dee Dee and a shawl for Aunt Bridget. She kept looking down, a mother's habit, because she had left her six-year-old son behind. Seamus had spent a cranky afternoon crying and kicking at anything and anyone who came within range. She'd put him in the care of Patricia O'Malley, a young member of the staff of Galway House, the home and school she'd opened for orphans of the endless Irish political storms. Nora wasn't surprised at her son's temper. He was always difficult when Jack was away.

As she walked in the crisp wind blowing off the Atlantic Ocean, she felt a guilty, floating sense of freedom. She craved an evening of her own, and she was sadly relieved to have a day or two away from Jack, who, in the past eighteen months, had not found anything to anchor him to the life on the West Coast of Ireland. Since moving from New York, he'd drifted vaguely through the rooms of the big house that had once been the center of a great estate and was now the home for eleven orphans. Jack was like someone recovering from a bad wound—each step a careful test of the water. And when he tried to make himself useful, he got in everyone's way. Now he spent most afternoons at the Harp & Fiddle, a nearby pub, buying drinks for the local loafers, or ruining Seamus's schedule by taking him off to play. It offended Nora's strict code of duty; she was still a prisoner of hammering childhood admonitions, that a person had to toil for his daily bread and that idle hands were the devil's workshop. Her greatest fear was to be counted shiftless. Nora didn't know what to do about Jack's growing unhappiness. Not that she had any doubt about what troubled him. They had grown distantly cool toward each other after the steamy passion of their affair ended. Without the undercurrent of emotional heat, they seemed almost bruised as they brushed against each other, moving around the large house.

In some deep way, she resented his homesickness. He didn't miss his teeming American city and policemen friends and backyard barbecue social life. The overwhelming and glaring truth was that he was conscience-stricken by what they had done. And Nora could not fail to take it personally, as a reproach.

Whenever he broke his black silence and spoke about "the incident," he agreed, in principle at least, that they had surely put the money to better use than the evil rulers of organized crime, who would no doubt have used the cash to finance more wholesale shipments of dope. But the principle was only a wispy theory, and it did not end the grinding argument Jack waged within himself. Nora refused to think of that now. She put the relative morality of all of her acts out of her mind—she had a knack for that kind of pragmatic amnesia; she'd learned it when she ran errands for the IRA and had to blot out the bombings and shootings. When necessary, she could erase all of the blood calculus of "The Troubles" and with an iron effort turn her attention to her immediate concerns, such as her present graceful glide down Hill Street, while dreaming about a cozy evening of overcooked lamb and soggy bread pudding and happy chitchat. The wintry weather was fine with Nora, as long as she was tucked snug into a warm coat and dry shoes. She was, for the moment, happy.

Dee Dee was hardly able to stop from laughing as she stood at the window, watching her niece make her way towards the house, with the light-hearted little-girl look of her Nora Kate coming home from school twenty years earlier. She might be bringing me an *A* on her card, Dee Dee thought. She looked as uncomplicated as a smile. Dee Dee was a little disappointed that her darling great-nephew, Seamus, had to be left at home because of the chill in the night air. But then she'd have a chance to gossip and giggle with her niece without the worry of the irrepressible six-year-old who seemed to enjoy best the game of dropping china from steep sideboards. She'd already set aside a piece of the pudding for him, and Nora could take it home. And another for Patricia.

Still, Dee Dee had nothing but affection for Seamus, even with all his yammering and racket and highwire antics. He reminded her of young Nora Kate, a wildfire posing as a child. Nora, when she was barely ten, performed pirouettes while setting the table for dinner, then, in the evenings, spun across Dublin rooftops, her face serenely indifferent to the danger, while Dee Dee watched and held her breath. Nora had the courage of a freefall skydiver. Going off to America on her own, then coming back with a fortune and starting up the school—it shocked and thrilled Dee Dee just to imagine the nerve a thing like that took. She could see that same daredevil glint in the eye of Seamus.

And, of course, Dee Dee could also see in him the hard traits of Michael, Nora's older brother, the legendary hero, the craziest militant in the IRA, a man held in awe by the ferocious gunmen and bombers of that trade. It was taken as a matter of faith that no Ulsterman could catch him and no British prison could hold him. After all, wasn't he the one who blew up Lord Louis Mountbatten's yacht, an act of such heartless fury that it threw the fear of God into the royal family? If there was any brilliant, unsolved crime listed in any police and Special Branch files, it was ascribed to Michael Burns in the IRA. He was judged a man without mercy, but they always added that there was no one better in a tight spot.

"She's coming," said Dee Dee to her sister, Bridget, who was sitting up in the wheelchair wearing a permanent scowl. Bridget had been glaring back at the world with the same dissenting scowl since her stroke twenty-two months earlier. Her expression never changed. And she didn't speak, unless you counted the low hissing sound that came out of the side of her mouth when she got excited. No words, just the broken steam pipe of spittle that ran down the side of her face. Bridget communicated by blinking, and the doctors said that was as far as she would go. Bridget had been a sour woman, and it seemed all too fitting that she should be struck with an affliction that forced her to bear witness to life without being able to utter a word of disapproval.

Dee Dee had the exact opposite personality. A pudgy woman with a sweet tooth and a sweeter disposition, Diedre was enjoying the first stretch of tranquility and true peace in her life. Until Bridget's stroke, she had been a willing servant to her older sister's implacable will. Even during the worst crisis of their lives, seven years earlier, Dee Dee had buckled to Bridget's cruel wishes for the sake of harmony. But it had cost them both dearly. Bridget had decided to make an issue over Nora's pregnancy. Nora wouldn't name the father, nor would she give up the child. As if that weren't enough, she boldly announced her plans to leave Ireland altogether and join the flood of Irish youth heading to America to seek their fortune. Opportunity and freedom, that's what she wanted. Or so she said. Mostly it was freedom from Michael and the IRA wars and Bridget's oppressive thumb. Dee Dee understood her niece wanting to escape.

Bridget, however, refused to let her go, not with the unborn child in her belly. Not to Godless America. Not without a home and job and place for herself. Bad enough that she was going to bear a bastard, but to risk the infant soul in a strange land was a sin, said Bridget. She threatened to expose Nora's IRA past to the police if all else failed. And they all knew that Bridget was not one to make idle threats. Everyone knew, too, that the undeclared subtext of the struggle was the child's legal status.

Dee Dee offered a compromise solution. Nora would stay in Ireland until she gave birth. Afterward, she would leave for America on her own. The baby would stay with Dee Dee and Bridget until Nora had established herself. Then, when Nora had a home and source of income, the child would follow its mother.

Dee Dee worked out the deal, but she was furious at her sister for forcing the cruel compromise, and something cold closed between them. Dee Dee could not escape the thought that her sister's stroke was more than an exploded blood vessel in the brain. It was the hand of God.

She had endured a lifetime of her sister's contempt, from morning to night questioning Dee Dee's competence and challenging her moral fibre and belittling her opinions. Now Dee Dee ran the ship; she did the shopping, cleaned the cottage, welcomed Nora home, accepted Jack into the family in spite of their unclear and unsanctified relationship. All Bridget could do was drool while Dee Dee cleaned her waste, washed her shrinking body, spoonfed her like a baby. The dirty work was a fair exchange for the late contentment in her life. It wasn't Bridget's mortification that pleased her, but the ability to open her house to Nora and Jack; she was certain her older sister would have closed it to them.

Dee Dee turned from the window and put her hand on her

sister's shoulder. "Oh, you should see our Nora Kate, Bridget. She looks like a little girl again. Remember? So light on her feet. So happy!"

The plane landed rough, bouncing twice before settling into a tipsy run along the tarmac. Manero and Valone fought off a surge of terror, then looked around at the calm expressions on the other passengers and realized that this was a normal landing for the commuter airline; they were the only people aboard who had paled and bent over with their heads in their laps, in the classic crash position. The flight attendant was about to say something comforting when Rocco Valone lost his dinner. He managed to get most of it into the paper bag from the back of the seat ahead of him, but some spillage was unavoidable. Sergeant Manero was concerned: this was just the sort of thing that would make them conspicuous. He would have been angrier if Rocco hadn't triggered a sympathetic nausea of his own. Every person on the plane studied the two retching policemen with horror.

After the plane taxied to a halt, the attendant tried to clean them up, but no matter how many moist towelettes she used on their slacks and jackets, the awful stench wouldn't go away. It just mutated into an unbearable smell of perfumed vomit.

The two detectives carried small bags, each with a change of underwear, an extra shirt, and some spare cash. They were met by a local contact—a young man dressed as a priest whose name they didn't know and didn't want to know. Enough to know that he was connected to the operation and would provide what had to be provided. The local man's eyebrows shot up when the two detectives approached. He could smell them from across the airport lounge. He put them in a car, handed them a map of the area, pointed out where Galway House was located, and reminded them that they had to drive on the left-hand side of the road. The safe house was south, near Cork, a good six- or seven-hour drive at night. "The necessary items are in the boot," he added. "The mother's going to be away at a dinner with her aunt. The boy'll be home with one of the staff. It shouldn't be any trouble—I've marked off all the key points." Then the priest made a quick getaway.

Manero drove a few miles, then pulled off the road into a deserted layby and opened the trunk. Even if the Ford was an English Ford, he refused to call it the boot. There were two old .38 caliber pistols inside the trunk and two boxes of ammunition.

"Christ," said Detective Valone, "I thought these people had modern weapons."

Sergeant Manero shrugged. "Gotta make 'em untraceable," he said. "What's the difference?"

"This stuff is from World War I," complained Valone. "My great-grandfather used better equipment in the Civil War."

"Your great-grandfather was stealing goats in Sicily during the Civil War. This'll do," said Manero, getting back behind the wheel, stuffing his pistol under his seat. "All we gotta do is snatch the kid. Remember that. The kid gets us the money. We got a live kid, he's worth three million. A dead kid is worthless. So we don't wanna hafta use these things. No shooting!"

"I'd feel better if I had something that worked," said Valone.

The map led them from the hills where the small airport was located towards the coast. It was dark, and Valone wondered where the Christmas lights were.

"This isn't Rockaway Boulevard," said Manero. "Christmas is actually a religious holiday in this country. People go to church, not shopping."

"You'd think there'd be more lights, if they were so religious."

Manero shook his head.

Valone handled the map while the sergeant squinted to see the road. It was getting late—nine-thirty—and Manero was already nervous. "How much farther?"

Valone scratched his head. "Maybe five miles," he said.

"Supposed to be a big church on the left, and then the main house is a mile ahead on the right."

"That's all they got in this country—big churches. We gotta watch out for that."

"St. Mary's of the Sacred Heart."

Valone was playing with his gun, chambering a round, unchambering it, rubbing the weapon to get the heft of it. It was heavy, and he held it out in front of him, trying to imagine what it would be like in a firefight. Guns had a life of their own in a fight, jumping around in your hand. Pulling one way or another. They were all different. He wished that he had a chance to let off a few rounds just to see what it would do. Just so the gun would introduce itself to him.

"Do you hafta play with that?" asked Sergeant Manero.

"I don't like going in without my own gun," said Detective Valone.

"Well, I'm sorry you don't have a chance for any foreplay so you could get to know this one, but how many times do I hafta tell you: we ain't gonna shoot nobody."

Still, Detective Valone kept the pistol grip in his hand, encouraging a tactile relationship. "I'm hungry," he said.

Manero, whose stomach was bouncing up and down near his throat, just grunted.

The dinner plates were still on the table, and Nora automatically started to clean up.

"Don't you dare!" said Dee Dee. "I'll do that later. You're a guest. Sit down and have something cheery."

They moved into the parlor and sipped port, putting Bridget's wheelchair between them so they could include her in the after-dinner conversation.

Nora fingered the stem of the wineglass, remembering how often she had washed this glass, and all the dishes in this household. Long ago. Before America. When Bridget was still in charge.

"I'm worried about Jack," said Nora, looking over at Bridget, looking for a reaction. She was convinced that there were times when Bridget was alert, paying attention and keeping score.

"Did you hear that, Bridget?" Dee Dee tried to make a point of including her sister in the conversation even if it was useless. "Nora and Jack are having a little domestic problem." Then she turned back to Nora. "What is it, dear? Is it the usual thing?"

Nora opened her mouth, started to say something, stopped, then shook her head. "Christ! Not everything's bedroom dramatics, you know."

Dee Dee looked hurt.

"Sorry. Sorry. Life's so odd. You know how you think if you can solve a problem, everything'll be all right?" Nora said.

Dee Dee nodded.

"When you have no milk, you think, well, if I can just get enough milk, there won't be anything else to worry about."

Nora saw her aunt look sadly at Bridget.

"Well, I can tell you now for a fact, there's always something worse to worry about. I've got enough laid by so that I don't have to worry about the milk or the landlord, or anything I can name, for that matter."

"Don't sound boastful," cautioned Dee Dee.

"I'm just talkin'," said Nora. "Nobody but you knows anything at all about me. I wouldn't dare tell a soul. But if I can't trust you, Dee Dee, well, who on God's earth can I trust?"

"I'm glad you feel that way," said Dee Dee. "What's the problem with you and Jack?"

"The man's just not fitting in. He's lost here. Seems such a small thing, now that I say it."

"I know what you mean. Sometimes I think it's better to concern yourself with the milk," said Dee Dee. "These other things, psychological things, are so hard to deal with."

"Well, that's not the truth, either. That's not our problem."

"Well, it's an adjustment, you know, a foreign country with

strange ways. He'll settle in. He's a good man, Jack. I like him."

"I'm glad for that. I like him, too. Though heaven knows he's not ordinary. I wouldn't mind a moody man. It's not the restless thing or anything like that."

"I don't understand."

Nora smiled and shrugged. "I'm afraid that I don't love him," and the smile on her face had a distant, dying twist of sorrow in its curl.

"Oh, dear."

"Well, these thing happen, you know. We had a mad moment and when we woke up, heaven help us, it just wasn't love. Though Lord knows what else it was. At the time I couldn't think it was anything but."

"I understand."

Nora looked at her aunt and wondered. Maybe she understood. She was always underestimating Dee Dee. "I like him," Nora said emphatically. "He's a good man." She shook her head again. "I admire him. There's no better man."

Dee Dee nodded. There was nothing to say.

"I wish that I could love him."

"Does he love you?"

Nora lowered her head and shook it.

"You spoke of it?"

"In a way. We both agree. We just don't know how to get out of it. But, no, we haven't spoken of it out loud. But there's no mistake."

They were quiet for a long time, drinking their wine, enjoying the heat from the gas fire logs, running thoughts in and out of their minds. Nora and Jack was a closed topic now.

"I've heard from Michael," said Dee Dee suddenly, with a large smile.

Nora looked up, alarmed. Michael appeared from time to time, but messages were not his way of communicating. He was a man who was always in hiding, thus in a permanent state of suspiciousness. Messages had to be entrusted to other parties, and that went against the grain.

"Well, not directly, I haven't heard," said Dee Dee. "A young priest came by this morning and said that he knew Michael and that I shouldn't worry about my nephew. Just a friendly Christmas card, you might say. A nice young man looking for the road to Donegal—the priest. Said he might run into Michael, you never know, and he would pass the word about the family. Wanted to know how you were—you and Seamus."

"And what did you tell this priest?" said Nora, feeling a sudden spasm of fear.

"Nothing," replied Dee Dee, seeing Nora's reaction. "Just that everyone was fine. I said you were running an orphanage in the old Carnaby House and were doing just fine. Nothing special. Common knowledge. I mentioned that you'd be here for dinner tonight and I'd pass along his greetings."

"Did he ask about Seamus?"

Dee Dee looked worried. "He mentioned him, I think. Yes, now that I think of it, he said it was too bad that I wouldn't be seeing the little devil tonight . . ."

This was not Michael's messenger.

Nora grabbed her coat and put it on as she flew out the door, without stopping to kiss either aunt good-bye. "I have to get home," she called over her shoulder. She fell on the ice, got up, and started running along the unlit lanes, overheated by a flaming sense of panic.

The scheduled flight was on time, but Jack Mann was straining in his seat, ready to bolt out of the plane and start running for the gate. He'd made arrangements at Heathrow and a rental car was promised. Let them be as quick as they are in their ads, he prayed silently.

His head was pounding, and he regretted the whiskey and water they had served on the Aer Lingus flight. He'd had time to think over the encounter with Moe on the short flight from London. He had worked at recreating every line, and then tried to understand the meaning. He had been forced to be rude to the woman next to him on the plane when she had tried to strike up a conversation. She'd turned to gaze out of the window at the empty clouds. He had felt a twinge of regret because he noticed that she was attractive as well as lonely. Someone between romances, he guessed. But he didn't have time for social work. He had to concentrate. He had to figure out the probabilities. And as his head cleared, so did the picture.

The part that kept eluding him was the motivation for Moe's summons to London. What was his role in this? Who sent him? Why? It didn't make any sense. The Mafia wanted their money back. That much he knew. But why would they send Moe to London? Unless it was to locate Jack, to draw Jack away from Galway. To isolate Nora so that they would have a clear shot at her, thus the money. Because by now, with all their connections, they would have put two and two together and know for certain that she had taken the cash and fled to Ireland. Any fool could figure out that much. How else could a struggling barmaid in Queens afford to fly home to Ireland, set her aunts up in a cottage, buy a huge manor house, and turn it into an orphanage? The tips even in America were never that big.

Jack's rental car was waiting and he got a quick start. He drove like a highway cop, overtaking a slow-moving Ford— some lost stranger weaving back and forth looking for land-marks. Impatiently, Jack honked and went around the car on the right. The Ford veered towards him as if the driver were unfamiliar with the left-hand rules of the road. Jack cursed and stepped on the pedal and bounced along the shoulder until he was able to regain the road ahead of the Ford.

The manor house was almost dark—the children were asleep—except for a light in the library. Jack left the door of the car open as he ran inside and found a scene not unfamiliar: Patricia O'Malley was reading a story to Seamus in the library. Seamus was pumped full of sugar and unable to sleep and when he saw Jack, he plunged down under the cushions, playing their game of hide-and-seek. Jack was sweating. He looked around the room as if there might be someone hiding in ambush. But then he realized that he had arrived in time.

"Where's Nora?"

"She's at Dee Dee's," answered Pat, who had a soft spot for Jack and was glad to see him, even if he did look like he had fallen off of a truck.

Just then Pat looked up, her face wide-awake, staring at something behind Jack. He turned and there were two men in the doorway, looking foul and mean, as if they had fallen off the same truck. They had pistols in their hands.

"Okay," said the smaller man, the one without the chin. "Let's go." He was pointing at Pat and Jack. "Where's the kid? Where's Seamus?"

"What are you talking about?" said Jack.

Sergeant Manero indicated Jack with a motion of his gun. "Cover him." To Patricia, he said, "C'mon, now, don't make any trouble. We all know what this is about so don't make us use these." He held up his gun.

Rocco noticed a movement on the couch and turned his gun from Jack to meet an expected threat.

Jack saw his opportunity. He lunged for the table lamp, thinking that in the dark he could at least disarm one of them. But Rocco Valone was quick. He fired once, hitting Jack in the fleshy part of the shoulder. Then Rocco turned back and fired at the movement on the couch. Young Seamus was rising out of the soft cushions. Jack saw where Rocco Valone's gun was aimed, and held up his hand to catch the bullet. The steel-coated bullet shattered his hand and kept going, right through Seamus's chest.

Jack fell to the floor and seemed to lose consciousness. The detectives let him lie there, bleeding, showing no sign of life.

Sergeant Manero recovered from his moment of shock, put his pistol to Patricia O'Malley's forehead, and pulled the trigger. Her head burst open like a melon.

Then the two detectives ran out of the house. As they drove off down the unfamiliar road, they passed Nora, who was running towards the house. They paid her no attention. Valone laughed. "Now I'm really hungry," he said.

"Dumb!" muttered Sergeant Manero fiercely. "Stupid, dumb, motherfucking asshole!"

He slapped the steering wheel with both hands, almost driving into a tree. "Why'd he hafta go for that fucking lamp? Dumb, shit, stupid, asshole!"

Detective Valone, who had retreated to the passenger door, was relieved that Sergeant Manero was angry at Jack Mann, not himself.

3

In his dream, Jack caught the bullet. It was white, molten metal, and it set the hairs on the back of his hand on fire. This must be a kind of nuclear energy, he thought, as the sulphuric smoke and the smell of burning flesh rose up and choked him. He was undergoing a meltdown. It seemed like a clinical and detached opinion in his dream analysis: What else but the sun's heat itself could have done this? It had to be a power that could burn through all the layers of the earth's crust until it found a home in the magma at the core of the planet.

He might have caught the bullet, but he hadn't been able to hold on to it. Despite all his determination and the greatest concentration of his will, the bullet was too powerful. He could see—in the medicated slow-motion memory of the actual event—the projectile splitting open his palm, which spewed forth a geyser of blood and bone and tissue. It then tore out of the back of his hand, singeing the hairs, before it continued, undiminished in strength or velocity, on its path of destruction. It was at that point that the image would go black and Jack would wake up screaming.

The nurses at St. Patrick's Hospital understandably thought that he was crying out in pain, and in a way he was, so they jabbed him with needles and sent him back into the hellish dream in which the bullet couldn't be stopped.

He was aware of Nora watching him, with a kind of gray grief, as he twisted on his high hospital bed and drifted in and out of consciousness. Her face was in the shadows of the room, but he could tell that she looked compressed, pinched, like a soldier on a battlefield presenting a minimal target. But he noticed her eyes, which contained a smoldering rage. The nurses tiptoed in and out of the room and he wasn't sure whether they were moved by concern for him or fear of Nora—so fierce was her presence.

When he awoke, finally, she was gone. He was jolted out of his dream by pain. His left hand, his catching hand when he had played outfield in precinct softball games, was in a hard plastic cast and throbbed with a life of its own. He turned to look at it and another spasm of pain cut like a knife into his right shoulder. Instinctively, he put his hand up and felt a large, thick bandage running from his neck to his chest.

Then he remembered.

"I'll call the doctor," said the man sitting in the seat vacated by Nora. Jack hadn't noticed him, ignored him now. He was shaking his head. Seamus, smiling, was emerging from the cover of cushions, then was flung against the back of the couch, which turned red with his blood. It was so quick that sudden death didn't even have time to erase the smile from Seamus's face. Just deflated his little body. Then he remembered the other sound, the gun firing against Pat's head, and the pictures went blank again, because that was the moment he passed out. Jack had no more memories—just the twin masks of death that flickered in endless replay before his eyes.

"You don't want a doctor?" said the man, standing now with one hand on the knob of the door, misunderstanding the meaning of Jack's head-shaking. He saw that Jack's face was filled with confusion and sorrow and took matters into his own hands. "I'll get the doctor."

The doctor was a haggard, middle-aged man with a rough beard that was turning colors like a leaf in autumn. He wore a long white coat and bifocals and carried a large manila envelope. He had a steady frown; his voice was full of occupational woe.

"I'm Doctor Norris," he said, looking up from examining the injured hand, meeting Jack's eyes with a look that certified his competence and nothing more, then returning to the hand. The tips of Jack's fingers were poking out of the end of the cast. They were held in a kind of open spread. The doctor touched them, and despite the fact that Jack's entire arm felt like one raw nerve, the doctor's touch was gentle, almost cool, and did not add to the pain.

The nurse arrived out of breath, probably caught on a break, thought Jack, and he could tell that it was this doctor's no-nonsense nature that hurried her up. Doctor Norris didn't even look up as she fussed with her tray of instruments. "Put something under this," he said, and the nurse stuffed a towel under Jack's cast.

"Do you know what happened to you?" asked Doctor Norris.

Jack shook his head. The man who had been sitting in Nora's chair was standing behind the doctor, peeking around him, listening.

"Who's he?" Jack asked the doctor. "A hopeful undertaker?"

Doctor Norris looked up and Jack could see a small smile cross his face, then vanish just as quickly. "Garda," he replied, going back to the swollen fingers.

"Inspector McCormick," said the man behind the doctor. He was a small man and he wore an inexpensive suit, but he was fastidious, wearing a carefully matched tie and handkerchief. And he was clean shaven.

"You were shot," said Doctor Norris. "Can you feel this?"

He touched Jack's thumb. Jack could sense a touch, but it was fuzzy, as if his hand had been asleep. "I can feel something," said Jack. "But nothing sharp or definite."

"That's fine," said Doctor Norris. "We're not hoping for great things yet. Just trace amounts of feeling are enough."

The doctor went across the hand, feeling all the fingers, registering no emotion—a cold professional. He fished an X ray out of the huge envelope, held it up to the light, then looked down at the hand. "Are you in pain?" he asked, still looking at the X ray.

"It hurts," replied Jack.

The doctor looked into Jack's eyes, pulling down the bottom lids. "I'd prefer to use as little medication as possible," he said, more by way of lecturing than conversation. "I want to see how much nerve damage you've suffered. Hard to tell if you're all doped up."

He stood back and felt Jack's wounded shoulder. "Course, we may have to go back in if you start to run another fever and it swells up again."

"Go back in?"

"Operate."

"You mean, you were in once already?"

"Three times, as a matter of fact. First time we just put the bones back in place. Didn't try to solve the puzzle. Second time we got artful and tried to match things up. The third time we had to clean out more debris. Tidy up the infection. You've been delirious with fever. Hell of a lot of damage for one bullet. But I've seen worse."

"How long have I been here?"

"Four days."

Jack was surprised. "I missed Christmas."

"The wound in the arm was infected, and that didn't help the infection in your hand. The body tends to take these things personally."

"What do you think? Will you have to operate again?"

"Probably. Almost certainly. Yes. But not immediately. We

put a lot of wires and supports to help the bones mend. The infection seems under control and the swelling isn't too bad. I'd say you're healing better than I expected. But sooner or later, we're going to have to remove some more of the debris and deal with the fine tuning and see how much of that hand we can get working. You'll be in this Fiberglas cast for another four weeks. Then we can have a more flexible cast. You won't have the hand back one hundred percent, but I think you know that."

"How much use will I have?"

"Sixty. Sixty-five, seventy. Depends."

"On what?"

"How hard you work. There's a lot of rehabilitation. It hurts. Some quit. You don't look like the type who quits. For now, you've got to rest. Let it mend. Eliminate all the infection. Spend the New Year with us. We'll try to keep the pain under control, but I won't promise that it won't hurt. After you get through with this one"—he indicated the policeman behind him—"we'll take some more X rays and see how it looks. Eat something. You look terrible."

Then he turned and left, the nurse trailing after him.

The inspector nodded and moved closer to the bed. He looked Jack up and down. "People don't appreciate the great damage a bullet can do," he said sympathetically.

"It can take out an eye, if you're not careful."

"But I understand that you're a policeman—one of us—so you know what I'm talking about."

"I was a policeman. I'm retired."

"Young to be retired."

Jack shrugged. "I was impetuous and in love, and besides, nobody appreciates a good cop. Especially in America."

The inspector took a pad and pen from his jacket pocket. With a ceremonial flourish, he turned the barrel of the pen so that the point appeared. "We need your help. You are our only witness. Can you tell us what happened?" he asked.

"Tell me something, Inspector. Was there a woman here?" Jack asked.

"You mean Miss Burns?"

"Yes. I could have been delirious, but I thought I saw her sitting there."

"She was here. Terrible ordeal for her. She left when they told her that you were going to live. There was some question about that for a while. Poor woman lost her son and that girl who worked for her, I don't think she could have taken it if she had lost you, too."

"Seamus is dead?"

"You don't remember?"

Jack shook his head.

"The boy was killed instantly."

Jack nodded. He remembered. But he didn't trust his memory anymore. He had to have everything confirmed.

"We were hoping that you could clarify what happened," said the inspector. "The boy was killed by the bullet that went through your hand. Apparently, you tried to stop it. Possibly not, but we're Irish and we like to put a romantic spin on our great crimes. Hell of a thing you tried to do—catch a bullet with a bare hand."

"I left my glove in America."

"What's that?"

"Nothing. Private joke. What happened to the other girl?"

"Ah, young Patricia O'Malley. She was murdered. Executed. Some brute put a big cannon of a gun to her pretty head and blew it off. There were powder burns on the skull. Cold-blooded bastards. We know that there were two of them because the bullets came from different guns."

"I'm sorry, Inspector, it's all a blank."

"Well, man, you must remember something. You were there. Tell me what you do remember." Jack could see a flare of temper. Unexpected in a man like Inspector McCormick. "What's the last thing you can remember?"

"Tell you the truth, I can't be certain what I've dreamed and what was real. It's all one big confused jumble right now."

"I can understand that, but you've got to make an effort. These people aren't done, you know."

"Inspector, I've had a great shock. I've undergone some trauma. Do you think this could wait for just a little while longer while I catch my breath?"

"Listen to me, Jack Mann, we've had a slaughter in my district and I do not intend to let it get away from me. You know that the longer you wait, the colder the trail will be. You've a duty. You're a policeman, by God."

It made sense. "What do you want to know?"

"Why did you rush back to Galway, to the house? From what we can gather, you were in London and you met an old friend from the county of New York. Poor bastard."

"What? Why do you say, 'Poor bastard'?"

The inspector looked up from his pad. "I keep forgetting that you were unconscious for a long time. You couldn't know that he was assaulted just outside of London. They found him in a vacant house two days ago. First they robbed him, then they murdered him."

"Oh, Christ!" moaned Jack, trying to turn his face to the pillow. But there was no way to turn without putting pressure on his wounds.

"Odd kind of robbery," continued the inspector. "They used a wire around his neck to kill him. Not many thieves use a garrote. Well, maybe it was a merciful thing after all."

Jack shot him a harsh look. "What makes you say that?"

"Well, you know he had a cancer," said the inspector. "Lymphoma. He was just finished with a course of radiation. Though it wasn't going to help much, from the reports I've seen. Maybe someone put him out of his misery, saved him a great deal of pain in the end. It's the church's way of seeing things, though I personally don't put much stock in it."

Cancer as a consolation. A hard notion to swallow, but there could be something to it. Still, it gave Jack something to explain his old friend's behavior. A dying man tricked into luring Jack out of Ireland. Tying up loose ends—that made more sense than betrayal. His old partner was looking out for him, he was certain. That's why they killed him. It was no mugging. Even with cancer, no mugger could sneak up behind Moe Berger and slip a wire around his neck. They couldn't do it and live to tell about it.

"Where's Nora?"

"We'd like to know that ourselves. She was here, watching over you—under instructions not to leave the county without permission—and the next thing I know, she's gone. Cleared out of the house this morning. Now where would she be going, leaving all those orphans and her staff?"

Knowing Nora, she could be off anywhere. "Did you ask her aunt? She's got an aunt, Diedre Burns, who lives on Hill Street in Galway."

"Miss Burns has taken charge of the orphanage," said the inspector. "She can handle things nicely, but she won't say a word about the whereabouts of her niece."

"Maybe she doesn't know," suggested Jack.

The inspector nodded, put away his pen. "You've been no help at all, Mister Mann. I suppose you know that, being in the same line of work."

"If I could I would."

"You see, two innocent people were murdered in my county," said the inspector. "Now I know that they have a lot of murders in New York City and maybe a child and a baby-sitter don't count for that much in such a hellish place, but they do here. They do here. I'm going to catch the killers, you see. If I have to chase them to the far side of the moon. I'll catch them. One way or another. With your help or without your help."

"I remember the pain," said Jack.

"You must've seen someone. Something."

"I saw a blur. Maybe there were two figures and maybe that's something I dreamed. I can't be certain."

"Tell me what you might have seen."

Jack shook his head. "It's all a blur. Light. Dark. And pain. That's what I remember."

"And the killers?"

Jack shrugged.

The inspector sighed. "Well, we'll have to pursue the case without your help, then, won't we?" He rose. "You probably think that you'll do some of your own investigating, maybe take revenge or settle the outstanding debts on your own, without bothering with us. Cut out the red tape, as it were. I understand that's the kind of copper you fancied yourself in America. No stomach for the routine. Probably why they made you retire so young. I'm a man who follows the routine. I don't trust people who throw away the rules. There's a reason for rules and routine."

He stood there for a moment, wavering between anger and contempt.

"Let me warn you, keep out of it. You leave this to us. You're not Garda. You're not even a citizen. You may even be a suspect, although I think you're probably more of a target. So don't interfere. Not that you're in any position to do much anyway."

He stopped at the door. "I don't have to tell you to stay put, do I?"

Alone, later, Jack lay in the darkened room, his uneaten dinner on the bedstand, and watched the shadows on the ceiling. Nora's disappearance left him swarming in confusion. Maybe she had been grabbed by the Mafia. Maybe they thought she would lead them to the money.

No. Not now. Not with Seamus in the ground. They had to know that before she gave them a drop of satisfaction, they'd have to pay. She'd give up her eyes before she left his death unpaid. Now the debt was theirs.

4

The stone Gothic church stood in the north of
Roscommon, close to the triangle of the bor-
ders with County Sligo and County Leitrim. It was a hard,
jagged country of deep lakes and sudden mountains, unsoft-
ened by the year-round mist. It was near enough to the Ulster
frontier that it served as a staging area for the soldiers of the
IRA's attack squads. And when the Provos were on the run
escaping south, they often stopped again at St. Michael's to
catch their breath. If their hands were stained with fresh blood,
the priests turned a blind eye and delivered absolution, along
with a hot meal and a bracing glass of whiskey. By some
unspoken agreement somewhere, St. Michael's had always
been in the hands of clergymen who were friendly to the IRA
and its wild, militant wing.

It was a small church, and only a handful of people sat for
spiritual reasons in the pews that dated back before the Great
Famine. The Roscommon natives were political Catholics and
had never budged from positions taken before they were born.

In fact, their beliefs were stones of insurrectionary faith, borne across the generations on the tongues of their fathers and their fathers' fathers. In the shops and streets, they spoke in Gaelic of four-hundred-year-old battles between the clans of O'Neill and Oliver Cromwell, of those ancient wounds that still ran red and were unforgiven.

In the rear of the church sat a young woman with a meek headscarf on her head, waiting for the priest to finish evening Mass. She looked like the latest in an old line of brittle Irish mourners—morbidly patient women, unbroken by all the slaughter and prattle around them.

Father Brian Daly had seen her sitting there, recognized her, then walked past her. Nora followed him out into the churchyard. She looked up at the sky and spoke as if she were alone.

"I have an ache in my heart, Father, and I swear by all that I once held holy that someone will answer for it."

"Have you been to confession lately, Nora?" Father Daly asked, sitting on one of the stone benches designed for biting piety instead of comfort. In back of the church were rows of trees, all bare limbs in the winter of western Ireland. The yard looked stark and grave under the shadow of a gray statue of the archangel.

Nora sat down next to the priest, patted his arm and smiled. "What have I got to confess, Father? That some maniac killed my son? That they executed my poor baby-sitter and wounded my dear friend and broke my heart? The only thing that I've got to confess is a dangerous grudge against the agents of my present misery. And I don't need any Hail Mary's for that."

"I heard about Seamus," he said, his voice softening. "I couldn't come to the funeral Mass, but I prayed for Seamus, as well as Pat, and I prayed for you."

Her head dropped for an instant; then she straightened and cleared her throat.

"I thank you for your prayers, Father. Much good I think

prayers will do against such people. But I really cannot talk about that now. I have to . . . I have other matters to attend to."

She looked frozen in her grief, as if she would break under any kind of pressure. Gently, the priest touched her shoulder and she flinched. "There's a great deal of comfort in faith," he said, and she knew that he believed it, depended on it. She had long since given up any hope of God or salvation.

"The church looks fine," she said, nodding at the repairwork on the roof.

"We got a big donation," Father Daly said cheerfully. "Some American money."

"Really?"

"You know how they are, these cleaned-up, fine American Irish. They run away and make their fortune and then they feel bad about deserting us—and us without a pot. So they come back on their fine, big tourist buses with toilets in the back—Would you believe?—park them right outside on the road and run to take a leak after Mass. Then they sit inside the bus and they look at us from behind the glass windows like we're monkeys. A grand trip back to their roots, with the toilet on the bus. A week or so is all they can stand. Then they go home to their fat jobs and send us a fat check because they feel bad for us, stuck here in the glorious Emerald Isle with hardly a potato in the soup, much less a traveling toilet. They tell their friends they've been back to the mother country, seen it with their own eyes, bless 'em. But you know, Nora Kate, there's always a bit of glass between us. Not many like you, who come back and stay."

"Come back and die. God, that I'd've stayed in America," she mumbled.

He heard and understood and let it lie.

There were a few flakes of snow in the wind. It was cold, and they were exposed, and so they got down to business.

"If it's Michael you're looking for, I haven't seen him," said Father Daly.

"It is."

"He's not someone who leaves a footprint, much less a forwarding address," said the priest, looking to see if there was anyone within listening distance.

"I have to find him. I didn't know where else to look. I don't want to hunt up the Provos. Most of the boyos I knew are dead or in Long Kesh, anyway. I thought I'd see Michael at Seamus's funeral, or nearby, or maybe get word where he could be reached."

"Why would he leave word with me?"

She flared at the priest. "He knows of the connection between us, Father, and, if you'll excuse me, apart from everything else, Michael is my brother! And he is . . . was . . . Seamus's uncle. There's that, apart from every other damned thing!"

"I didn't mean . . ."

She knew that his intent was always harmless. He was not a cruel or even a thoughtless man, but he could be clumsy. She looked at him and felt some tinge of pity. He was not young. Middle-aged and starting to get paunchy and muddled. Not the man who had stopped in Hill Street. Dee Dee had said a young priest had stopped by, and she wouldn't have described Father Daly as young. She would have said a "nice" priest had stopped by and ate up all her cakes and talked her ear off, but she didn't mind a bit. Middle-aged, dumpy, and a little befuddled, at best.

"Is there a young priest helping you in this parish?" she asked, trying to make it sound casual, wondering if Michael had recruited someone else.

"Young? No. Just myself and Father McCluskey; you'd hardly call him young. He's on retirement. Frightening man. When we're at dinner, I have to keep looking at his chest, just to make sure it's still moving."

"A young priest stopped by a house near me—this was before Seamus was killed—and said he had greetings from Michael," she said. "I didn't actually see him, but the person he spoke to described him as young."

Father Daly shook his head. "That's not likely. First of all, Michael wouldn't send a priest to contact you. He'd come himself, if I know Michael."

"I didn't think it was Michael, either," said Nora, shivering from the cold and from coming up empty.

"Let's have some tea," suggested Father Daly, getting up, taking Nora's arm.

"No, thanks all the same," she said, pulling away. "I have to find Michael."

Nora had always liked Father Daly. When she was running errands for the IRA, when she still believed in the possibility of a United Ireland, he seemed one of the reasonable volunteers, a man who truly hated the deadly tactics while he loved the cause. Not like the psychopaths and thrill-seekers who cheerfully planted bombs in public parks and counted dead babies as victories, then went out to a pub and sang gay songs about Michael Collins and all the other dead Sinn Fein martyrs. Not like the cold killers who planned murder with the precision of surgeons. Not like her brother, Michael.

Father Daly had an abiding sympathy for the cause, but he had no heart for rejoicing in the deeds. And neither did Nora. If there was anyone she could talk to about her doubts when the violence had become routine, it was Brian Daly. They had sat often in the church rectory and sipped tea and consoled each other about the blind alley in which they found themselves. That was ten years ago, and he had put on the weight and some sorrow since then, but he hadn't changed much— just a little more weary and a little more resigned—and Nora didn't want to cause him any more anguish.

She started out of the church courtyard, tightening the headscarf against the weather. Father Daly caught up with her, panting slightly at the exertion.

"Listen, Nora, I know that you're not in it now, and that's for the best." He looked around, checking the empty street. "I never thought that you belonged in the thick of it."

"And you did?"

"Well, that's the chauvinist part of me I can't shake off. I can handle it. Yes, I belong in it because I'm needed."

"Because you're a man!?" she exploded.

"Because I'm a priest," he said with indignation. "I'm a spiritual chauvinist, not a male chauvinist. A priest has to stay with his flock, even if it's going straight into hell. You were always too squeamish for the work. Though you'd've made a hell of a priest."

She laughed. "So would you," she said.

They stood by the churchyard gate, blinking up at the snowflakes. He was having trouble with whatever he had to tell her.

"You don't have to help me," she said.

He nodded. "Ah, but I do. You've suffered a terrible blow—I cannot be blind to that, ignore the suffering—and I would do anything to help."

"Do you know where I can find Michael?"

"Let me ask you something, Nora. Are you after revenge? Because if that's the thing you're after, I don't want to be a part of it. And you won't find it very satisfying. First of all, it won't bring Seamus back. Second, you'll only do yourself harm. To your soul. Even if you don't believe in such a thing anymore, I do, and I wouldn't want to answer for that."

"Father, nothing and no one will bring Seamus back. Not you. Not your God. Not anyone or anything. I've taken all the blows that man or God can deliver. There's nothing left to hurt. Nothing. I don't mean to be disrespectful, Father, but that is a very important truth: there's not a thing that can touch me. Not anymore. They shot my whole world out from under me, man. Do you understand that, Brian? They killed my child. They shot him in the chest and blew open his heart. I used to bend over the crib and kiss that little chest, like it was a holy relic. My baby! What sort of madmen would do such a thing?"

"I can't answer for it," the priest replied sadly. "It's a cruel thing and I won't try to explain it. Not to you. I don't understand—I accept on faith that there must be a reason. There must!"

He circled around, slapped a tree, put his hands in his cassock pockets and leaned close to Nora's ear. "I'll tell you this much. Michael's off on a mission. That's as much as I can say. So there's no use prowling after him. You won't find him in Ireland. He left yesterday."

She nodded. Thought about it. Yesterday. Three days after the funeral. He could have come, unless he was saving himself for an important purpose. She looked at the sky. "Do you know where?"

Father Daly shrugged. "I know that he's on a mission. That could be anywhere. Besides, it's not the sort of thing they would tell me. I only know that he spent a night and then he was gone. I didn't ask questions. It's Michael, for heaven's sake. Who could pry anything out of him, of all people? I can't even imagine British Special Branch questioning him. He'd frighten them to death."

She laughed.

"There was something odd," said the priest. "He was staying in the attic safe-room and I brought up his dinner on a tray. Not much. A bit of stew and a slice of chocolate I saved for him. He was reading a batch of newspaper and magazine cuttings."

"What's so odd about that?"

"The kind of cuttings that he was reading. You expect Michael would be studying the biographies of the Brit cabinet. But they were cuttings about the cinema. Madness? I couldn't help but notice: they were all about the American awards ... You know, the movie things where they give people these great, big, ugly statues that they have to hold up and wave. Oh, what's the name?"

"The Academy Awards?"

His face brightened. "That's it! He was reading a huge stack of cuttings about the Academy Awards. Can you imagine Michael interested in movie actors?"

No, she couldn't. Not in the least. The last thing that he looked at when he went to a theater was the screen. He went into dark theaters to hide or to kill time. He could tell you more about the people sitting around him than what was taking place on the screen. If Michael was reading up on the Academy Awards, there was a point to it. It was important, and she intended to get to the bottom of it.

Nora reached out and shook his hand. "I know what this costs," she said. "Uh, tell me, Father, what time did he leave?"

"I don't know, but I did overhear that he had to be at Shannon at five."

She nodded, kissed him on the cheek and set off down the road, hurrying to meet the bus that would take her to the train that would bring her to Dublin.

On the second night of his hospital stay, when she was alone with him, Nora had heard Jack's semiconscious ravings. He had spoken of the killers. Cops, he had called them. Wise guys from Brooklyn or maybe Queens. But Americans. He'd mentioned it only once. But that had been enough for Nora. In her shoulder bag she had her passport and enough cash to finance her trip back to America, where she would find Michael and her son's killers.

Inspector Timothy McCormick looked down at his vest and frowned. He had spilled some tea on it, and he was convinced that it was ruined. He rubbed the stain with water, but it only got worse. But it wasn't the tea or the stain that troubled him. It wasn't even the fact that it was New Year's Eve and the headquarters of the Galway County Police sagged under the gloom of a holiday. The hallways echoed with the absence of the usual turnout, the decorations seemed cheerless, and the mood was grudging. What bothered Inspector McCormick was his inability to find Nora Burns and the widespread indifference of his superiors.

"Why aren't you out celebrating?" asked the chief superintendent, pausing as he passed McCormick's office. The chief was rushing off to a party of his own.

"One or two details," replied the inspector, standing up; he had an old army habit of coming to attention when a superior officer came by. Some thought that he was obsequious, but the real reason that Timothy McCormick showed them all the courtesies and professional etiquette was to deflect his superiors' attention from the fact that he had mutiny in his heart. He didn't approve of the prevailing sloppy approach to work, the time-serving, the paper-shuffling, the strict obedience to form over substance. He thought that his superiors should all be helping to find Nora, not to mention the men who killed her son. That's where she was, he was certain—hunting them down. In many ways, he thought, he felt the same urgent anger that she did. Her disappearance, along with Jack's amnesia—real or fake—made her the crucial link with the killers. He hadn't made up his mind about Jack. He seemed all right, and he had the wounds to justify his story. But McCormick suspected that he was holding something back, which is what any good cop would do. Keep a spare gun in your pocket. For now, his only hope was to find Nora Burns.

When he looked up again, the chief superintendent was gone, off to his New Year's party, taking whatever air was left out of the headquarters building, in the heart of downtown Galway near the Great Southern Hotel. The last sentries on duty sensed the change in tone and came by and offered Inspector McCormick a holiday toast.

"*Slainthe,*" he told Sergeant Meacham, one of the oldtimers who had volunteered to stay behind and let the youngsters out to celebrate the New Year. He raised a glass and sipped at the ale.

"You could use a bit of cheer," said the sergeant, and McCormick drained his glass, then held it out for a refill.

Mattie Nolan came in with a notepad. Inspector McCormick had forgotten that she was still working. "Will you look at the time, Mattie? There's a holiday, for heaven's sake. You've still time to find some sober lout to buy you a stiff drink."

She smiled at him indulgently, as if he were an idiot. "There's no one sober between here and Cork," she said, and he nodded and turned away. He didn't care to acknowledge the torch that she carried for him, had carried for the eight years that she worked for him. It wasn't a question of getting along. If anything, Inspector Timothy McCormick and Officer Mattie Nolan got along too well. Too much alike. They finished each other's thoughts and felt each other's moods.

Most people would have said, if the question came up, that she was not a pretty woman, not in a conventional sense. But there was something exotic about her. In Paris she would have made herself beautiful. Her interesting nose had a little twist to the left of her face, and her mysterious eyes blazed or turned to frost, depending on her mood. She went out of her way to conceal her erotic possibilities. She tied her hair back in a bun, wore plain business suits, and maintained a starched personality in public.

Inspector McCormick accepted her, along with the torch, because she was so efficient and loyal. He did not know how to move the relationship past the business stage without damaging it. In his work, he needed loyalty. He needed Mattie.

The phone rang, and she picked it up. "Inspector McCormick's office," she said crisply. She listened for a moment, took some notes, then said, "Right. . . . Give me your number and I'll be back to you in five minutes. . . . Yes, I know what time it is. It's nine-fifty. I'll be back to you before ten and you can get away to your celebration."

She was smiling when she hung up. "We've found her," she said. "She was aboard an Aer Lingus flight to New York."

Circulating Nora's picture to airport ticket clerks had paid off.

"She would slip us, that one," said the inspector. "When does she get in?"

Mattie shook her head. "She's down already; noon, our time," she said. "Knowing her, she's already leased her own flat and invented a cover story."

"Well, we can certainly chase after her," said McCormick. "I think we'd best be after her. If she's on the heels of the villains who killed her child, we'd better beat her to them."

"She used the Virginia Haig name," replied Mattie. The Garda knew the name from a false passport Nora had used during her IRA days. The airline clerk had put it together with the snap.

"We are dealing with a woman with a brain in her head," said McCormick. Then he looked over at Mattie: "Are all your documents up to date?"

5

New Year's Eve, 1991

The new waiter stopped in his tracks, avoiding a public disaster. He teetered just in front of the outstretched leg of a diner blocking the way to his station in the third-floor Grand Ballroom of the Waldorf-Astoria Hotel. He carried a heavy tray of seven main courses, and the diner's leg would have sent him sprawling—tray sailing, dishes flying, revelers scattering. And it was no accident. It was a clear provocation, because the leg's owner was watching the waiter's face, looking for a reaction so that he could carry this thing to its limit. The waiter simply stared at the leg, willing to wait until the customer—a young, strapping car salesman who invariably got ugly after four drinks—removed the obstruction.

"Hey, Sam, move your leg!" said the salesman's male table mate, a good-natured number-cruncher who worked in the same car dealership. He would have let the incident run its normal course—which would have required him either to make abject apologies for his friend, or else to take him home bleeding—except that he'd noticed something unusual in the eyes of the waiter. A hint of murder.

"Yeah?" said the salesman, staring at the waiter with some belligerence. "Suppose I don't want to move my foot? What about that?"

"C'mon, Sam," said the salesman's date, the attractive owner of a beauty salon. She was embarrassed by her escort's behavior. "Move your damn foot!"

The waiter, who called himself Michael Miller, had an instant to decide how to react. In spite of long years of training and iron discipline and his own best judgment, he wavered between breaking the salesman's nose and backing down. It was only a passing thought, a human temptation, and then he was in control again. But the dangerous thoughts did not vanish entirely. He was almost forty, getting old by the strict standards of his lethal trade, slowing down by daily increments, and now and then he had to swallow a latent animal outcry against the inevitable moment when he would become physically unreliable. But not yet. Not now. This was no time to make his last stand. He lowered his head and marched in a semicircle, flanking the car salesman's leg to reach his station and deliver the seven dinners. Only three quarters of an hour until midnight. The people who paid three-hundred-dollars-a-plate wanted the meal over by the time the nets opened and the skyful of bright balloons was released, signaling the New Year. They wanted to welcome in 1991 with a full belly.

The salesman's triumphant laughter burned Michael's ears as he worked his way around him. Why do I let this bother me? he wondered. One more American thug! Such a childish, overrated nation! No inkling of what the world was like, how hard times could be. Happy-go-lucky clowns with a willful desire to see things go their way. Gifted only in luck. He would have enjoyed taking the man into a quiet room and questioning him, asking him why he went around poking

sticks into people. Didn't he know that he could be badly hurt
playing such dangerous games? He put that thought out of his
mind and got on with his job.

The room, which rose into two tiers of balconies, was deaf-
ening, with horns and shouts and the background music from
the orchestra—sentimental tunes from a time when New
Year's celebrations inspired high emotion and soggy sentiment
rather than modern-day excess in the use of drugs and the
intake of liquor and the boundaries of sex. God, he hated such
limitless people!

The crowd was dressed for a rowdy soiree. They all wore
shiny, playful cardboard hats that glittered under the mirrored
lights. The women were decked out in swank formal gowns,
and the men were stuffed into rented tuxedos. Only on closer
inspection was it clear that this was nobody's A-list. The social
set, the smart, backroom boys and their third wives celebrated
the New Year in private mansions or more chic, undiscovered
rooms. In the Waldorf ballroom were the leftover strivers, the
middle-class bridge-and-tunnel set—small shop owners from
Queens, middle managers from Long Island, car salesmen
from Brooklyn—who were under the impression that they
were celebrating in high society.

At a vantage point where they could see the floor without
being noticed, stood the headwaiter, John Dunlap, along with
the shop steward for the hotel waiters' union, Carmine Paolo.

"He's not gonna make it," the headwaiter said, watching
Michael reluctantly change direction to avoid the belligerent
car salesman.

"C'mon, give the guy a chance."

"Look at him," Dunlap said. "He wants to eat that guy's
lungs."

"Wouldn't you? That guy's a prick. I know him."

"You know him?"

"Not him, personally, but guys just like him. Look, John,
you been out on the floor on New Year's. There's always some
asshole wants to start a fight."

"And your new guy looks like he wants to give him every opportunity."

"He's handling it! He's walking around."

Dunlap shook his head in deep skepticism. There was something disturbing, something he couldn't quite put his finger on, about this new man. During the afternoon interview, when Carmine brought him in as a replacement and demanded that this Michael Miller be put to work, John Dunlap had wanted to say no, he had enough help. It wasn't true, he was always shorthanded on New Year's Eve; but his intuition had told him that this one was trouble. He'd sensed the same thing that the car salesman's number-crunching friend had seen: Michael Miller was no waiter. He lacked the essential quality, a kind of noiseless modesty that all waiters had to display. He didn't show a talent for submission.

Dunlap had seen the flash of danger again, in that split-second hesitation on the ballroom floor; he recognized the urge that Michael had suppressed. He knew that Michael was weighing the cost of punishing the customer. Earlier, when they were in the locker room getting dressed for work, he'd noticed that the new waiter was perfectly capable of breaking any car salesman in two. In street clothes, Michael Miller looked thin and not very large, but with his shirt off, he was all gristle and muscle. And when he got into the kitchen, he lifted the trays loaded with seven main courses as if they were made of tissue. It took a strong man to remain steady under that great weight. Michael never even broke a sweat.

"Why's it so important that he has to work?"

Carmine said, "Ah, my uncle's wife, you know, I must've told you about him, the one who died? Well, now she's sick and Michael—that's her only son—he has to pay the bills. They got no insurance, nothing. I promised my uncle before he died that I'd look out for my aunt and my nephew. You can see that he's a worker. You got to admit that, Jo Jo. He's holding down that station. I couldn't handle it."

It was true. Dunlap had deliberately given Michael a heavy

station, expecting him to quit by nine. But Michael showed no signs of fatigue. He was ahead of the veterans, the ones who were in great shape and got into speed and endurance competitions with each other. Even they were falling behind the new man.

Carmine had lied. He couldn't tell Dunlap the truth: he had gotten a direct order to put Michael Miller to work in the ballroom. The order had come from a man to whom he owed important favors—protection when he couldn't live without it, pressure on bosses during negotiations, forgiveness of loans at double-digit daily compounded rates. The order had come from a man who owned him. Carmine wouldn't say it had come from the mob, but it had come down from someone who could have him murdered. Of that he was certain. No questions. No backtalk. Just do it. He didn't know why, and he didn't want to know why.

He was grateful that it was such an easy order to obey, and that this man who called himself Michael Miller—and he didn't believe the name for a minute—could hold up his end on the floor.

Forty-eight city blocks north and four avenues west, on Ninety-eighth Street and Columbus Avenue, Michael's sister, Nora Burns, examined a furnished room no bigger than one of the closets in Galway House. There was a private toilet with the room, but no bath and no shower. To bathe, the owner said, Nora would have to use the larger and better equipped bathroom down the hall. The one shared by the whole Duggan family.

Nora didn't mind. All the drawbacks that the owner, Patrick Duggan, named seemed small in the light of her recent calamities. She nodded and peeled off three hundred dollars in twenties, two weeks' rent, and Duggan—a small man with a big belly poking out of his torn T-shirt—smiled. He took it as a personal compliment that she had decided to stay at such an inflated rent. Not that he thought she'd last long. She had to be one of those illegal Irish roses who came to America with a thousand dollars tucked into their blouses. The poor things never realized that such a puny sum would run out in a month in New York's pricey world. They would soon be driven to desperate measures, taking lowly, off-the-books jobs and sleeping in shifts, living five-in-a-bed to survive. According to Patrick Duggan's practical beliefs, these pretty flowers fresh from the auld sod had to be plucked while they were still under the spell of the American myth. You couldn't let them wait. He'd take his three hundred dollars and let the third week run out before he threw her out onto the street.

What he didn't know was that Nora Burns had more than $250,000 hidden in the cheap suitcase on her bed. Along with the cash, her real passport was sewn into the lining. The name she traveled under now was of a school friend, Katherine Kerry.

She could tell from the way Patrick looked at her that he was measuring his chances. She knew that she was an appealing woman—even with the grief in her face—and there would always be some man who would, as a matter of pride, attempt to break through her distant, unapproachable manner. Invariably, she would have to end up deflating his ego.

"Thank you, Mister Duggan. I'll be resting now," she said, ushering him to the door of what was now her room.

"Don't you want me to tell you a few things about the neighborhood?" he asked, flustered by her quick dismissal.

"Not tonight," she replied, and tried to smile, although her smile had a brittle, knifelike quality.

He stopped at the door. "It's New Year's Eve," he said.

"I know."

"A few friends are stopping by. You're welcome to join us."

"Another time," she said, closing the door.

"Another New Year's Eve?" he said, standing in the corridor.

Nora was aware of the date. She'd counted on it. Coming into the country on New Year's Eve had been a conscious, deliberate thing. The immigration and customs inspectors would be less attentive to a false passport when they were sore and bitter at having to work a holiday. The battered valise would not be searched by grudging officials who would rather be home swilling beer. It was no accident, arriving in the middle of the festivities. It was what she'd wanted.

She looked around the room, with its faded, flowered wallpaper, its plastic flowers in a cracked vase, and a sagging dresser in the corner, and she felt safe. No one would look for her here. Not with frayed carpets and a broken chair in an unregistered room where no cooking was allowed and the landlord wore a torn undershirt. She could begin her search for Michael tomorrow. Michael would help her find her son's murderers. He owed her that much. They were Americans, she was certain of it. Some instinct told her so. They were after the money, as she knew, deep down, they would be. The voices she had heard that night were American. And Jack's flickering memory was of cops. It was the only thing that made sense. Mafia. After their money. They were on this continent somewhere. They were in this city. She had time. As they said, "Revenge was a dish best eaten cold."

She lay down on the bed with its stained covers, feeling the lumps in the mattress, wondering how many starry-eyed Irish immigrants had wasted their dreams here. How many spirits had old Paddy Duggan helped crush in lieu of the rent? She looked out of the window. It was snowing. Not hard, but smooth, white flakes floated past her window. Seamus would have squealed with pleasure and run outside to play. She could see him flying into a snowbank, and his face—all red with excitement—turning to see if she was watching. She could hear the laugh, like a hiccup, that always made her laugh as well.

She thrust that thought aside, the way she ruthlessly shut thoughts of Jack out of her mind. Jack would survive, and Seamus was dead. And so, in many important ways, was she.

*   *   *

The car salesman felt woozy and left the party at the Wal-dorf-Astoria just before two in the morning. His date had gone home an hour ago. He'd told the number-cruncher he'd be back in a while, but he needed the air. He didn't take his coat or his hat. He wanted to feel the weather in his face. He didn't mind getting his tux wet.

He came outside onto Park Avenue and suddenly slumped into the arms of the doorman. He laughed, allowed himself to be lifted to his feet, and staggered south, inhaling as much air as his lungs could hold. He didn't notice the figure trailing him in the shadows. He didn't worry about such things because he was big and able to take care of himself. Muggers and street thieves avoided him, even when he was drunk; he looked like a cop, with his big shoulders and aggressive belly. He'd once thought of taking the test for the police department, but first came the army, then the job pushing cars, and times were good and so was the money and when he thought about it, when a friend on the job called him to come down and take the test, told him that a new class of recruits would be selected and he was bound to be high on the list, he remembered that he hated taking orders, so he let the deadline pass.

At Forty-second Street, as he entered a deserted tunnel of the Pan Am Building, his head stopped swimming and he sensed someone following him. He could hear the scrape of shoes and feel the heat of breath close behind him. When he turned, the knife-edge of Michael's stiff hand struck him in the windpipe, breaking his trachea, cracking his neck, and killing him instantly.

The man who called himself Michael Miller went into the dead man's pocket, removed his wallet, kept the cash and scattered the rest of the contents over the car salesman—one more New Year's Eve crime victim.

"Mind your foot," he said pleasantly to the dead body.

What Michael didn't notice, because he hadn't been back in New York City for a few years, were the two men perched on the girder above the tunnel. They were homeless drug addicts, and the girder was where they lived. The city had become filled with homeless voyagers like these since Michael had last been there. Now they lived in constant motion, moved from surface to surface by the relentless tide of police nightsticks. The two men above the tunnel had seen more than one street-killing from twenty feet above the pavement, and they were accustomed to a certain level of violence. But they had never seen a genuine kung fu black belt in operation. They exchanged looks of utter fear and remained very still. They didn't want the scattered credit cards. They didn't want the blade of that hand slicing away their lives.

Michael felt better. It wasn't simply the answered insult that buoyed his spirits. That was of no consequence. He felt good about himself. Michael had needed to know, when he slipped out of the ballroom on the heels of the salesman (explaining he needed a bathroom break), how well the weapon would work in battle. His reflexes were still good. His timing was fine. His body—though scarred and rearranged in the years of combat—was fit, thanks to his daily routine of exercises. He was as clinical and ruthless when it came to judging himself as he was when testing the mechanical operation of his gun. If he didn't hear the perfect click, he knew that the weapon was rusty or out of alignment. In the last analysis, he was the crucial weapon. And, from time to time, even the deadliest killer, the best-trained soldier begins to suffer little rust-spots of doubt about how he will act under fire. The car salesman had awakened his temper, made him question himself, forced the test.

Now that he had tested himself, he was almost satisfied. The stealth was there. The hand still had the speed and the strength. The eye was accurate.

And, perhaps most important of all, the spirit was willing. He looked at the corpse of the car salesman with the same indifferent satisfaction that he felt when looking at a target on a range with a well-grouped burst of holes. He should have felt invigorated. Even elated. But the clean kill of the loutish car salesman didn't drive away the feeling that had been growing inside him lately like something heavy and alive. Not that he hadn't made all the moral calculations—surely Ireland was worth a few innocent casualties. But now and then, more and more frequently, he could see the faces of his victims, and he felt—in a tangible and vivid way—an inexplicable hesitation. A small stammer of regret. There were nights when he woke up sobbing. He'd thought that proving himself against the car salesman would cure that. But it didn't.

The mission required that he click like the well-oiled automatic pistol he wielded in a fight. This was no small, annoying attack to grab a cheap headline. His intent, after all, was to stage a wholesale massacre of American celebrities. Moreover, he intended to perform the slaughter in the full glare of the public.

On Tuesday, March 26, the ballroom of the Waldorf-Astoria Hotel would be packed with movie stars and politicians, socialites and tycoons. Everyone important who, for whatever reasons, could not or would not attend the Academy Awards ceremony in Los Angeles would be at the Waldorf, attending the East Coast version of the Academy Awards dinner. And if his plan worked as he expected it would, they would all die. The mayor and the governor and maybe even the vice president—small fry. De Niro and Hoffman and Streep and Diane Keaton and Cornelia Guest and Bill Blass. All 750 of them. It would shock the world, maybe as nothing else before had ever shocked it. All those movie stars, all those *People* celebrities, all those eye-bugging shutter hogs would be gone in one devastating moment. The country would be thrown into political and cultural turmoil.

Kill one or two politicians and movie stars, and the press got indignant and the politicians got angry and studies were undertaken and experts were consulted so that it wouldn't happen again. "Nightline" attention! Hold a few hostages and interest rose, then waned. The world's attention span was a very tricky thing and besides, there was always a fresh supply of woe. But take out hundreds of the celebrities—in one giant, mad act—and the coping machinery would break down. The public would finally see: Ireland would be united or the world would never sleep with both eyes shut again!

When Michael came back to the floor of the Grand Ballroom, John Dunlap was waiting. The headwaiter took Michael's arm and said that he had done a splendid job under the worst circumstances. Not only were New Year's Eve crowds impossible, but the sheer volume and confusion were almost more than the most talented waiters could cope with. Michael had outperformed the best.

"I just wanted to thank you and say that you're welcome here as long as you want a job," said Dunlap.

"Thanks," said Michael. "I appreciate that."

Then Michael went back to his job, cleaning up tables, bringing fresh water to the parched diners, helping drunks back to their seats. John Dunlap watched him for a moment, then looked down at his hand. It was cold and wet from touching Michael's sleeve. Well, he thought, explaining the oddity to himself, maybe there was an open window in the bathroom.

6

Thursday, February 7, 1991

The consulting rooms for the chief surgeons at St. Patrick's Hospital in Galway were new, or at least recently refurbished to give them a barren high-tech surface. Each pastel office buzzed with the toxic sound of Muzak, a suffocating addition that designers of airports and modern offices somehow thought humanized arid public areas. The architects and consultants had good, solid studies to back them up, showing that the pastels and tuneless melodies reassured frightened patients. However, for the most part, they had the exact opposite effect. Most patients sat there in a state of controlled alarm.

In contrast, Dr. Joseph Norris's office was cluttered and chaotic, like the abandoned headquarters of a defeated army. There were medical reports and loose charts and random X rays scattered like shrapnel over the counters. It looked as if the generals had fled with uneaten food still on the table, which was not an entirely inappropriate thought since there was usually uneaten food on the desk. A radio drowned out the speakers with jazz. The ashtray overflowed with the stubs of the cigarettes that the orthopedic surgeon smoked to the bitter end. The atmosphere of brimstone and disorder was dramatically different from the antiseptically pure offices of the more state-of-the-art surgeons. Jack Mann found it strangely reassuring.

Dr. Norris himself, in his shabby white smock, stood at the backlit X-ray screen, squinting through smudged bifocals and a plume of cigarette smoke at the skeletal pictures of Jack's hand. Jack tried to peer around him, failing to detect any latent truth in the murky shadows and clouds that made up the essence of the X rays. It was always baffling. It amazed him when a doctor showed him a spot—or what he said was a significant shadow—on an X-ray picture, expecting him to recognize the flaw, or, at any rate, the difference that was, according to the physician, as plain as the nose on your face. He nodded dumbly and pretended to see whatever it was that he was supposed to see, the thing that was being clucked over gravely, but the truth was that he could have been looking at a surrealistic place mat, for all the meaning he could detect.

"Hmmm!" said Dr. Norris, stubbing out the cigarette on his desk, missing the ashtray by an inch. This was not the clear-cut answer Jack was seeking about whether or not he could leave the hospital.

"Here, have a look," said the doctor.

Jack stood next to the doctor and gazed at the X ray of the hand.

"Just look at that!"

Jack looked.

"Frankly," said Dr. Norris, "I'm quite impressed."

"That's good enough for me," said Jack.

"You see the difference, don't you?"

He slapped an old X ray—one taken two days earlier—in the metal clips on the screen. Jack looked first to the right, then to the left, then back to the right again, and on to the left, so that it appeared he was watching a slow tennis match; he saw absolutely no difference.

"This bone here was all fragments when we first opened up that hand," Dr. Norris said, taking great pride in just how badly shattered and destroyed Jack's hand had been. "Splinters, really. See, I tucked it together and got the splints on— you can see that here." He pointed to a blurred section in the middle of Jack's palm; Jack could see only skimmed milk.

"Amazing!" Jack said with false enthusiasm.

The doctor turned and saw the blank ignorance on Jack's face. He pulled down the negatives. "You don't deserve me," he said. "I've done a miracle on that bloody hand. In the old days they would have cut it off."

"Joe, you're a magician," said Jack good-naturedly, folding himself into the leather chair—a piece of furniture that was comfortable, thus out of sync with the plastic decor of the rest of the hospital. "Of course, in the old days they often confused magic with witchcraft, and there's a good chance that they'd've burned you at the stake."

The doctor smiled and lit a cigarette with the stub of the last, keeping the chain alive. "Still very fragile," he said, jutting his chin at Jack's hand.

"But I can get out of this place?"

The doctor ran his hand—the one holding the cigarette— through his sparse hair. For an instant Jack feared a hair fire, but then he saw that it was an old habit and Dr. Norris had it under control, and what's more, enjoyed throwing a scare into his patients.

"You can leave, but I recommend against it. We're having lamb stew tonight."

"That's the thing that's going to kill me—the food," said Jack.

"All cooked by a fine Irish hand. Well, I can see that you don't like plain food. Ireland's not known for the gourmet cooking, I'll grant you that. But I can understand. You want to get back to your delicate American cuisine where you can feast on your famous greasy fried beef and badly prepared potatoes."

Jack didn't say anything, because he was not supposed to leave the county, much less the country. This doctor was like a lot of them in the Republic—touched with a streak of romantic rebellion. If the Garda wanted Jack to stay, well, then, the man should go. And the good doctor would lend a subversive, helping hand.

"You'd better take a copy of your X rays with you, in case we have a fire. I wouldn't want you to go to some American doctor and have him think we're all uncivilized pagans. Tell him to call me and we'll talk about it. Or, better yet, he can fax me, and then he can call me; it'll give him something to tell his colleagues about, faxing Ireland. The number is on the envelope."

"Do you have a fax machine?"

"Certainly not! I wouldn't have any such thing in my office. They never work. And even if they do, then what? Huh? Have the man call me and I'll explain the mechanics of the operation I performed so brilliantly and famously."

"You'd better give me some pills for the pain," suggested Jack, and Dr. Norris filled two large jars with codeine-based tablets, then wrote out prescriptions for more, along with a note for any nervous airport officials.

Before he had left New York to find Nora, Jack had set up an account in an American bank. He had signed a signature card under another name and Moe had regularly deposited his pension checks into the account. They had used an alias to evade the tireless Mafia hunters. The checks were deposited to the account of Barry Stein, Jack's dead nephew. He carried his nephew's identification. The latest statement listed $48,-678.94 in Barry's name. Jack also had some cash he kept within reach for emergencies—an act of foresight, considering the kind of life he led. He would not wind up helpless on the streets if he went to New York. He would carry only essentials in a small overnight bag because he didn't want to travel with anything bulky.

"I have to find her," he told Dee Dee, who was the one who informed him that Nora had gone to America. Nora had given her aunt an emergency contact address—a bar in Queens where she had once worked as a cocktail waitress—but had warned her to keep it secret. Dee Dee would have, too, from anyone but Jack. She couldn't take seriously Nora's gloomy pronouncements on the relationship. Not after Jack's attempt to save the child. Not with her own affection for the man. Surely, Nora couldn't have meant Jack when she had said, "Tell no one."

And there was good reason for concern about Nora's state of mind. The sudden departure on New Year's Eve could only mean that she was looking for trouble. Dee Dee thought that Nora would be after revenge.

"She's looking for Michael," Jack said. "I'm sure of that. If she went to America, it's because he's there."

Nora also knew about the mob and the money. She would grasp in an instant that if the killers came from anyplace, it was America.

"Do you feel up to the trip?" asked Dee Dee.

His hand elevated to alleviate the pain, his face drained of all blood, his strength sapped by guilt and worry, Jack could only smile miserably. "The only thing that I feel up to is a nice nap," he said.

"Where can I reach you?"

He said that he'd call, keep in touch, but he had no idea where he would stay. He knew the bar where Nora said she could be reached, but he couldn't use it as a forwarding address. He had to play it by ear.

"I'll call," he said. "I'll let you know."

"Take care of yourself," she said when he was at the door, looking dog tired. "I've grown fond of you."

He leaned over and kissed her on the forehead.

Bridget's chair was turned away. They didn't want to look at her face when they spoke secrets.

It was hard riding the bumpy train to Dublin, but he numbed himself with pills and Bushmills. He was not certain whether the combination was potentially lethal, but at this stage of his life, he didn't much care. One way of dying was as good as another. He was traveling along a thin, risky ledge of danger and it was no time to look down.

On the airplane, the attendants took pity on Jack's outsized cast, his wounded shoulder, and feverish look and put him in an empty seat in First Class. They fed him champagne and pâté and kept casting worried looks in his direction and draping napkin-sized blankets over his legs when they thought he was asleep. There were headwinds, and the flight lasted nine hours. By the fifth hour, the pain in his hand was beyond the reach of pills, champagne, or the solicitous attention of the crew.

"A pillow," said one of the stewards, and Jack put it under his arm. Then another. And he prayed that he would pass out. They would arrive in America early in the evening of the ninth, a Saturday, and the only way he could get to see a doctor was to go to an emergency room. He knew what that was like on a Saturday night in New York City.

On his way home, New York City grew in his thoughts: his education on the streets, his determination to succeed and his career as a cop. He drifted in and out of a twilight of half sleep, remembering the one particular stakeout that changed the course of his life. It's not every life that has such a sharp, clear-cut moment, even more rare to be able to locate and pinpoint the defining instant, but out of the flickering effects of the liquor and the drugs, Jack was able to become again a plainclothes New York City policeman teamed up with Moe Berger. It was a summer night—August of 1981—and it was his own personal turning point. He could have become a high chief within the department, or remained one of those outsiders who peck at the flaws like hawks. It was a conscious choice.

He was somewhere over Greenland when he found himself parked around the corner from a Manhattan dope den. Nineteen-eighty-one was a golden year in his professional and personal life. His wife, Natalie, had not yet been struck with the cancer that would kill her, and his career was on an upward track. A friendly inspector whispered in his ear that if he played his cards right, he was marked for quick promotion. The powers of the department had placed an asterisk next to his name in their short list of future commanders. All he had to do was to avoid mistakes, or, as his mother had told him when he was a little boy, "be nice."

But the command scouts had failed to detect that streak of stubborn defiance in Jack's nature. Sooner or later, it was bound to show up. As it turned out, it appeared on that day in the summer of 1981 when he and Moe were cruising the streets of upper Manhattan, with no particular destination. As cops do, they routinely scanned the street for thieves or burglars. Out of the corner of his eye, Jack saw an old junkie in desperate withdrawal, bouncing up and down in a doorway on Amsterdam Avenue. "You never know," said Jack, who parked the cruiser and approached his old snitch, while Moe stayed in the car.

After a few moments, Jack came sauntering back, got in the car, started it up. It was two blocks before he spoke. "That's Jose," he said. "Just got out after eighteen months at Riker's. Stone junkie, but tame, you know? He steals car radios. Can't stand violence."

They were driving south at a slow clip. Moe let Jack tell his story in his own time.

"My man is clean, but he does not want to go back to the joint—not before he has a chance to party a little. So, in exchange for some time, he said he would give me a world-class dope den."

"When you say world-class, are we talking Western Hemisphere or truly global?"

"A supermarket that feeds five hundred addicts a day," said Jack.

Moe whistled.

If true, it was one of the biggest drug markets in Manhattan. So, for the next two days, Jack and Moe circled the abandoned building that Jose fingered as the A & P of dope, on 110th Street. There was no doubt about it—lookouts on the rooftops, guards prowling the streets, and a steady supply of folks who arrived at the fortress in a state of high anxiety and left with that familiar air of calm.

They sat in the unmarked cruiser watching the watchers watching them. The unmarked car was as conspicuous as a blinking light. "You know what's funny?" said Jack.

"Words that start with a 'K,' " answered Moe.

Jack ignored him. "What is funny is that nobody seems concerned about cops. I mean, they know we're here, but those lookouts and guards don't give a shit about us."

"I know what you mean. Sort of offends your professional pride."

"They're here to guard against rival gangs. That big, fat guy with the MAC 10 has been eyeballing me since we parked here. He's saying 'Fuck you' with his eyes."

"He can't talk that way to us!"

"These guys act like they got immunity."

Jack and Moe marked the lookouts, the strong points and the escape routes and were already counting the commendations they would win for this one. This was a king-sized drug market. Bound to be promotions and pictures on the front of the *Daily News*.

Jack and Moe went back to Borough Command to ask for backup in order to stage a coordinated raid on this massive drug operation. They met an embarrassed silence, a clearing of throats. They were told to forget it. This was a Narcotics Task Force operation, not to be touched.

Jack couldn't believe it. Moe could. He tried to explain it to Jack. This was the way it worked with the CIA who protected

Colombian drug cartels, and it worked that way with local branches. The Narcotics Task Force gave immunity to chosen drug dealers in exchange for cooperation. The dealers were supposed to turn in the high-level suppliers. Mister Bigs. Only they never gave up any Mister Bigs. Instead, they gave the Task Force a few pathetic low-level dealers. Meanwhile, the supermarket continued to flourish.

Ideally, the cops were supposed to get the better end of the bargain. But in the corrupt and greedy eighties, cops needed cash and became partners with drug cartels. They skimmed off mortgage payments and swimming pools and tennis courts and annuities.

Jack and Moe listened to their Anti-Crime Task Force commander, the borough commander, and the Narcotics Task Force commander, who all issued strict orders against interference with the 110th Street drug market. The A & P, they all agreed, was vital to win the war against drugs. Jack had a more cynical version. He was convinced that envelopes filled with cash flowed through the police command with the exact same regularity as the dope flowed through the city.

Fuming, Jack and Moe left Borough Command, had coffee, and were unable to speak. Then, without a word, they knew what they had to do. They got into their unmarked cruiser and drove to the drug den. They circled the block once, twice, three times. On the fifth circuit, Jack, who was in the passenger seat, picked up the radio and called in a "10:13," the signal for a cop in trouble. He gave the address of the drug den. Both Moe and Jack knew that the call would bring down every sector car in the borough of Manhattan, as well as every special unit on the street. Cops would drop a mother in the middle of childbirth to answer a 10:13. It was the one radio call that never failed to draw an instant and all-out response. The reason was simple: cops who heard the call of a cop in trouble were putting money in the bank; they wanted everyone to come when they were in trouble.

Parking around the corner from the drug market, Jack and

Moe waited less than a minute before the first cruiser came
screaming down the wrong way on a one-way street. They
looked at each other and smiled, put the dome light on their
unmarked car, and went roaring in with the Marines. The
dealers never knew what hit them, but a hundred cops closed
in from all sides. The lookouts with their street automatics ran
for their lives. The guards threw down their MAC 10's and got
on the floor with their hands behind their backs—they had
been through this before and knew the arrest procedure. And
the dealers in the empty apartments of the abandoned building, who thought that they were protected, were caught red-
handed with dozens of kilos of cocaine and heroin.

It was the perfect answer to the obstructed raid. Jack and
Moe knew that the swarm of precinct cops and the special
units who'd respond to the 10:13 could not ignore the flagrant
drug violations taking place right before their eyes. The protected market was closed down for good. It became a famous
raid, for which the Task Force claimed credit. They told the
media that the raid had been a meticulously planned operation, with split-second timing and steel-trap execution. Then
they laid out the confiscated bags of dope and weapons on long
tables for the benefit of the newspaper and television photographers. They ran the handcuffed dealers through the "Perp
walk" for the benefit of the reporters. And the district attorney
and the mayor and the Task Force commander held a joint
press conference, calling the raid the largest victory in the
never-ending war on drugs.

Jack and Moe were not allowed near Borough Headquarters. They were sent home while the brass and politicians took
the credit for the raid.

It was that one act, that stakeout, that decided Jack's career.
He couldn't be trusted. No one could prove he radioed in the
phony 10:13. After all, it was a major drug bust and calls were
flying left and right, and in the excitement even veteran cops
tended to get excited and overstate the case.

But the commanders knew whom to blame. Very quietly

the asterisk for quick promotion was removed from the name of Jack Mann. He took his place on the outside looking in.

"We'll be landing in ten minutes," said the stewardess, touching Jack's bad shoulder, awakening him with a fresh bolt of pain.

"You think I could get a wakeup glass of champagne?" he asked.

The stewardess shook her head. "All out," she said. "Sorry."

Jack could see America coming up outside of the port window of the airplane. There was the Statue of Liberty, and floating nearby was an oil slick making its way into the Hudson River from the storage tanks in Bayonne.

7

On Thursday, the seventh of February, Nora was called into the closet-sized office of the proprietor of the bookstore where she worked on the Upper West Side of Manhattan.

"Listen, Noora, I gonna have to save some money," said Pedro Gomez, the owner of the secondhand bookstore on Broadway at 112th Street. The bookstore specialized in textbooks, catering to the students at nearby Columbia University, but had fallen victim to the collapsing dominoes of the economic freefall.

The owner ran his hand across his mouth, and shook his head miserably. "Business is very bad," he said. "Very bad. I may have to let myself go." He giggled out of sheer nerves.

He didn't have to tell Nora how bad business had become. She was the cashier and bookkeeper and knew the exact size of the gap between operating costs and profit. It wasn't bad management—Pedro worked long hours and watched the merchandise like a hawk. It was simply bad times. The whole economy hovered between recession and depression that winter as the Americans waited to hear about the savings and loan industry or the Middle East battlefront or the domestic interest rates. But the economy was inconsolable. Even when the war news was good, it couldn't seem to rally the public's faith in hard goods, and business continued its long, painful slump.

"I understand, Mister Gomez," she said, smiling.

She liked Mister Gomez. He was a rare gentleman who respected her work ethic, as well as her privacy. She felt bad for him. He was a faithful family man, thunderstruck by the failure of the American dream. He had worked for years as a building superintendent, saved every penny to buy the store, and now was watching it die.

"I don't know what else to do, Noora."

"It's fine, really. But what if I continue to come in and help out?" she offered. "You don't have to pay me until things pick up and you can afford it."

"No! No! No!" he said angrily, and she realized that she had offended his sense of manhood. "If I can't afford to pay you, I'm not going to take advantage."

She couldn't tell him that she didn't need the money, that the job had come as a life vest when she was drowning in self-pity. She had arrived in America full of wild, unfocused wrath.

The only tangible plan she had was to find her brother, Michael, who would instruct her and help her take her revenge on the people who killed her child. So far, she had had no luck. She had tried to make contact—going out to the Queens pub called the Shebeen where there were IRA sympathizers who might know how to reach him. But the pub was run by a new owner, Jerry Callan, and he said that he didn't even know if Michael was back in America. Nora asked him to keep his eyes open. She said she would check in from time to time in case Michael showed up.

If she couldn't find Michael—and he could make himself vanish when he wanted—she would act on her own. By now she was certain that the Mafia and the murder of Seamus were connected. Someone sent them to Ireland and arranged matters so that Jack would be away. Someone clever and cunning and unscrupulous. It had to be some Mafia kingpin who wanted his filthy money back, who was willing to sacrifice her son to make a point: no one steals from the mob and gets away clean. Only, she had a point to make herself, and she was determined to find the bastard and pay him his full share of the debt.

She was patient. By heroic acts of will, she slowed herself down and lashed herself to a daily routine. Mornings she got up early and showered before anyone else in the apartment was awake. She took breakfast at a small shop on 100th Street where the counterman came to know her. Her bagel and coffee and orange juice were waiting when she came through the door at eight in the morning. The counterman's name was Tony. He liked the compact assurance of her manner and smiled when he saw her. His was a sloppier, less disciplined life and his attention to Nora was happily free of a romantic dimension. The extra service was nothing more or less than a salute.

After breakfast she walked north to the bookstore and took up her station behind the cash register. The job itself, taking cash, running credit cards through the charge machine, and answering questions about stock on hand, required very little thought. It allowed her to rest.

Except for those moments when she saw Seamus playing in the back of the store; she almost called out to be careful and not pull down the books. And then it would come back to her, that he was dead.

At lunchtime, she walked four blocks to the university. The guards at the gate knew that she worked at the bookstore and let her onto the campus without a student pass. She carried a bag with a sandwich and a container of apple juice. She sat on the steps and watched the students going back and forth to class. Sometimes they held hands with a blissful, faraway look on their faces, and she had to turn away, so poignant and sweet were the lost emotions that came rushing at her. She didn't mind the cold, welcomed it, because the sting reminded her that she was alive, a member of the race.

Sometimes the students shouted at each other in passionate, abstract debate that had no real force behind it. She watched and listened and chewed her sandwich slowly and then walked around, picking up literature from the tables of radical feminists or AIDS advocates or social anarchists who seemed to belong to another place and another time. Even their politics seemed theatrical to Nora. Americans were too lighthearted to be true radicals. She thought that if they really meant it, they would be more . . . worried. But that was the paradoxical fact about Americans—the great mass of the population didn't seem to be capable of serious rage.

For dinner, she ate in one of the Chinese or Mexican or Cuban restaurants that were sprinkled like exotic seasoning along the Upper West Side of Manhattan. She sat at a table, always alone. Occasionally, someone would try to strike up a conversation, send a drink to her table, or make some other clumsy attempt to break through her solitude. She was polite, but resolute. She eavesdropped on the lovers and the friends, the business people and the married couples. The talk was unselfconscious and full of details about American style and habits. She drank it all in.

Afterwards, she would go home and read for a while, avoiding the ever-hopeful landlord, offering, when she could, a consoling word to his martyr wife. When she opened the door to her room, she was overcome by the odor. It was Seamus in his pajamas after a bath, smelling of lemon lotion, his red, bristly hair sweet with shampoo. Then she would lie awake and plot her revenge.

The State Department sent a formal letter, suggesting the closest possible liaison and cooperation with Inspector Timothy McCormick, an expert in counterterrorism from the Irish

Republic, while he was in New York working on a double homicide that seemed to have a New York City link. The Irish Garda, suggesting that this was strictly routine, was determined to prove that the murders in Galway were not the work of the IRA. Thus, a high-ranking, veteran inspector (who'd managed to convince his superiors that it was a worthwhile expense), together with his assistant, were dispatched to solve the case. The official letter was sent to the office of the New York City Police Commissioner, with copies to the mayor. The police commissioner, a man wed to the close-mouthed system of stonewalling everyone who did not carry a New York City police badge, passed the letter on to his chief deputy in charge of protocol, who greeted Inspector McCormick with all the warmth of an ex-husband. He allocated to him and Officer Mattie Nolan an office near the pressroom at headquarters—an assignment which was an open display of contempt and disrespect. Of necessity, a deputy inspector had been assigned to work with McCormick, but the Irish policeman had come to realize that the deputy inspector was under orders to cooperate in the most minimal fashion.

For most of January, Inspector McCormick and Officer Mattie Nolan had been unable to get information about Moe Berger, Jack Mann, Nora Burns—or anyone else who might be connected with the deaths of Detective Berger, young Seamus, and his baby-sitter. McCormick could not figure out why. When the name appeared in the newspaper, and he asked an innocent question about the infamous Don Iennello, the head of New York's most powerful crime family, he got stonewalled. The newspapers seemed to have fuller versions of the don's identity and antics than high-ranking policemen.

When he took Deputy Inspector Bob Reymond to lunch one day to talk about the case, and perhaps learn the reason for the lack of cooperation, he was stunned by the American's cold candor and strange logic.

"Look, Tim, let me ask you something. You ever been down

to court? I mean, the criminal courts, the arraignment parts. You ever take an hour and sit there and listen?"

They were at Sweet's, a fancy fish restaurant at the South Street waterfront piers near police headquarters. Around them buzzed talk of mergers and buyouts and stock options. Inspector Reymond bent over the table so that they would not be overheard. "You ever check out that court scene on Center Street?"

The waiter placed Reymond's red snapper in front of him, then served McCormick's codfish. The waiter was discreet and knew the sound of conspiracy, and so he left quickly.

"No," replied Inspector McCormick. "Never have, although we do have our criminal courts in Galway and I can't think they'd be much different."

Reymond nodded. "Ummm, good snapper!" He wiped his mouth. "Well, you're wrong, my friend. You people have a few bombings up north in Belfast and you think that's a big crime wave. Christ, we got drive-by shootings every night in Brownsville. We got crack killings every single day. The crime here is nonstop."

McCormick nibbled at his fish. He could taste chemicals. He was accustomed to fresher fare. The food in America was bountiful, but lacked freshness.

"Here's what you find here in court. Numbers. Large, relentless numbers. The courts are overwhelmed. The judges want to get rid of the cases. Not just postpone them. Get rid of them. Dispose, is the word they use. And they do it in any nasty way that they can. Some lawyer comes in looking for justice, it makes the judge mad because now he has to handle some complicated defense and it slows down disposal. Some wise guy defendant insists that he's innocent, and it makes his defense lawyer mad. You know why? Because it's gonna make the judge mad and the prosecutor mad and the damn bailiff mad because they won't get a quick disposal. So the defendant, who knows all this shit and may or may not be innocent, is mad, too.

"You know what that means? It means that every single day, everybody walks into court mad. Before the first word is spoken, before the first page on the first indictment is turned, everybody is pissed off at everybody else. They are all pissed because before this day is out, some asshole is gonna say something or write something that will slow down that big, grinding wheel of the criminal disposal system."

Reymond stopped talking and turned his attention to his fish, held up his hand for fresh beers, and allowed the dust to settle. Reymond's concept required some digestion for Inspector McCormick.

"You've fine descriptive gifts," said Inspector McCormick after they were down to the bare bones of the meal, waiting for coffee and tea. "I can see, just from what little time that I've spent here, that it's true. There's a wild anarchy in the air. You have to be a bit mad to live like this, begging your pardon."

"No offense."

The coffee and tea were served, and then Reymond had an urge for a piece of cheesecake. Inspector McCormick was watching his diet for the sake of Mattie Nolan. Something had happened during the assignment. He and Mattie, perhaps moved by the exotic change in climate, or the undertone of risk, had recognized the depth of the emotion between them. It was not something that they could bring out into the open— not with all the danger and high purpose of their assignment— still, their love now had standing. It was an accepted fact between them, not requiring public vows or private declarations. They betrothed themselves to each other through small gestures: Tim McCormick watched his weight and Mattie Nolan took care of his laundry and kept his hotel room alive with fresh flowers.

"Here's the thing, Bob. I don't question a word of what you've said. But here's the part I can't get through my head: it was one of your own that got murdered in London. Moses

Berger. He was a detective! An active New York City Police detective. Now, he was the partner of the fella in Ireland, Jack Mann. It's not just a coincidence—you don't think that. Wouldn't you want to get to the bottom of that? When one of our people catches it, we don't leave it alone. Not till someone's in the bloody box."

Bob Reymond looked around, then said, "Moe Berger, according to the official reports, was killed during a mugging. He was not on official business. He was not acting on behalf of the department. As far as we're concerned it was an accident. Period."

"You don't believe that."

"I believe what they tell me to believe. Weren't you listening to me? The thing I told you about court? It's a microcosm. The police department is the same way. They don't give a shit about Moe Berger or Jack Mann or Seamus Burns. They want to dispose of the cases so that they can retire in good time. Get their pensions without any open questions or undisposed cases on the books. I think we caught that disease about numbers in Vietnam. Body counts."

Tim McCormick held up his hand. "Some milk for the tea," he told the waiter. When the waiter was gone, he said to Bob Reymond, "I don't know what it is in this country, but a man always has to ask for milk with the tea."

He had concluded there was no point going on with Bob Reymond. Reymond was marking time, waiting for his pension. In fact, Inspector Timothy McCormick had come to the conclusion that there was no hope at all of any help from the New York City Police Department, or any other official agency. The death of Moe Berger did not stir a breath of wind with his American colleagues. And they didn't care about Seamus and Pat, or even Jack Mann, for that matter. Inspector Tim McCormick would be able to do his job unmolested by official watchdogs. He and Mattie were on their own, which was the way he preferred to operate. No help and no interference.

The realization had a calming effect on his stomach. He ordered a piece of cheesecake.

She decided. It was time to make her move. The loss of the job forced the issue. On a mild evening in early February, Nora put on her coat. She strolled through the Columbia campus and out onto Amsterdam Avenue. The whole world seemed caught at some ripe moment of transition—not quite daytime and not yet night. The food carts parked outside the gates with tasty hotdogs and shish kebab were starting to pack up as dusk moved in. The day students were heading home and the evening students were starting to arrive.

She headed for Harlem, and when she hit 131st Street, she began to slow down. White people didn't usually stroll in Harlem after dark. Not unless they were police decoys traveling in pairs, or desperate junkies, or plain suicidal.

The street vendors passed her, wheeling their carts back to their sheds, squinting at the odd sight of her. She could feel herself being watched, and she tracked the potential threats as they appeared on the screen of her warning radar. When she saw a police team, she sped up so as not to arouse suspicion. They wrote her off as a junkie hooker who deserved whatever was waiting to happen to her. They didn't look closely enough to see that she was an unbroken member of the middle class.

"Honey, you best get into a cab and go home," said one black woman from a second-story window. "Ummm, ummm." She shook her head.

At 137th Street, a man with a wine bottle in a brown paper bag started laughing. His friends turned to see what he was laughing at, and Nora flushed.

At 138th Street a young man fell in behind her. He was still in his teens, but old enough to know the streets, if she could believe what she read in the newspapers. She kept track of him in the reflection of the shop windows. He had his hands in his pockets as he bounced along behind. She let him get within thirty feet, then, in an unlit portion of the avenue, she whirled, whipped out her six-inch knife, and came at him so fast that he had no time to react. She grabbed his hair and laid the blade flat across his throat.

"If you take your hands out of your pockets, I'll cut you from ear to ear," she said.

"You crazy?" he said.

"Maybe."

She marched him into a doorway and frisked him. She took a small roll of bills, counted it, keeping her guard up. With one hand, she searched through his wallet, inspecting the credit cards and student ID.

"You robbing me?" he asked in utter disbelief. "Oh, man, I do not believe this. Are you going to rob me?"

"Well, you were going to rob me, weren't you?" she said, pressing the blade closer so that he could feel the metal against his skin. He was a nice-looking youth, just beginning to sprout a mustache, and he was frightened. She kept her own face averted.

"I was just walking," he said. "I was curious. White lady in Harlem. What is it you want—dope? You looking for a dope dealer? I can't help you get no dope. I'm a college student."

"I'm not after dope," she said.

"Well, I can't help you with anything kinky," he said.

"I don't want anything kinky," she said.

"What do you want?"

"A gun."

"What?"

"A gun," she said.

"So you'll be able to practice your trade with state-of-the-art technology?"

"You sound like a college student."

"What makes you think I know where to get a gun?"

"They say you can buy one on any street corner."

He laughed and she released her grip a little. He tried to get away, but she grabbed his hair and flung him back, face against the wall. She didn't want him to get too good a look at her. She didn't want him to be able to identify her. The youth was impressed by her strength.

"I need a gun," she said. "I don't need an argument or a lecture on social conditions. I need a gun. I won't tolerate any attempt to try to steal my money because then you'll have to kill me and that will bring down every kind of heat. You understand what I'm saying?"

"You a cop, am I right?"

"I'm not a cop, and I'm not dirty. I just need a gun! It's not going to get anyone into trouble."

"Guns have a nasty habit of getting somebody in trouble," he said.

"This is no joke," she said.

"Okay. I get the idea. You gonna kill your old man? 'Cause if you're gonna waste your old man, I'd suggest poison. Poison is hard to detect, 'less you're lookin' for it. Guns leave holes and cause suspicion. Just academically speaking, you understand."

"I'm really running out of patience."

"Shit! You're running out of patience! You come up here to Harlem thinking every nigger has an arsenal in his hall closet and you're running out of patience?! God, you white people really kill me!"

"I'm wasting my time."

"Hold on. Maybe not." She relaxed her grip a little more. "My friend, Junior, he deals some guns, but, man, they are expensive. What's coming my way?"

"I'll pay what it's worth. Tomorrow. At seven-thirty. Across from the Amsterdam Avenue entrance to Columbia at 114th Street. I will give you one hundred dollars for arranging the deal. I will pay your friend four hundred dollars for an untraceable automatic .25 pistol with five clips of ammunition. It has to be real, it has to be in very good shape, it has to be untraceable. You got all that?"

"I got it."

"And, listen, my friend, I won't be fucked with. Do you understand?"

He nodded.

"Now I'll walk away and you don't look around or try to see my face. I know what you look like and that's enough. I'll watch you and your friend and if I think it's okay, I'll approach you. Remember, if you're there tomorrow, it's one hundred bucks for you and four hundred for your friend, Junior. If you try to mess with me, I'll kill you. If I don't, my friends will. You're a nice kid; don't ruin your life. I just want the gun."

She stuck his billfold and the money back in his pockets, then started to leave.

The youth knew the sound of business when he heard it. He didn't try to see her face or turn when she walked away. He hoped that he could find Junior and work out the deal in time to meet the lady on Amsterdam Avenue. After all, he could use the money for tuition. It was going up every day at City College.

8

Tuesday, February 12, 1991

The chemist could be trusted. That's what the contact swore up and down: this was a stand-up guy who'd suffer burning coals before he'd give up a customer. They could put out his eyes! That was when Michael knew that he couldn't trust the contact or the chemist. Michael understood that everyone broke under pain. The only variable was the amount. Because of what he had had to go through for this mission, he had even come to recognize the canker of unreliability in himself—a pulse of conscience, midnight doubts. An operational hesitation that only he could detect, but that would one day be fatal.

Michael trusted no one. Not even himself, now.

The chemist's lab was on the fringe of Staten Island, in a shack under a web of bridges and overpasses, on a dry spit of sand in a marshy wasteland. The blur of toxic odors coming from the leaky oil storage tanks and the burning landfills and the illegal dump sites masked whatever noxious potions were whipped up by the chemist.

"Call me Waldo," he said cheerfully, ushering Michael into a soft chair. "It's not my name, but I like to be called Waldo." After they were done with the introductions and were drinking coffee from glass beakers, Waldo confided that he had previously made a nice living as a consultant to amateur drug dealers. But, like everyone else, the drug dealers were becoming more and more difficult and violent, and Waldo preferred another line of work.

"You know something? They don't even know how to cut the dope," he said with professional disgust. "And you can't teach them. I blame the schools. Kids come out of high schools with a diploma and they can't spell. I tell them two parts of boric acid to one part of this or that, and they try to write it down. You should see, like spiders crawling on a page. I saw one kid, and you know what he wrote? He wrote: 'Por it, Sid' when I said boric acid. Pathetic. They come out of school and they're illiterate. I'm telling you, this country is going to the dogs. If we don't straighten out the school system, we're gonna be in big, big trouble."

He was a man well up in his sixties with thick glasses and a fringe of white hair. Under his white smock he wore a clean shirt and a plain blue bow tie. The bow tie seemed to Michael a sign of character. He looked bookish, like a strict and prim teacher. It was said that he was smart enough to hold down a science chair at Princeton, and Michael could well believe it. But Waldo preferred the open market. That's what he told Michael. This way, he had his own hours, answered to no one, and spent as much time as he wanted taking vacations, traveling. But even in that, he could not escape the fact that he was an outlaw. "The wife and I went to Hong Kong last summer. Great food. Great scenery. One of my customers wanted me to look him up, you know? Inspect his lab, see the business. But not me. I don't mix business and pleasure. Great restaurants in Hong Kong. You ever been there?"

"I try not to mix business and pleasure as well, Mister Waldo. So if we could . . ."

"Oh, sure, sure," said the chemist.

"Don't take offense."

"No offense. No offense. It's nice to meet someone who has his mind on business. That's me—strictly business."

Waldo took the beakers of coffee, washed them out in the sink, then dried the insides of the containers with a towel. "I don't use the paper towels," he said. "Environmentally unsound."

"You're an environmentalist," declared Michael.

"You work around here, you see what we're doing to this planet. A shame. A real crime. Oil spills. Rubber fires. Landfills that will burn until the end of the twenty-first century." He shook his head. "Put a little back, that's what I say. I hope you don't use paper towels."

The chemist carefully flattened out the moist cloth dish towel, hung it over a wire near a Bunsen burner to dry, and sat down again. "Now, what can I do for you, Mister Michael?"

"I need something special," began Michael cautiously.

"You wouldn't be here if you didn't. You come with the best recommendations. My own son-in-law couldn't come with better recommendations."

Michael had received explicit directions to the lab, which was at the end of a dirt lane. His rented car was parked outside, with the trunk backed up to the door. "I'll be right back," he said, then went out, checked to see that he wasn't being watched, and brought the box from the trunk back into the lab. He laid it down on an empty table and made certain that the door was locked.

The chemist came over and peered into the box. Nodded. "Fire extinguishers," he said. "Industrial type. CO_2. Uh-huh."

"I think that the carbon dioxide can be taken out of these two gadgets," said Michael.

"Uh-huh, uh-huh. Nothing easier. Matter of fact, we could use it on some of the tires burning in the meadows. Won't put them out—nothing will, they'll burn forever—but it won't hurt."

Michael smiled. "I'd prefer if we could be a little more discreet. You could empty them out here." He looked around the immaculate lab hidden behind bars and locks, reinforced walls and doors, undetectable in these acres of debris.

"Nothing simpler," Waldo said. "So now you got empty cylinders. Now what?"

"I want you to put something else in them."

"Cocaine, am I right?"

"No. Not drugs."

"Thank God for that. So what are we gonna put in these empty cylinders?"

"Serin."

The chemist was stunned. "That's a nerve gas!"

"That's right."

Waldo stood away from Michael. He took off his glasses and wiped them with a handkerchief he kept in his back pocket. Then he looked at the cylinders.

After a moment, Michael asked: "Can it be done?"

Waldo looked up, and his face had grown more serious. "Of course, it could be done. It's very dangerous, but I could open up the cylinders, put a capsule with a Serin charge inside and have it work on the same release principal as the fire extinguisher. That's all very possible. How long would it be stored in the container?"

"A few months," Michael said, not willing to disclose too much about his plan.

Waldo nodded. "Possible. Possible. You have to know how to handle that stuff. Very dangerous. Very unstable. If it gets loose, you could wipe out Newark. Not that wiping out Newark is such a bad idea."

"How soon can you have it done?"

"Depends. Actually, I could get ahold of some on the commercial market—they use it in dyes. But I'd have to be very careful so that it wouldn't be traced. I wouldn't want to attract unwanted attention. I assume you want this kept between us."

"That is an essential part of the deal."

"I understand," said Waldo, who stared with deeply sober interest at the fire extinguishers. "I could assemble them myself, but that would take a few weeks. I would have to be very careful. Very careful. You understand how deadly this gas is? A drop, not even a drop, a particle of moisture can kill instantly. If you released the contents of both cylinders, my God, you could kill hundreds of people."

"I won't need a protective suit for myself."

"That would be dangerous. You should have one, just in case. There could be an accident. It could release in transit. Better to have a suit. Even if it's going to be used by remote." He looked up. "It will be very expensive, my friend."

"Besides the expenses for material, what would be your fee?"

The old man thought for a moment. "It would cause great destruction, you see, so that the police would be looking for anyone with the technical expertise. Very few people would know where to begin. The police would lock up anyone with a chemistry set. I would have to have enough money so that I could vanish completely."

"I'd insist, Mister Waldo."

"So, for making all the arrangements and disrupting my life, such as it is, I would have to have a minimum of $150,000," he said, and his voice trembled.

"Let's say $200,000, including the expenses."

Waldo was so impressed by the sum that he put out his hand, then hesitated when he realized that the hand he was about to shake would be thick with blood.

Michael had brought in a small attaché case. He opened it and handed it to the chemist. It had one thousand hundred-dollar bills inside. One hundred thousand dollars impressed Waldo, who shut the case, and locked it in his safe.

"I'll have the balance when you're done," said Michael.

He wrote down the phone number of a booth on Hudson Street in Greenwich Village. "Call me here in a week. Eleven in the morning. Exactly. If the phone is busy, keep trying. If it doesn't answer, keep calling every day at the same time. Now give me a date when I can count on delivery."

"I'll call. We'll talk. I can promise it, let's see, on March sixteenth," Waldo said. "It's Saturday, the day of the St. Patrick's Day parade. The police will be distracted."

"And after that we will not see each other again," Michael said. Waldo nodded. "I cannot stress too much that this is a secret," Michael continued. "No one must know about this. No one. Not the people who sent me here. Not your wife. Not your son-in-law. No one on God's earth."

For the first time, Waldo showed an appreciation of what he was up to, as well as a flash of temper. "Do you think I'd *want* anyone to know?"

It was fifteen minutes until airtime and the "talent" for the local television news program were wandering backstage, reading to themselves out loud. This was the standard practice for on-air news performers who had to calculate stories in broken heartbeats of time. Suddenly, the chorus of fires and basketball scores and war updates was interrupted by the voice of soundman Max Gross, who pushed his way past the high-tempered sportscaster, the always-insincere anchorman, and a half-dazed correspondent.

"Where is she?" cried Max, who knew very well where she was; his outcry was the foghorn blast of a battleship under full steam, clearing the channel. The program director looked up from his notes just as Max Gross, too senior to fire and too beloved to hate, knocked them out of his hands to scatter over the set.

Bonnie Hudson, who had reached her early thirties with a composed indifference to her lush feminine appeal, gritted her teeth whenever she heard herself referred to as "the Channel 9 Weatherwoman." As Max Gross crossed the studio floor looking for her, she was in her usual spot between newscasts— bent over the "A" wire of the Associated Press. This was the teletype printer that brought the crime news straight from the cop shop. Police headquarters. After five years of trying to master the theatrical bubble of delivering television weather news, she still cherished a wild hope that one day she would once again cover crime stories, the way she had when she was a police reporter for the squeamish tabloid *New York Newsday*. She missed the great soap opera of family massacres and all-out car chases—the city's riotous and rampant passions spilling out into the streets. She wanted to sit again on the electric edge of all-night poker games at police headquarters, waiting for the alarm bells of big-time crime stories and the city bursting at the seams.

Not that she was completely ungrateful to television. During her stint on the air, her salary had been boosted to six figures, and her following in what was designated as the tristate area had blossomed from a high-cult lunatic fringe to a trendy mass, all of whom repeated as a kind of urban mantra her daily sign-off, "Hey, it's only weather!" She got good tables at the best restaurants and seats for shows and ball games, and all the rest of the celebrity perks. What she missed was the grit of hanging around with men who didn't wear makeup to work.

She was late for her own makeup and she had not even glanced at the weather wire. She had no idea what the forecast was going to be tonight, although it was drizzling a cold rain when she came to work—a fact which, according to her own personal view of weathercasting, was a vital clue to outdoor conditions. Her suit was wrinkled and her hair was less than kempt, but by the time they hit the air with her segment, she would at least have run a comb across her scalp.

She looked up and Max Gross stood there, gasping for air. He smiled and nodded, then pointed to the fire door. There, his left arm in a cast, looking wet and wounded, was Jack Mann. Bonnie dropped the piece of wire copy and ran across the studio, scattering the program director and the anchor and the sportscaster and the dippy correspondent, who jumped out of her path, having been run down once already.

"You son-of-a-bitch!" she said, staring up at him, her fists clenched. "You dirty, rotten, miserable, ratfuck, son-of-a-bitch prick bastard!"

He didn't say anything. Just smiled. Then he opened his arms and she folded herself in his embrace, closing her eyes. It had been almost five years since they had seen each other. She was starting out as a weather forecaster and he was still a working cop. They worked together on a story, and although tender feelings were aroused, he was married at the time and far too honorable to make a pass. By the time the job was over, his wife was dying, and whatever romantic opportunity there had been, had passed. They had gone their separate ways.

"Hey, we gonna get a weather segment tonight?" asked Harvey Levy, the managing editor, as Bonnie rested in Jack's embrace.

"She'll be all right," Max Gross said, watching from a fatherly distance. "Give her a minute."

With his good hand, Jack stroked Bonnie's hair. "You wanna get coffee after?" he asked.

She nodded. There were tears in her eyes when she looked up. "Moe was killed and you were shot and I thought you were dead! Every time I tried to get some details, all I got was bullshit."

"I'm fine."

"I'm not," she said, and she broke away to glance at the weather wires that Max handed her and submit to the pancake of the makeup man and the hairdresser's comb.

"Wait for me!" she cried to Jack, as the stage manager and news director led her to the set.

"Now for the weather with our own perky weathergirl, Bonnie Hudson," said the ever-bubbly anchor, Chuck Childers. "What have you got for us, Bonnie?"

"Contempt, Chuck."

The camera came back on his red face, and he forced himself to laugh. "That Bonnie!" he quipped.

The weather map came up on her left, as it always did, but she was disoriented and she pointed to a picture of Donald

Trump in a visual on her right and said that we were in for a bad cloudburst.

"You better take an umbrella," she said. "But that's no good, because it's gonna be pretty windy and you'll blow ten bucks, unless you have one of those expensive Bloomingdale's umbrellas, and then you get into major debt."

She looked over, saw that she was pointing to Trump, turned to the camera, smiled, and said, "Like him."

Chuck Childers was leaning back in his chair grinning. Bonnie turned to the weather map. "Now that we've caught up with the latest Donald Trump financial update, I can tell you that the weather is no different. Lots of wind, lots of wet, temperatures in the midthirties, which isn't so bad considering that we're in the midst of winter and should be huddling near stoves and drinking hot chocolate. As for the five-day forecast, it's gonna be cold, cold, cold, cold, colder. But, hey, it's only weather. Chuck?"

She always made it sound like "schmuck." At least, that's the way he heard it.

"Thanks, Bonnie," he said gamely, slightly pissed at her quick recovery on the Donald Trump visual.

There were few customers at Rusty's bar on Third Avenue and they found a table in the back. They hadn't spoken in the cab over.

They ordered beer and were left alone by the waiter, who restrained himself from saying, "Hey, it's only weather."

Bonnie sat back and ran her eyes up and down Jack in the dim light of the bar. "You got old," she said finally.

"That's what happens," said Jack. "Wait around. Couple of years, you'll be old, too."

Bonnie was hungry and waved the waiter back to their table. She wanted a cheeseburger and fries. Jack ordered ribs. Rusty's was famous for ribs.

Jack filled in the details about what had happened with

Seamus, but she seemed to have a rough idea already. "They were after the money," said Bonnie.

"How do you know?"

"I kept in touch with Moe."

"He spoke to you?"

"We had dinner before he left. I've kept track of you through him."

"He never said anything."

"I asked him not to."

She smiled and started packing away her food. He had always admired her appetite, and he took some pleasure just watching her eat.

"You gonna be alright?" she mumbled through a mouthful of meat and cheese and bread and ketchup.

He looked at the cast on his left hand. "Hafta find a doctor," he said. "Orthopedist."

"Does it hurt?"

"Only when someone asks me if it hurts. I'll be okay, if my Irish doctor isn't a quack."

"We'll find an American quack."

She went back to her beer and her fries and they were quiet for a moment. Silence was never awkward with them, and Jack found that amazing and comforting.

"Do you know where to find Nora?" she asked.

He shook his head. "Christ, is there anything you don't know?"

"I don't know where to find Nora."

"How the hell do you know about Nora? Oh, yeah. Moe."

"There's always a woman between us," she said, smiling. "There was your wife and after she died there was Nora."

He nodded. "Maybe I'm afraid of you."

"You think I'm gonna whack your arm?"

He laughed. He couldn't manage the ribs with his bad hand and Bonnie cut up a few pieces for him. He still didn't have much of an appetite, what with the pain pills. He ordered another beer.

She found herself being shy.

"I can still talk to you, can't I?" he asked.

"Only if I know what's going on. Just don't talk down to me. But, yes, I like the sound of your voice."

"I'm worried about Nora."

"You call that talk?"

He shook his head. "I think she's out of her mind with grief. Seamus's killing drove her over some edge."

"Somebody killed my kid and I'd be tough to live with, too. Not just my usual hormonally impaired."

"Yeah, but you don't know her. She's really in a very dangerous frame of mind."

"So you want to find her. Isn't this where we left off?"

"I have to find her. I can't walk away from her, knowing what I know, having been through what I've been through, and not try to save her from, I guess, a kind of suicide."

She looked confused. He reached across the table. "Look, there's been nothing between me and Nora for a while. Not . . . personal. I'm fond of her . . . We went through a great upheaval together and our emotions got confused. I thought it was love. She thought so, too. Now I know better. It's like being in a war together. People who go through a major trauma tend to exaggerate the feelings that they have. They confuse big emotions with big affection."

"You sound like someone who's full of shit. Some date-raper."

He laughed.

"So, you're not in love with her?"

"I'm fond of her. I admire her. And I can't abandon her . . ."

"You still sound like a prick."

"That's gender solidarity. She knows how I feel. She feels the same. You wanna make a big thing about it, okay, I can understand that."

"You understand shit. God, men are such assholes!"

He looked at her and his face softened. "Women, on the other hand, are perfect saints. Each and every one. You show me someone with female chromosomes and I'll show you a potential saint."

She was eating his ribs. Steaming.

"I have to find Nora and I have to find her brother," he said.

"Michael?"

"How do you know about Michael?"

She looked up, feigning innocence. "Oh, there's an Irish cop over here looking for Nora and Michael, and I have a way with Irish cops, in case you have forgotten." She batted her eyes. "I've had a few private conversations with him . . ."

"McCormick! An inspector, right?"

"The same."

He slumped in his chair, winced when he reached for the last slug of beer.

"Do you have a place to stay?" Bonnie asked.

He shook his head.

"I'll sleep on the couch," she said. "Tomorrow we'll get a famous bone doctor, and then we'll go after our Nora and Michael. One of us is bound to cut out your heart."

9

Monday, March 11, 1991

It took a lot of work to find all there was to know about the city's leading mobster, Don Daniello Iennello, and to nail down a connection between him and the killings in Ireland. Nora spent days inside the public library, cranking through old newspaper microfilms.

It took stamina, rereading star crime reporters and columnists who wrote colorful stories about the don and the two-and-a-half-year-old robbery in which $2,926,000 in cash had been stolen from a Mafia payroll.

The people who lost so much cash have long memories, wrote one of the leading columnists with good contacts within the mob. *You can bet that someone is going to have to account for every penny, and it won't be some graduate CPA, and it won't be like a trip to the IRS, where sloppy deductions are simply disallowed. When you mess up your bookkeeping with the mob, they disallow your life.*

The don, Nora had learned, traveled inside a moving stockade of bodyguards, trailing undercover police teams and lurking photographers. A walk down the street became a parade.

Nora became one more anonymous spectator, gaping at the circus.

The newspapers and local television stations in New York City thrived on reporting seemingly inside accounts of Don Daniello Iennello (known as Joey Sharks because of all the loan sharks who worked for him). He was, according to those self-proclaimed expert crime reporters—who were hired like retired generals or academic economists to inform the public about the Byzantine crime world that was beyond normal human comprehension—the most important Mafia kingpin on the East Coast. He controlled gambling, prostitution, loan sharking (of course), protection rackets, and the distribution of dope in rich chunks of Brooklyn, Queens, the Bronx, and Manhattan. A hometown duke. And besides, his crimes were never depicted as anything truly sinister; this was merely a half-tamed neighborhood character who'd happened to strike it big by working the shady side of town. A winner of the underworld lottery. The public got a kick out of the way he thumbed his nose at the government and the way cops seemed to go out of their way to grovel and smile at him and show him something approaching the proper amount of respect.

Just being that prominent, with his picture in the newspapers every other day and his lawyers being quoted about the injustices he suffered, was enough to arouse envy among his rivals. The other Mafia dons were as touchy as movie queens when it came to star billing. But Joey Sharks didn't get to the top by being stupid. He was cunning, and he had managed to gull some small segment of the public into believing that, on top of everything else—fighting off rabid grand juries and ambitious prosecutors and vicious Italophobes—the don was seriously ill. He had envy and pity going for him.

It was true that two years back he had suffered a small stroke and still walked with a cane, which he waved menacingly at the police surveillance units that clung to him like anxious parents. They picked him up in the morning when he left his apartment in the Carroll Gardens section of Brooklyn, fol-

lowed him to the social club on Sullivan Street in lower
Manhattan. There, as soon as the door closed behind him, he
tossed aside the cane and took his daily wakeup dollop of two
shots of whiskey.

Although the don was small and thin and approaching his
seventieth birthday, he had the strength of a young dock-
worker. With one swing from his knobby fist, he could (and
often did) knock down the thick young men planted around
him. And he had more than enough energy to satisfy the string
of bubble-gum chewing young blondes who were left for him
like complimentary fruit in various hotel rooms around town.

If strength and cunning were not enough to protect his
dukedom, he was also ruthless. When he detected a threat, or
merely felt vaguely uncomfortable around an associate, he had
the man killed. No hesitation. No appeal. And no regrets. *Bing!*
Bodies with single bullet holes behind the ear turned up with
clockwork regularity in various empty lots and abandoned
cars from Throgs Neck in the Bronx to Bath Beach in Brooklyn. The newspaper and television crime specialists would
cover the murder, then speculate about five different possibilities for the rubout: "There are some people who say Tommy
Telephone was killed for blah, blah, blah, and others who say
it had nothing to do with blah, blah, blah, but might be connected to some unknown past grudge."

That was safe, because there always was an unresolved
grudge with these gorillas. The post-doctorate crime reporters
would cover the funeral, narrowing the possibilities for the
murder down to two or three, based on unnamed, but "reliable" sources—usually some overwhelmed police lieutenant
who spent his days updating a big, impressive genealogical
chart covered with pictures. Some of the faces were covered
with red *X*'s. The *X*'s, the police mob expert would explain
to the thrill-seeking reporters, represented death. But the "reliable" sources were just as baffled as the crime reporters,
reading the meaningless reports from the surveillance units

and listening to locker room gossip. The truth was they had no idea who was doing what to whom or why.

Of one thing they were all certain: Joey Sharks, the don, was getting away with murder.

Nora had read seventeen library books about the growth of the Mafia in New York, and the status of the crime families who ran everything from construction to City Hall. They all fingered Joey Sharks as the most powerful don. She scoured the newspapers and memorized the quirks and habits of the don and his chief bodyguard, Benny-the-Blinker. She knew that the don spent the mornings counting his cash in the Sullivan Street social club, then issued commands which were secretly transmitted by Benny in person because every phone within a mile radius was tapped by one or another federal, state, or city strike force. The don had lunch at Pepino's, a small, family restaurant on Carmine Street, where he ate pasta and fish (he was wary of cholesterol—the don took no chances of a silent hit on one of his arteries) and then dallied in one of a dozen hotel rooms with one of a handful of willing Mafia maidens.

He had dinner at Scargulio's, a favorite also of the Manhattan District Attorney, senior police officials, and overpriced lawyers. Joey Sharks had his own banquette in the rear of the restaurant. Everyone had their backs to the wall at that seashell-shaped table. Next to him was plunked the catch of the day, the particular creamy blonde with whom he had spent the afternoon. The don had a few unbending rules. He insisted on his privacy, at least for the first fifteen minutes. During that time he and the blonde sat undisturbed by the maitre d' or the waiters, or even his bodyguards or lawyers. From talking to lawyers and court officers gawking with her as she waited on the street near his headquarters—men who liked to boast and shock with their knowledge of the don's intimacies—Nora heard that the blonde's head would disappear under the table where she would do things for the don that his long-suffering wife would never do.

When he was finished, the don would zip up his pants, wiggle his finger for the waiter to bring him a glass of anisette and tell the blonde to get lost. Benny-the-Blinker, the chief bodyguard, would slip her two hundred dollars for cab fare back to Brooklyn or Queens or whatever sour section of New York she called home.

Nora had already consummated her deal for the .25 automatic pistol. At the appointed hour, the college kid from Harlem had shown up with his friend, Junior, who had tried to charge her five hundred dollars. But as the college kid said, she was one tough lady, and if she said four hundred dollars, that's what she would pay. Still, she gave the college kid an extra hundred because she liked him and wanted to help him on his way through school.

In the weeks she had possessed it, she had gotten to know the gun. The gun felt fine and the action worked well and the ammunition looked new. She had no place to testfire it, but she carried the gun and the spare clips in her purse as she followed Joey Sharks around town. At the first opportune moment, she planned to kill him. It was the only thing she could do. He killed Seamus. If not him, someone working for him. Maybe they didn't mean to kill Seamus—because that wasn't a smart way to get their money back—but after thinking about it, there was no other possible motive for what had happened. It was not a robbery. The Garda would have caught ordinary bandits. It was not the IRA. Michael's reputation alone would have blocked that. No, there was no doubt about it: this was an attempt by the Mafia to retrieve their stolen money. She had come to the unmistakable conclusion that Seamus had been murdered on Joey Sharks's orders. She had picked her villain, and it was this thin little rodent who ran most of New York's rackets.

On that March morning, a gray Monday, she paralleled the

don and his entourage as they were making their way to the social club from west Broadway. Suddenly, the hulks were chasing off a camera crew who wanted to film the don in full limp, and the police surveillance units were still absorbed with their coffee. "Now," she told herself, seizing the opportunity the way some running backs sense daylight. The loaded gun was in her pocket. She clicked off the safety catch and stepped off the opposite sidewalk, ready to make a dash. She could get two or three shots in his chest—where they had shot Seamus—before anyone had time to reach her. It would cost her her life, but she didn't mind. In fact, she preferred it.

But as she stepped off the sidewalk, blind to the rest of the world, tires squealed and a cab horn blared in her ear, sending her reeling back in shock. She missed being run down by a breath. The don looked up, muttered something about dumb dames, the police glanced up from their coffee, and the bodyguards came rushing back, pulled by the urgency of the horn and tires. The chance was gone.

She didn't notice a photographer from the *New York Post* who snapped her picture as she reeled back, startled, from the sound of the cab. The picture appeared on page one of the next day's newspaper, twinned with a picture of a surprised Joey Sharks. The caption ran across both pictures and said: LOOK OUT!

Mattie Nolan slammed the paper on Tim McCormick's desk, knocking over a cup of white tea. They had been packing up, getting ready to go back to Ireland, having run out of breath in the chase for Nora or Michael Burns.

"Will you look at that?" he cried, wiping the hot liquid off his slacks.

But he could see that she had the steam up.

"Will you look at that!" she said, smacking her hand on the front page of the newspaper.

The trouble was that the tea had eaten into the paper

and the picture was no longer lucid. "Yes, well, now you've ruined the paper, too," he said. "I seem to be afflicted with spilled tea."

Officer Mattie Nolan stormed across the hall to the press-room and ripped a *New York Post* out of the hands of Billy Spector, the house man covering headquarters. He could see that Mattie was in a state of excitement so he said simply, "Help yourself," as she marched back across the hall.

She laid the paper down, put her finger on Nora's face and waited until Inspector Timothy McCormick made the appropriate connection.

"Good God!" he cried.

"If we're lucky," she said.

He took a moment to read the story.

"We should tell someone," he said finally.

"Who?" Mattie asked. "They think we're dotty already. You want to tell the commissioner? You want to tell the don?"

"Maybe Inspector Reymond," suggested McCormick.

"Inspector—Tim—we're out on a limb here," she said, taking up a wet towel to wipe the stain from his pants. "No one believes us."

He shook his head. She held up her hand to stop him, but he had something to say. "No one believes *in* us," he corrected.

"Well, there's a fine distinction."

"Remember that weather person? What's her name?"

"Bonnie. Hudson."

"She's got a head on her shoulders. You know that Jack is living with her. Did I tell you that?"

"You did not."

"I mentioned it. Not that it makes the least bit of difference. Except to prove a point."

"What's that?" Mattie asked.

"We'd best not trust anyone else with the information. We can find Nora on our own."

"How do you know that Jack's living with her?"

"Oh, I've been monitoring things," he said casually. "When

you were shopping, I went through the building. Talked to some of the neighbors. Nice people. Love to gossip. Seems she's been asking about an orthopedic doctor. Now, she has no broken bones that I can see."

"You didn't tell me?"

"I meant to, Mattie. I didn't want to trouble you if it wasn't important."

"That's not it," Mattie said, flaring.

"Oh, and what would it be, then?"

"You like her."

He was smiling. "Is that jealousy?"

"It is not."

"There's no cause. True, I happen to like the girl, but she doesn't hold a candle to you."

He could see Mattie soften. "The man keeps deep secrets!" she said. "You keep secrets from me?"

"I'm deep, Mattie, dear."

"Now why would you want to follow Jack Mann? Why wouldn't you just bring him in and question him?"

"Well, I wanted him to lead me to Nora. But, most important of all, I don't think he knows where she is. I think he's looking for her. He went to the Shebeen and asked about her."

"Why would he be looking for her?"

"To stop her. To protect her. They've got thick secrets between them, too."

"We know she's after that mobster."

"That's an easy guess. It's no accident that she's out there on Sullivan Street. She was after killing him, for certain. It's what we feared most."

"You mean, Nora has no help? Will Jack be able to find her now?"

Tim thought a moment. "I'm not certain. She's acting alone. With her bloodlines, that makes her about as dangerous as they come."

10

The mob henchman grabbed Nora under the arm and pulled her away from the oncoming cab, then, with a reproachful shake of his head, handed her off to the civilian on the sidewalk who said that he knew her. Michael made certain that the newspaper cameraman had turned back to catch the reaction of Joey Sharks before he showed himself. He didn't want any photographs. He led Nora away from the commotion.

That familiar grim look was on his face, and Nora knew better than to argue with Michael. She'd seen that same expression in Belfast when he was slipping through British checkpoints after blowing up an army barracks, leaving arms and legs scattered like so many blown leaves. She'd seen it in Derry when he was on the run from another bloody operation; that was the one that had cost six toddlers their lives and cost him, finally, his sister's participation in the IRA. She could no longer see the sense of an army that blew up children. She could not, after that, separate the expression on Michael's face when he was in the middle of an action from the torn limbs of the dead tots. That look was a cold, bottomless glare without any heart. And it didn't give anyone else room to appeal. She cited her pregnancy with Seamus, but it was Michael's pitiless eyes that drove Nora from the IRA. Anyone else would have been shot as a wartime deserter. But she was Michael's sister, and they let her go in peace.

It was not so easy to unshackle herself from Michael. He was her brother and he would never let her go entirely. He used her when he found it necessary. In the last botched mission in New York, when she had been working as a barmaid, she'd let him talk her into running errands and passing messages. Thus it was that she'd gotten herself entangled with Jack Mann, as well as the cursed three-million-dollar mob payroll, which she'd stolen with pride for the sake of the orphans. That they would come after the money—all the way to the rough coast of Ireland—was something she'd refused to seriously consider. Until after the death of Seamus.

Nora allowed herself to be dragged away from the social club on Sullivan Street, although she wanted to stop her brother in his tracks and unleash her grief like thunder. She wanted to force Michael to tell her how he found her (although so great was his legend that even she believed in his magic powers to find anyone he wanted) and where he'd been and what had taken the place of family on his agenda. Above all: she wanted him to explain to her how he could have any other thought except exacting revenge for his nephew's murder.

At Canal Street they got on the first northbound train that came along. They were just another couple riding rapid transit in the middle of a workday morning—dangerously steamed at each other—and just waiting for some innocent stranger to fall between them and say or do the wrong thing so that they could both turn on him together.

Neither of them wanted to speak first, and so they let the pressure build as the stations went past. A transit cop walked through the cars, noticed the silent flame, stopped and waited for a moment, as if that would either provoke them or calm them down, then decided that it was some domestic thing. He couldn't deal with them all, not on his salary, and so he kept going to the next car, looking for the easier, less complicated crack whackos.

A one-legged homeless man selling *Street News* came through the car, and a smart-assed Hunter College student said that he was "faking it." Michael put five dollars in the homeless salesman's hand. The student moved to another part of the train.

At Sixty-eighth Street, Michael got off, and after a slight hesitation, Nora followed him. He waited for her, then walked up the long staircase and out onto Lexington Avenue. He led her to a cafeteria on Madison Avenue at Seventieth Street and presently they sat at a small round table, cooling like the tea.

After a while, she put her elbows on the table, looked across at her older brother, and said, "You never sent a bloody word."

He looked around. "I couldn't," he replied.

"Oh? Another mission, is it? Who's it to be this time, Mother Teresa? Is she the next to be martyred on the world stage so that the politicians and philosophers and theologians and editorial writers will get it into their thick skulls that Michael Burns will stop at nothing? Wipe out the planet, if he has to."

His lips didn't move. "Keep your voice down, for Christ's sake."

"Or what?" she said loudly. The two beefy construction workers taking their coffee break at the next table turned around.

"And what the fuck are you looking at?" Michael said, rising out of his chair, ready to squash their hard hats on their hard heads. They were both larger than Michael, both top-heavy from hard lifting, and both had been out on the street long enough to recognize something well beyond their own capacity. They blushed and turned away, looking down.

Michael, unsatisfied, got up, threw some money on the table

for the tea, and deliberately knocked over one of the construction men's coffee cups as he stalked out of the restaurant.

On the street, Nora laughed bitterly. "I suppose brute force
is the only thing that works nowadays," she said. "Lord, did
you see their faces?"

He took her arm again and aimed her west. She went,
helpless under the propulsion of his will. "God, Michael, I
swear, you could frighten the devil himself."

"I do, every day," he quipped as they made their way into
Central Park. "I just look in the mirror."

As they walked, she grew more and more calm and settled
in Michael's protective cusp. She was still furious, but told
herself that it was unfair: after all, he didn't kill Seamus. He
simply didn't prevent it.

"What did he say?" Bonnie asked.

Jack had been to the doctor, who had X-rayed the hand,
tested the motion, and said the healing was going fine.

"I have to get to work on the physical therapy," he said,
looking at the lumpy tissue in his palm, "and work on this, if
I don't want the scar to stay there."

Bonnie pushed away the newspaper, making room for herself, and examined the hand. He was sitting on the bed in her
apartment on Fourteenth Street, and she was still slow with
sleep, still in her nightclothes. One of the big advantages of
working on evening television was the opportunity to sleep
late. She didn't have to be at the studio until five in the
afternoon. It was just past noon.

"What about feeling?" she asked.

"It's still pretty numb. Pins and needles. He said it's very
slow, the nerves grow a millimeter a day, or something like
that, and I have to be patient. Not expect much."

"You can't feel this?"

She bent down and kissed his palm.

"It's hard to tell," he said. "I don't know if I feel it or maybe
I just want to feel it."

She ran her mouth along his hand, then took his fingers in her mouth, one by one, sucking them seductively.

"I have a sense-memory of something; a definite tingle," he said.

"What about this?" she said, her voice grown husky, and she put his hand under her nightgown and rubbed it along her breast. "Do you feel anything now? I know that I feel something."

He bent over, reaching for the strap of her gown, almost gone in Bonnie's half-lidded mood, when his eye fell on the front page of the late edition of the *New York Post* that he'd bought when he got out of the subway coming back from the doctor's office. He'd grabbed it out of habit, without examining the front page, then tossed it on the far side of the bed when he came in. It lay there, unfolded now, with the front page staring back at him.

"Nora!" he shouted.

That jolted Bonnie, who slapped his hand away from her chest and sobered instantly. Jack lunged across her body (causing a momentary misunderstanding on the part of Bonnie), grabbed the newspaper and held it up.

"You're reading a newspaper?" she cried.

"Nora!" he repeated.

"Italian women kill for less," said Bonnie, working herself into a snit.

Jack held up the newspaper, trying to communicate, as if he'd lost all language skills. "Nora!" he said emphatically, showing Bonnie the picture—as though he were trying to make contact with a primitive tribe. "This is Nora!"

She didn't quite get it still, stung by the abrupt interruption of what she clearly thought was her own moment. "You mean to say that you read newspapers during passionate interludes?" she shot back, trying to clear the fog of lust.

Again, he held up the front page. "This is Nora!"

She faced the front page, stared at the picture. "You mean, that's Nora's picture?"

"Yes! Yes! That's her."

"What's she doing on the front page of the *Post?*"

"I wish I knew."

That's when the phone rang.

There were clusters of cardboard shelters like tents in the section of the park where Nora and Michael fell into a kind of rapid, power-walk. An army of homeless, helpless souls had encamped out of sight of the main paths where they would have given offense to the yuppie joggers and been chased by police. For some as-yet unknown reason, they seemed to Nora to be always asleep. Or maybe just pretending to sleep. A way to be undisturbed. Like, let sleeping dogs lie. They were curled on stiff boards under paper blankets, depending on their fetal defenses.

"America!" Michael said with sarcasm, noticing where the bulk of Nora's attention fell.

Nora didn't say a word.

"The streets are paved with gold, they used to say," said Michael, nodding at the Hooverville, with the cardboard box flaps blowing in the wind. "Do you remember? No, you're too young. America, there's the place! The streets are paved with gold. And we believed it. Our Uncle Tommy went off to Chicago to make his fortune and he came back a broken man. This was after the war, in the forties. Late forties. I was just a kid. Sitting on Da's knee and listening to Tom talk about things being no better in America than they were in Belfast. No gold in the streets, but lots of greed and useless work to keep a man poor.

"The whole town was in the room, or so it seemed to me. They'd come to see him. Like he was a celebrity. People climbing the walls to hear how Tom Burns had gone to America and made his fortune and come home to gloat a bit, and why not? Da was sipping on some ale and sucking on a big pipe and I was listening to all the fairy tales of childhood. But he wasn't sayin' anything like that. He was sayin', and I was listening carefully, that the big shots ran the country, just like anyplace, and rode around in great big cars and had mansions in the country with swimming pools in the backyard and they ate beef cooked on outdoor barbecues, never mind the poor bastard workers who were just as bad off as the rest of the world."

Michael and Nora came into a clearing. The ballfields of the meadows stretched out below, clear in winter, with only a handful of vagrants scavenging for empty cans. A police car was parked on a promontory, and the two officers were dozing, not unlike the vagrants in the Hooverville, thought Nora.

"It was amazing," Michael said. "Here was Tom talking about the misery and the struggle and this woman pokes her son—I believe it was Maggie O'Toole, whose husband was a tinker—she pokes her son and with shining eyes, says, 'You hear that, Kenny? They drive around in big cars and have swimming pools in the backyard. I told you America was grand.' "

Nora snorted. Michael smiled.

"I looked at Da and he just winked at me. He knew that the poor bastards just heard what they wanted to hear. Living on dreams. And why not? If you can't dream about making your fortune in America, well, you might as well stay stuck in the Bogside; you might as well join the EEC."

"Well, you heard, didn't you?"

"I did. I made up my mind right then, at the age of six, that I was going to stay in Ireland and fight for my place. There were no streets paved with gold. Not in America. Not any-place at all."

"So you paved the streets with bombs."

"I thought . . ." He paused and Nora was almost touched by his momentary confusion. His voice was lower now. "I don't know what I thought."

He put his arm around Nora. She could feel the pistol in his belt. He couldn't see the one in her pocket. He brightened.

"Listen, Nora, darlin'. What did you think you were doing there on Sullivan Street?"

"Come to pay my debts," she said with a flinty family sound. "I don't like outstanding bills."

"And how do you know you've got the right party?"

She stopped and looked him full in the face. "Oh, it's him, all right," she said with force. "I can just look at the wee man and know that I've got the right one. He's the only one I can be certain had a hand in it."

"And even if you're right, what will you do?"

"Kill him," she said, and he had no doubt that she meant it.

He started walking again. The cops might be waking up, scanning the park for troublemakers. A man and a woman in heated discussion might be stopped with or without a pretext. Cops didn't need a reason. Some scent about them might arouse suspicion. And he had a gun in his belt, and Nora might have anything in her coat pocket.

"I want you to stay out of it," he said.

She shook her head.

"Just for now. Just until I do what I have come here to do. Then I'll help you find whoever killed Seamus. It might be more complicated than that crippled bastard downtown. Now, tell me where I can find you. When I'm done, and it won't be long, we'll do the job together."

"Why didn't you come to the funeral?" she asked. "Or even send a word of comfort, why?"

"I couldn't." His hard voice cracked, and he looked away. They were moving briskly and he picked up the pace. She rushed to catch up. She grabbed his arm and looked at his face. She was wrong. He didn't have the neutral look of a spectator. She could see pain. "I couldn't," he repeated, and she could see that, for him, giving the explanation was like squeezing out a kidney stone.

She gave him her phone number. He repeated it. Memorized it, and started to walk away.

"Wait a minute, Michael." They were nearing Columbus Circle now, where they had their pick of subways, buses, or cabs. He stopped and turned. "I've got another question." He came back and bent close to hear the question.

"What were you doing down there?"

"Where?"

"On Sullivan Street. Where you found me. What were you doing there?"

"I knew you'd be there," he said. "I was there to protect you."

He was lying. She knew her brother. He was a man who stood up straight in a firefight with soldiers, but when he had to tell his sister a bald-faced lie, he shivered and floundered just enough so that she knew for certain.

When he turned and left, she decided to follow him.

11

They were in the bathroom. Bonnie was sitting on the wicker chair, watching him slowly maneuver his safety razor across the rough stubble on his face. She didn't have to get ready since the call from Inspector Tim McCormick had been friendly, but firm: he wanted to meet Jack, not Bonnie. She was boiling with questions she didn't dare ask.

From the mirror over the sink, Jack saw the silent reprimand smoldering in her eyes.

"You look pale," she said crisply, as if she was already counting him lost and listing his defects.

He reached over and picked up the glass of liquor on the sink and emptied it in one gulp.

"That'll put some color in your face," she said sarcastically.

He turned and smiled. Then, going back to his shaving, he opened a gash in his chin, cursed, and plugged it with toilet paper.

"If you want me to go . . ." she began.

"No, sit there," he said. "I think we may be onto something California-mystical here. I'm bleeding and I'm pale. Amazing. You knew it before it even happened."

She rose quickly and lunged out of the bathroom, slamming the door behind her. Then she came back in. Stood there, with her back to the door, her hands on the knob, her eyes rolling somewhere between tears and flames.

"Tell me about Nora," she demanded.

He looked at his face. Bonnie was right: it was pale. And there were secrets sunk into his cheeks. Funny, how he had avoided seeing the lengthening lines and deepening craters that had changed the planes of his face. The long exile from his homeland, which he had recognized only when he returned to New York, was apparent in the sunken sockets of his eyes. Living off the fruits of an ambiguous fortune with the resulting twilight of guilt was there in the face, along with the shadows that came from too much liquor. And Nora was written there, too.

"I don't think I can tell you about Nora," he said, sitting on the lip of the bathtub, hardly aware of the hard, narrow ledge digging into his rump, immune to comfort, or maybe seeking the discomfort. He stared at the wall straight ahead.

Bonnie plunked down in the wicker chair. She asked: "Because she was that . . . significant?"

He couldn't bring himself to say no. Not for Bonnie's sake. But for Nora's.

"You were in Europe," he said in confusion, as if that might explain things. "On vacation. You were away."

"I remember," she replied.

He shook his head. "We weren't even friends at the time. It was frantic for me. I went a little nuts. What did Moe say about it?"

"Moe never told me the full story. He said it was too complicated."

It was. No one knew the intricacies of the drama that had begun in the parking lot of La Guardia Airport on a rainy

125

night in November of 1987, after the IRA had decided to
finance an operation by hijacking an armored car. Unbe-
knownst to the IRA, the armored car had held a three-million-
dollar Mafia payroll.

By the time he'd entered the case, Jack was no longer a cop.
He had quit the department three years before and was working as a private detective, picking up scraps of work. Through
the airport foul-up he came upon the wild IRA plot which was,
in the end, a plan to blow up the Prime Minister of England's
airplane. The leader of the IRA operation was a legendary
figure named Michael. He had a sister who worked in an Irish
pub in Queens. Her name was Nora, and she was useful as a
courier. Michael had won her support by promising to bring
her son to America.

The plan might have worked, except nobody had counted
on Jack, who tossed a wrench into the works. He'd become
obsessed with the case, pursued it beyond any reasonable
limits. For reasons buried in childhood training and a crucial
misstep at a New York airport, he had to redeem himself. It
was a deep, Catholic need.

Eventually, Jack tracked the IRA connection to Nora, although he wrote her off as an innocent bystander. Nevertheless, they became romantically enmeshed. Not knowing the
details of the plot herself, she led Jack to her brother. When
everything fell apart, she fled. Only Nora didn't escape empty-
handed. In the smoke and confusion, she took the disputed
three million dollars—money the mob considered theirs,
money that the IRA lost to Jack, money that she and Jack
would share in operating an orphanage. Jack had followed her
to Galway where he slowly discovered that he had mistaken
excitement for emotion. His passion for Nora had turned into
nothing more than respect for her work.

Bonnie would never grasp it. Not with all its emotional
complexity and facets.

"I'd like to know," Bonnie said in that pugnacious style he found so endearing, "just where I stand."

"In the toilet," he replied, looking around the room.

She started to leave in high temper, but he stopped her. "Just kidding," he said. "Sorry."

The problem was that he did not know how to explain. He thought that she should be understanding, but he was living under her roof, swilling whiskey before noon, and holding out on mysterious secrets. If she didn't trust him, he didn't blame her. But she simply didn't know how desperate his life had become when he left the police department. How unfit he was for the world when he didn't have the authority of a badge and a backup.

"Being a cop does not prepare you for humility," he said. "It teaches you to grovel before superior officers, but that's not the same thing. Most cops are two different people. They lick the boots of the chiefs, and then they go out looking to get even. If they don't take it out on the next poor bastard who crosses them, they take it out on their wives or their kids. Being a cop prepares you for revenge, but not humility."

"I don't understand," she said.

He shook his head. "I'm trying to tell you how lost I was when Natalie died. I thought that I was a grown-up, that I could manage my life, but I had no idea of what a child I was. Natalie had taken care of my personal life—not just doing the cooking and cleaning, but setting the agenda, choosing the friends, deciding how we lived. And the police department set the table for my professional life. I went to work in the morning and it was a job. A job!

"I kept the streets clean. I arrested bad guys. I made people feel safe. At night I came home and Natalie told me about the kids she taught, how terrible life was if you were black. She educated me about the world outside the Irish Catholic limits of the department. She was a Jew, and she had a good heart, and I saw things through her eyes. I didn't want to get into this because I realize that it's painful for you. God! It's painful for me. But all these things gave my life a kind of symmetry. I knew what was what. And then, overnight, Natalie was gone."

"Sounds rough."

"Yes. It was . . . unbearable. What made it bearable was meeting you. We met at the wrong time, as far as getting together. I couldn't be unfaithful to a dying wife. But the thought of you put me to sleep at night and kept me awake in the day."

She was quiet for a long time. Then she asked: "What about the drinking?"

He looked over at the nearly empty glass, picked it up, gazed into it, and came to a quick and resolute decision. "I have just stopped," he said, putting down the glass firmly.

"Not your drinking," she said picking up the glass and draining the last drops. "Mine."

He laughed.

Tim McCormick was waiting outside. He had a copy of the newspaper in his hand. When he saw Jack, he hailed a cab.

"I saw it," said Jack, getting in, grunting at the twinges in his shoulder and his hand.

"How's the mending?" asked McCormick.

The cab started up and Jack let out a sigh as he let the acceleration push him back in the seat. "Oh, there's pain," he said. "Some days, when it's cold, it hurts like hell."

"You can't expect to get shot and not pay the piper," said McCormick.

"How the hell do you know?" asked Jack.

McCormick shrugged, seemed embarrassed.

"You've been shot," guessed Jack.

McCormick nodded. "In Ulster. An ambush. I was taking a course—something to do with counterterrorism. They didn't teach the terrorists. On the way to class one day some young, brave IRA boys—not old enough to shave—they stood up in the road and opened up on the passing car with M16's. Sprayed the car back and forth, then replaced one clip with another and opened up again. I was hit in the stomach and leg. I was out for quite a while. I still have trouble with a thick steak."

They were heading south towards police headquarters. The streets were crowded with pedestrians spilling off sidewalks obstructed with tables where peddlers were selling everything from false Rolex watches to designer knockoffs. Dresses. Ties. Computers. Shoppers stood sideways at the tables, as if they weren't really interested, while the merchants were busy watching for theft. Inspector McCormick never tired of the pace and variety of the New York City street bazaars. He stared out of all the cars and buses that he rode in as he traveled through the city. He didn't like the underground for that reason—you couldn't see the great, moving carnival.

The air was always fragrant with the scent of cooking food from a thousand countries. A World's Fair every day. It was alive with the spiels of fast-talking characters and back-talking natives. The cab was swerving in and out of traffic as it headed down Broadway, while the Indian driver yelled and cursed at pedestrians and motorists in wild, indiscriminate bursts of temper and frustration. The driver didn't pay attention to the conversation in the backseat. There was no point, because it was always upsetting and baffling. The Americans spoke of deals and business and the sorrow of their own individual plight, no matter how blessed they were, and occasionally spewed out hatred of foreigners like himself. They were insensitive to his presence. As he had become, over the years, insensitive to theirs, driving like the wind, as if that would wash the talk out of the air. He only listened for the trigger words that would push his foot down harder on the gas pedal, not realizing that he was becoming, every moment, a diehard New Yorker.

"We should have a society, a social club," said Jack. "The formerly shot."

"Can't," said McCormick.

"Why not?" asked Jack.

McCormick smiled. "Because fellas would die to get in."
Jack groaned.

They reached the headquarters and Jack watched it go by.
He didn't ask. Not because he trusted McCormick, but because he knew that McCormick wanted him to ask. He knew
the tricks and tactics of old cops. His breathing grew heavier.
McCormick's got her, he thought. Somehow, he grabbed Nora
and he has her in a room and she has unraveled. In her
mourning, she has given me up, blamed me for the killings,
and implicated me in the theft of the money. McCormick will
turn me over to the Mafia in exchange for help in solving the
killing. Or, maybe they have caught the people who killed
Moe and Seamus and Pat, and McCormick's going to put me
on a plane back to Ireland. Or turn me over to Michael for his
own revenge.

They turned left after City Hall and ended up outside of
the rebuilt waterfront. This wasn't a spot for the rubber hose,
thought Jack, relieved that he was not about to face some
physical ordeal. He didn't feel up to it. If Tim McCormick was
going to work him over, it would be in the back room of a
remote precinct house. Jack's breathing grew easier. They paid
the Indian driver, who grumbled something—probably a
Hindu curse—and burned rubber as he drove away. McCormick stared for a moment, not quite accustomed to the spontaneous and inexplicable retaliations of New Yorkers for
crimes committed one step back. They were paying for the
offenses of previous passengers.

They entered one of the seafood restaurants in the mall.
Inside, Officer Mattie Nolan was holding a table. She smiled
when she saw them, and Jack could see the uncomplicated
pleasure that Inspector McCormick took in the sight of her
freckled face.

They got through the introductions, and Jack guessed at the
length of the emotional rope between the two Irish police
officers, although he knew better than to mention it. They
were Irish and reticent and would allow the affection between

them to sharpen, like a picture in developing fluid—taking its
own sweet time.

The food came and it was overcooked and overpriced, but
that was what happened at Disneylike reconstructions. You
paid for the sailing ship that never left the pier, and the smell
of the waterfront, even if it was mixed with spilled oil, and the
geometrically cobbled streets and the rebuilt old-thyme shops
that looked too new to suggest anything but a theme park.

"Well, we know that she's in New York," began Jack, breaking the ice.

"We know more than that," said McCormick, staring
glumly at his blackened bluefish. Then he looked up. "We
know that she's found her Mafia villain."

How much did they know? Jack wondered.

"What do you think?" asked McCormick, pumping Jack. "I
mean, do you have opinions about what she's up to, who's
helping her?"

"I don't even know what you two are doing here," Jack said.

McCormick looked around, checking to see that no one was
listening. "It's very simple," he said. "Two children were murdered in a very brutal crime. My chief agreed that it was a
crime that should not go unpunished. And there's another
reason."

"What's that?"

"Well, we wouldn't want you Yanks to get the idea that this
was some homegrown terrorist thing."

"You mean, you didn't want the IRA blamed?"

The inspector nodded.

"And he sent you to America?"

McCormick shrugged. "We're following leads. Nora Burns
obviously has some clues about the murderers. You might,
yourself."

Jack did. But he wasn't going to tell McCormick. His story
sounded fishy. Policeman's intuition told Jack that McCormick was holding back, had other reasons for his presence. He
just wasn't smart enough to figure it out.

How much did McCormick know about the money and the mob?

He'd made all the wrong choices after Natalie died. In an act of despair, he'd quit the police department to become a private detective. It was nothing like he'd thought it would be. Instead of playing Sam Spade and cracking glamorous cases and raking in hefty fees with lush expense accounts, Jack found himself chasing sordid gossip on cheating wives for sleazy lawyers. Or else he was taking orders from half-wit go-betweens who acted as if a former cop hired as a bodyguard was someone you sent out for food. He grew grateful for lousy assignments that took him out of town where he stayed in bad hotels and ate greasy meals so he could pocket some expense money. Overnight, he became poor. From a working cop with a reliable paycheck and a good credit rating, he became a deadbeat who missed mortgage payments and was unable to pay the rent on an office.

It was at that point that the money fell into his hands. The IRA, through Michael, arranged a truce with the Mafia. Nevertheless, the ledger remained open. The ruling mob families honored the agreement with the IRA—allowed the plot to fall apart. But they counted the debt as an open wound. They had been publicly insulted by a gang of thieves who had gone unpunished. They insisted upon full satisfaction, in the course of time.

Revenge. Spite. It was the engine that kept them all moving. The Mafia still wanted their money. Nora wanted revenge over the murder of her child.

"Do you know about her brother?" asked McCormick.
"Michael? I know that she won't speak about him."
"We think he's in New York," said McCormick.
Jack looked shocked. "I really wouldn't know," he said.
The waiter, who had told them that his name was Jason, thus hoping to create a personal obligation, was back smiling

his bright presence and running through the desserts. He seemed a little disappointed when all they wanted was tea. "Don't forget the milk," called McCormick.

"What do you expect of me?" asked Jack when they were alone again.

McCormick bent over the table. Mattie Nolan leaned back, protecting his back. "We want you to help us," said the inspector. "We want you to help us find her."

"Even if I could, why would I betray her?"

McCormick studied Jack's face. He was measuring his man, deciding what was going on behind those kindly eyes.

"You know the girl," said the inspector. "You know where she might turn. We're strangers here. We want to help her. After all, she didn't kill Seamus."

"Why not use the New York police? After all, they have the resources."

"We have Earl Gray, English Breakfast, decaf, blackberry, orange pico..." Jason was back, rattling off the choices because he had been so flustered at their utter disinterest in sweets that he had neglected to present the selection.

McCormick looked at him as if this was another form of New York snobbery—which it was.

"We'll have Earl Gray," Mattie Nolan said.

"Do you have Lipton?" Jack asked perversely.

Jason's face showed first horror, then a slight but unmistakable sneer. "No," he said staunchly, as if he were trying to bear up against this sort of outrage. "We do not carry Lipton."

"Earl Gray," suggested Mattie.

"Something freshly brewed?" said McCormick, coming to Jack's defense.

Jason asked if they would like to see the manager.

"I'll just have coffee," said Jack, turning back to McCormick and Mattie Nolan.

"Caf, decaf or cappuccino?" offered Jason.

"Plain Nescafé," said Jack.

Jason had given up all hope for a tip and marched away in

a huff, intending to call his former employer—the manager of a French restaurant on Lexington Avenue, where he had been appreciated—at his very next break. The recession must be over by now, he thought.

When they were alone again, McCormick said that the New York City Police Department was unreliable. He could not count on them, and neither must Jack.

"What do you mean?"

Tim McCormick and Mattie Nolan looked at each other and silently seemed to decide to confide in Jack. "It is our belief that Moe Berger was murdered," said McCormick. Jack did not look shocked. "It is our further belief that he was murdered on the orders of a Mafia family trying to recover stolen money."

Again, Jack blinked but looked otherwise unshaken. "So?" he asked.

"The people who killed have no scruples. None. They'll kill Nora. You. Me. Mattie. Anyone."

Jack nodded.

"You must help us," said McCormick.

Again, Jack nodded dumbly, unable to absorb it all in a single lunch. But this he knew: he had to find Nora soon.

Watching Jack walk away after they separated, Mattie Nolan said: "I think the man is completely in the dark."

McCormick nodded. "I hope to Christ you're right."

12

From across Park Avenue Nora watched Michael go into the Fiftieth Street service entrance of the Waldorf-Astoria Hotel. She had followed him from Central Park with professional caution, doubling back over streets, boarding buses when she thought he might be suspicious, then jumping off to catch up. She was still good at this business of trailing someone.

Nora had been one of the best-trained trackers in the IRA and knew the subtle tricks of moving smoothly through city streets; as if you were in the water, her handlers used to say, so as not to attract attention. She glided past store windows like a tourist, or kept her head down like someone on her way to work. Nora was proud of the fact that she could stay undetected behind almost anyone. She wasn't sure about Michael, because of his usually high awareness, but he seemed changed now, almost unguarded. As if he didn't give a damn. Had the great soldier of poster-sized virtues and legendary

caution grown unaccountably sloppy, incomprehensibly careless?

Around her on the west side of Park Avenue a crowd had
gathered to witness one of those New York fights that sputter
to life without any warning—or sane or reasonable cause.
Layers of hidden, sullen agendas had simply broken open with
rage. Without a word, the crowd had formed. The spectators'
faces were numb or curled with the contempt of the safely
uninvolved. The blank faces of subway riders, thought Nora.

They bore witness in their warm topcoats, carrying leather
cases, as if some all-out street action would rescue them from
their dreary routine. The fight had gone from shouted insults
to physical menace. The principals were a meter maid and a
woman motorist who was brandishing a cut-down broom handle like a club. The meter maid was black, and the woman
with the club was white, so the confrontation had ethnic texture and some factional rooting began to develop along racial
lines.

"Calm down, lady! It's only a ticket," said someone in a
Brooks Brothers voice.

The white woman was blazing. She had shed her thin mem-
brane of cordial passivity when she picked up the cut-down
handle that she kept under her driver's seat for last-ditch
protection. She was a woman closing in on forty, growing a
little thick around the middle, but not quite ready to submit
to age or fate or the relentless hydraulic lift of a municipal tow
truck.

"Shoot the bitch!" cried someone else in the bundle of
passersby, thinking, no doubt, that meter maids were armed,
or, if they weren't authorized to carry side arms, that someone
in the crowd could provide a weapon. "Shoot, dammit!" The
voice had a black ethnic sound. When Nora looked, all the
black people in the crowd seemed businesslike, well turned-
out, and above such intolerant goading. But she had heard it
plain and the voice sounded like it meant what it said.

The crowd formed a tight circle, like a boxing ring, giving

shape to the battle. A truck trying to force its way east blew its horn and the people in the crowd turned as one and stared the driver down, as if to say that the street fight on Park Avenue outranked his delivery schedule. The truck inched forward anyway, forcing part of the ring to move grudgingly. These were practical people who recognized the physics of metallic truck tonnage against raw flesh. Some messengers on bicycles stopped, walking their bikes around the perimeter for a better view, then stood up on their pedals, grinning at the break in their endless war with midtown traffic. The messengers whistled and cheered and hooted like dogs (the new version of a cheer that Nora found repulsive: "Hooo! Hooo! Hooo!" with clenched fists clawing at the sky). They were not aligned with one side or another—just eager for someone, anyone, to strike a blow.

"Hit 'em!" she heard. "Kill the bitch!" It was impossible to tell whom they wanted dead.

Nora smelled sauerkraut and saw that a man with a pushcart was working his way around the rim of the crowd. There was another man following the pushcart, a man with holes in his head for eyes—an addict enjoying a moment when someone was worse off than he. He was jumping up and down, crying for blood. He smelled of urine and wine, and the steam puffed from his mouth as he yelled for justice and vengeance. Nora was paralyzed by the force and frenzy of the participants, but more than that by the people's quiet, inert hate. They continued to watch with cold-blooded detachment.

The woman with the club made a move, and the meter maid retreated, but she was too late. The club grazed her face, drawing blood, leaving a line that could not be recrossed. Nora identified the car that belonged to the woman. It was a station wagon from New Jersey, a suburban car with mud on its skirts and smudged windows. There were two children in the back-seat—one no older than five; the other, two—their hands pressed against the side window. They were both screaming and crying in the depths of the fear that they had been taught for the dreaded city.

"I told you, I was just dropping off my husband!" screamed the white woman with the club, who knew she had gone too far, but reared back and whacked the meter maid on the arm. Nora could hear the bone crack. The crowd backed off. A howl of pain emerged from the meter maid.

A cop, who had been standing in the shadows of the building, waiting to see if this would resolve itself without his intervention, was roused into action. He plunged through the crowd, radioing for backup as he moved the people out of the way. The woman with the club paused when she saw the policeman, then brandished it anew. "I was just dropping off my husband and she wanted to tow my car away!" she cried, as if the policeman would see her side, recognize the pure innocence of her position, see for himself how easy it was to get caught up in some escalating, irrational nightmare gone haywire, and let her go. But things had gone too far.

"Drop the bat," he said in a flat voice. His next move, Nora knew, would be for the gun. The woman recognized the ominous tone, too, and let her weapon fall to the gutter.

"Should have shot the bitch!" called a voice, and Nora still could not pick out the owner. It could have come from anyone.

The cop had handcuffed the woman and was radioing for the Bureau of Child Welfare to come and take possession of the children in the car. In a while an ambulance fought through the traffic and the paramedics put a temporary splint on the meter maid's arm, which was bent into an odd shape.

"Could I just call my husband?" asked the woman motorist. The cop shook his head. Against regulations. "But he works in that building!" pleaded the motorist. She nodded at an office building one hundred feet away. The cop kept writing in his memo pad as a squad car and a sergeant pulled up, lumbered into the scene, and took charge.

The crowd didn't have to be forcibly dispersed. The drama

was complete. "Show's over," said the police reinforcements unnecessarily, and the people moved on. They had seen it up close—not on the five o'clock news—and would look for it tonight, although, as it turned out, it was too small for the small screen. Just one more outburst on the street. No one shot. No one falling from a building. Only a meter maid with a broken arm and a housewife pushed off the ledge of sanity by urban pressures and stuck with an assault charge. The two screaming kids in the back of her car would end up in the city's stone cold care system until the authorities contacted the husband, who had been one hundred feet away all along. The car would be towed—and dented—and stored on a city pier.

Nora was as dazed by the trajectory and inevitability as the rest of the New Yorkers. She had witnessed a modern passion play and would store it in the dark closet of modern consequences. Pay the two dollars, was the appropriate parable. Never mind whether or not you're innocent or justified: the price of not paying is too high.

Nora shook her head and went into the hotel across Park Avenue. What was Michael doing at the Waldorf? She had noticed the cheap black shoes he was wearing. Not like the carefully crafted brogans he usually wore—shoes, like the rest of his wardrobe, so elegant and expensive that he was unnoticeable. Why was he wearing blue-collar shoes? And plain black pants? She looked at her watch and saw that she had spent only fifteen minutes standing across Park Avenue.

The doorman stationed under the great marquee pushed the revolving door for her, smiled, and saluted. The lobby was crowded with the late lunch crowd and women with Bergdorf Goodman or Saks Fifth Avenue shopping bags. She walked up a small flight of stairs leading to the main lobby, then stopped at a cluster of comfortable chairs and couches in front of the registration desk. That club chair would give her a fine view of the long corridors, yet there would be concealment. She wore a headscarf Michael had never seen, her face was half hidden by a plant, and she held her chin in her hand for further camouflage. The concierge passed by without taking notice of her.

An hour later, a bellboy stopped in front of her chair and handed her an envelope, then turned and left before she could react, deny, or fish out a tip from her purse. Her name was written on the front of the envelope in Michael's handwriting. The note inside was brief.

Meet me in front at 10 tonight.

Four blocks west and four blocks north, two young plain-clothes policemen in an unmarked car watched Don Iennello limp into the Hilton Hotel. Doormen held open the side door under the glare of the don's bodyguards. A passage appeared in the lobby as the don's people ran interference. Tourists were shocked, but consoled themselves that a sick man had to be given some room. They didn't know that they were being pushed around by the henchmen of Joey Sharks.

"It's New York," said a woman from Utah to her blustering husband, who wanted to file a formal complaint with the hotel's management—after all, they also paid good money for their room. His wife grabbed his arm. "Honey, it's New York! What can you expect?"

This seemed to explain matters to her husband. At least it mollified him, and he allowed himself to be pulled away.

Outside, the two plainclothes policemen in the unmarked car watched the commotion in the lobby and smiled at each other. "Who's today's babe?" the one in the passenger seat asked his partner.

"Staten Island," said the older partner behind the wheel, the one who had been on the job for ten years and was beginning to think about Florida, and who was checking his stocks in the *New York Times*. He'd lost thirty points on his main blue-chip stock since the Gulf War began.

"Staten Island" was a relatively new member of the don's harem. She was a hefty blonde with plenty of bounce in her, thought the cop in the passenger seat. He was starting to lose his hair at twenty-seven and he had late-night fantasies about the don's life. The thoughts came as he lay next to his pregnant wife in a Long Island suburb. Staten Island, he was sure, had plenty of bounce and a streak of adventurous wildness. His twenty-four-year-old wife smelled of milk and turned away with Catholic horror at his erotic suggestions. "You been readin' those magazines?" she said.

Staten Island was on the eighteenth floor of the Hilton, dressed in a baby doll nightgown and floating on a chemical bed of uppers, downers, cocaine, and whiskey, ingested incautiously as she waited for the don. She was eighteen years old and dreamt of owning her own boutique, which the don would bankroll in the aftermath of her willingness. She did not believe the stories about his stinginess.

The don took the elevator to eighteen, then walked down two flights to the sixteenth floor where he was ushered into a small room fogged with smoke. He sent all his lieutenants out, and when he was alone with the two detectives, he waved his hands in the air. "Open the windows," he ordered, sitting down in one of the chairs around the cheap coffee table. He gazed at the flower print on the wall and wondered who was running the fashion end of the hotel. He would put people in the pictures, if he were running the joint. Lush women with ripe bosoms and lean, lecherous men. Get 'em started, he thought, if they came in for a matinee like he did.

Detective Sergeant Vincent Manero nodded to his partner, Detective Rocco Valone, who leaped to open the window. But it wouldn't budge. Rocco slapped the frame, but it was frozen in place. Sergeant Manero came over and tried to help, but even the two of them couldn't move the window.

Joey Sharks was scanning the room for bugs and cameras, a habit impossible to break. He muttered, "No wonder you two geniuses screwed up so badly on that little job."

The two of them were grunting so strenuously that the don

feared that they would soon break a windowpane. "Hey!" he cried. "Cut it out, *gimbones!* Open the fuckin' air conditioning. Christ, they hire rocket scientists these days."

He poured himself a tumbler of whiskey from the bottle on the coffee table, drank half, took a handful of salted nuts and dropped them in his mouth.

"I think they seal the windows," said Sergeant Manero.

"Siddown," said the don, and the two policemen looked around, then plunked themselves on the bed. They folded their hands in their laps like obedient students.

"You mind?" asked Sergeant Manero, nodding in the direction of the liquor.

"Help yourself," said the don.

When Rocco didn't budge, the don said, "You, too."

They sat for a while, drinking deep, and the room was thick with tension.

"Now. You had something to tell me?" the don said. The two detectives bent closer. The don shook his head, sighed, laughed. "This fuckin' airport business, it never goes away."

The chinless sergeant got up and walked to the window. He held his hand over the air-conditioning vent and shuddered. "Cold," he said.

"Shut it off," said the don. "But no more cigarettes. I got to save myself." He smiled, thinking of Staten Island bouncing two floors above. Then he stopped smiling. "What I still don't get is how you two clowns fucked up the job. That's what I don't get. A little snatch. Nothing complicated. Two of New York's finest fuck it up! How do you explain that to your grandchildren?"

The two detectives blushed, and looked around for the hidden microphones. "Coulda happened to anyone," said Sergeant Manero lamely. "That guy, Mann, he went for us."

"A simple fuckin' snatch, and we got all the inside dope; we got the mother out of the house so we don't have to worry about her." In spite of the business grief, Joey Sharks was enjoying himself, watching the twisting of the two cops. He hated cops. Always would. He always took pleasure in making cops squirm, even if they did work for him. As far as he was concerned, a cop was a cop. Period. There was no such thing as loyalty or trust. If they betrayed the police department, they'd betray him. In fact, cops were babies when they got caught. They turned in a minute. They wore wires and testified and sang you into the joint forever. Babies! He'd seen them cry like babies. Full of bullshit guilt, wanting whoever was in charge to like them again. There was no class of people who wanted to be liked more than cops. That was why he was convinced that sooner or later, no matter how many oaths they took, he'd have to put one between their eyes. A matter of business. Strictly.

"So, the only one you have to deal with is the fuckin' baby-sitter and you guys screw it up." Joey Sharks shook his head theatrically. "I got guys holdin' doors for me coulda handled it better. And if I have you guys whacked, you know what they'll say? They'll say two highly decorated veteran detectives were found dead execution-style in their own unmarked car."

He laughed and the two cops laughed, but he had made his point. "But, you know," continued the don in an almost contemplative manner, "I'm not a killer." This launched the two detectives' eyebrows. "It doesn't come naturally to me. It's a sign of failure," he said in his best lecturing voice. "I regard myself as a thief. That's my real talent. When I was just a little kid in Bari, I stole fruit to eat. Then I stole money to buy fruit to eat. Sometimes I had to have someone eliminated because they were a threat to my livelihood. I didn't want to get caught and go to jail." He shook his head. "So, once in a while, I had to kill." He leaned closer. "But I never liked it." He fell back in his chair. "Never. It's a very ugly thing. And then you get people coming for revenge and the killing doesn't stop. Stealing, people don't mind. You gotta eat. They gotta eat. They understand."

Sergeant Manero waited until the don finished. When he

was certain that he would not interrupt or offend, he said: "If I may Don Iennello, this Irish inspector they sent over here, he works out of headquarters. We know him. He trusts us." The sergeant smiled. The don smiled, too; it was one more proof that cops cannot be trusted. "He told us that he found Jack Mann."

The don sat up straight. His eyes narrowed. His arms gripped the chair. "This is the same cop who screwed everything up, am I right?"

Both cops nodded.

"He's here, in New York," said Sergeant Manero.

"Kill him," said the don without hesitation.

Manero shook his head. "If he's here, she's here."

"The mother?"

"Nora. And if she's here, we still got a shot at the money," said the sergeant.

The don stopped. The smell of money was like perfume.

"We can get the money," he said, as if it were his idea. "We get this Jack Mann. You two. You owe me. You get him and you work on him. You convince him that he should help us."

"He may be hard to convince," Manero said.

"I gotta tell you how to do your job? You follow him. He takes you to the mother. The mother is dangerous, but this guy, he's gonna help us. You made that other *strunz* break, that Jew."

The two detectives nodded.

"I want the money," the don said. "I don't care who you hafta kill. I don't care how many fuckin' bodies you leave behind. You get me the money, you don't hafta worry about a pension."

"We have a few leads. Nothing definite. But we can get to work on it," said Manero.

The don was sweating—and he'd almost forgotten about Staten Island bouncing two floors above. After an unsatisfactory hour with her, in which he had to smack the pretty blonde until she cried, just to arouse himself, he left the hotel in a hurry. The two plainclothesmen assigned to monitor his movements missed the detectives who sneaked out earlier, but noticed the concern in Joey Sharks's face. "She musta bounced him up against the wall," said the younger one. He was filled with envy.

But the don was not thinking of Staten Island. He was sure something was going wrong.

13

Harvey Levy was trying to make Bonnie Hudson understand just how things stood with her. She hung by a thin thread. He was trying to present the news in some friendly fashion, since he knew that Bonnie had a hair-trigger temper.

"You know, they would like you to use the maps," said Levy. He was head of the news division of Channel 9.

The weather maps had become a sore point between the management and Bonnie Hudson since her return from a brief fling at an even more suffocating network job. No matter how artful or cute the graphics department made them—using pictures of Bonnie in a rainhat or in snow gear or in a bathing suit—she ignored the maps.

Bonnie and Harvey were in his office. Five television sets tuned to five different stations flickered silently in a specially built cabinet. They were lined up in a row where Levy could see them. Bonnie could watch the reflection in the window behind him. It was a dark, long room with plaques and pictures and awards on the walls. Most of the awards were for work he had done as a newspaper editor and represented the only achievements of which he was proud. It was on his last newspaper that he had discovered Bonnie Hudson, whom he regarded as the best of a dying breed—a fierce enemy of all unchecked authority and wanton stupidity. She was also a subtle beauty who couldn't be bothered with endless fussing with her makeup or her hair. "Any reporter who looks well groomed isn't doing the job," was her anthem.

To Harvey, she was a talent who knew exactly how female she was, and precisely how smart she was, yet understood the underlying tragedy that in the male-circumscribed world she lived in, those longitudinal and latitudinal lines would never intersect.

When his own time came and Harvey gave up on the possibility of journalism and left the *New York Newsday* newspaper, he plucked Bonnie from her exile in the police shack where she was being harassed by the shaky bookkeeper-style managers of the paper. They were all careful men who would never grasp her vivid talent nor the obvious reasons why you couldn't name the cops you went drinking with on the expense accounts. Because there were no other openings in the television station, Harvey put Bonnie on the air as a weathergirl (which is what the management insisted on calling her) and to her shame, she was good at it. She never stopped asking to wear a press card and go back on the street, where she could chase real stories.

"They want me to use the maps?"

He nodded. They wanted maps.

"Harvey, Norman Schwartzkopf uses maps," she replied. That acid tone ate through the argument and told him just what she thought of the idea.

He wanted a drink. The doctors said he couldn't drink anymore, and that seemed an appropriately hellish payback for someone working in television. No liquor, no fire in the belly. But just now, sitting across an empty desk from a woman who saw straight through to the parched heart of things, he needed something to moisten the way.

The corporate executives of Channel 9 were not just unhappy with her weather segment, they were actively looking for a replacement. To be sure, Bonnie was popular with a quirky faction of the audience, but they were people on the fringe of the important demographics. Her fans did not matter when it came to selling airtime to beer sponsors and car companies.

Behind the unhappiness with Bonnie was the fact that the suits were trying to clean up the station's image so that they could unload it. Buyers were always finicky about messy nonconformists.

Harvey lifted himself with a sigh, went over to the bookcase and plunged his hand behind a row of books at eye-level.

"It's behind Chaucer," she said.

"Most things are." He smiled. He put the bottle of Glenlivet behind *The Canterbury Tales* because he knew no one at Channel 9 would browse in that fancy Middle English neighborhood.

He poured a generous slug of liquor in his coffee mug. He held out the bottle, but Bonnie shook her head. After a long swallow, he leaned back, clutching the mug in both hands.

"You know, they're selling the station," he said, forgetting his pledge of discretion.

Bonnie shrugged. "I'm trying to sell my apartment," she said. "Everybody in America's trying to sell something, to get out of debt. We're all overextended, cash-poor, going into the toilet."

"Well, these guys hired a media consulting group."

He looked at her and they both laughed, because neither believed in media consultants, focus groups, or public polls. People lied or told the pollsters what they thought they should say, or gave what they regarded as the correct answer. Nobody knew what they thought anymore until the polls came back. People were polled and advertised and intellectually addled into wide-awake unconsciousness. Journalism, Harvey and Bonnie had both agreed in one of those late-night conversations that hovered somewhere between a long lament and a random seduction, was an intuitive, sensuous art. You knew it when you saw it. Some people got it and some didn't. The media consultants didn't. Never.

"Bet they loved me," said Bonnie, who was, at the moment, preoccupied. What the hell was Jack up to? How did it connect to Nora's mysterious absence and what the hell was the Irish cop doing here? Where did Don Iennello figure in? And what, in God's name, was Harvey blathering about?

Harvey nodded. "They called you 'unprofessional.' "

"They're right, I suppose," she said with a shrug. "I mean, according to their own dim lights."

"In particular," he said, ignoring her outburst and reaching into a drawer of his Mission desk and pulling out a folder, "they said you had an erratic approach to the weather."

Bonnie was amused. "Well, the weather is a pretty erratic thing, when you come to think about it. One day it rains and the next it doesn't. I'd call that erratic. Wouldn't you call that erratic, Harv?"

Harvey sat there for a moment, took another slug of whiskey. "They like the maps, you know. Especially the ones with the moving clouds," he said. "They are convinced that people put a lot of faith in moving clouds. It makes them think that . . ."

". . . you can actually do something about the weather," she said brightly.

He looked down again at the report. "And the exclusive color radar—you keep making fun of it."

"Everybody's got exclusive color radar. How is that exclusive? Every station. Even radio stations have exclusive color radar. Harvey, have you taken leave of your senses? We both hate exclusive color radar."

"Okay. But you do make fun of the weather map," he said.

"Well, I happen to think that weather maps are silly, which is very close to being funny."

"No, you know what I mean. Like, during the Gulf War, when the Pentagon was holding daily briefings and using maps of the area, remember what you said? You said that our weather map was a secret battle plan and we were going to be invaded by elite battalions of weather arrows and high-pressure ridges."

"It was a joke! Look, I know I can be a tad unusual. But I always tell the weather. Always. There's not one program where I don't say whether you should wear a coat and bring an umbrella or mention the temperature. I just don't think it's crucial to dwell on what's going on in Tulsa or on the Pacific Coast. Or how many low-pressure systems are moving in what direction and influencing the jet stream, which, as we both know, is a bullshit myth anyway."

"We got a lot of calls about the map thing. One even from the Pentagon—some lawyer-soldier who said that you might be in violation of . . . I don't remember, something."

"Loyalty," said Bonnie, who was accustomed to legal threats. After all, she usually spent her two and half minutes on the air insulting the anchor, the corporate executives, and the Republican administration in Washington, whom she blamed for pollution, global warming, acid rain, and toxic dumps. One night three weeks ago, she'd gotten so carried away that she'd blurted out that IQ points were seeping through the hole in the ozone layer.

"How do you know?" interrupted the indignant anchorman, Chuck Childers, when she uttered what he called "that unsupported claim." He actually believed it.

"It's the only way I can explain your career," she shot back on-camera, before she could check her tongue. Then, as if to say, to hell with it: "Chuck, our nation is at war; information is scarce. Shouldn't we reassure the public that our smart bombs are being guided by smart anchors? By the way, what is your IQ? Or, if you don't want to tell me that, what about your SAT scores?"

Childers had tried to laugh, but it had caught in his throat and he'd sounded like he was strangling.

"Why'n't you ask me?" the idiot sportscaster had asked.

"Because I don't have to," she'd replied.

Off camera, Max Gross had buried his face in his hands as the anchor and the sportscaster both became mute. Bonnie had smiled into the camera and whispered her nightly mantra: "Hey, it's only weather!"

Before Childers went back on a set with her, he made Bonnie swear that she would treat him as though he were bright, or at least competent, and not probe into his IQ or SAT scores. The wounds were still fresh.

Harvey Levy, who'd calmed the roiling waters after that incident, now sat up tall behind his desk and cleared his throat. "Look, the media consultants said that their surveys show that the public does not want bitterness and contention on the set. The public wants a happy family. The public wants weather."

Bonnie agreed. They were entitled to weather. "I'll see that they get plenty of rain and some wind and maybe some sunshine. Every goddamned day! Rain or shine."

Harvey tried to smile, but she was incorrigible. "You gotta pretend to behave," said Harvey, feeling the effects of the liquor. "I'm tellin' you, they got a contract out on you."

"Who? The Mafia?"

"Might as well be," he said. "The suits."

"Harv. *You're* the suits."

She got up, took some tissues from the box on his desk and wiped her skirt. On the air they wouldn't be able to see the stains from an orange she had eaten earlier. Then she stopped and looked at Harvey.

"They're really trying to sell this place," she half-inquired, half-declared.

Harvey didn't say anything.

She nodded. "Then why not let me chase a story? A real story."

"Jack?"

"Jack. Something's going on out there—I can feel it—and nobody's after it. Why not let me chase it?"

Harvey Levy shook his head. "They want weather," he said. "They want moving clouds and Canadian highs and stationary lows."

Bonnie had known she would be turned down before she even asked. Not that it was Harvey's fault. Not that it was anyone's fault. It was the way things were now, with news propped up with a painted smile. Good news. Even the bad news was only good news turned upside down. Crack mothers were selling their babies, budgets were busted, high public officials were crooks, drive-by killers weren't even teenagers yet. And the highest-rated shows were celebrity shock TV shows. Or real cops arresting small-time dealers. And on the front pages of the newspapers was the latest celebrity midget, Madonna, whose only apparent talent was for being annoyingly famous. And disgustingly filthy. A brazen, sleazy performer with no taste except for vulgarity. The public wallowed in her unabashed sluttishness.

"I can be a good reporter," said Bonnie, and Harvey's rueful smile drove her away.

On that night's weather segment—in the chatty moment when they were supposed to noodle at each other, with the anchor delivering a good-natured rebuke or, perhaps, thanking her for the weather—she told Chuck Childers that the station was up for sale and he'd better sell his hairpiece. Childers began to scream like a tenor and the station went to black for two full minutes, until she could safely get out of the studio. She didn't care. The switchboard lit up and Harvey Levy, who had been watching the segment in his office, returned to *The Canterbury Tales*.

At the polished bar of a pub on Cross Bay Boulevard in the borough of Queens, Jack Mann was on his third diet cola. So far, he hadn't seen an opening to grab Callan, the owner, a thick man, younger than he looked, who had given in to his gut. He laughed and called it an occupational hazard. The bar was called the Shebeen to evoke a wild, outlaw glow from those true Irish rebels who had fled to America and settled in this eastern part of Queens. The grandchildren still told sentimental versions of the bloody Rising, and cursed the British occupation, as if they themselves lived under the boot. They were soft sympathizers, but useful when it came to contacts and logistics. The contempt in which they were held by the provisional army gunmen was always modified by their willingness.

A lot of the Shebeen regulars worked the freight or maintenance shifts at the airport, and there was some built-in larceny in that. They'd always come home with some spilled goods that would become part of the airlines' acceptable percentage of wastage. A box of shirts. A CD player. A case of whiskey. It was the price of doing business. The other patrons of the pub, cops or firemen, turned a blind eye to what they regarded as the harmless felonies of their drinking companions. As the poet said of the Irish, their love songs were sad and their war tunes were happy, and they spent their evenings singing along with the jukebox while the wives stayed home and tended the brood. The usual course of the evening was that they started out marching bravely to "Kevin Barry," and grew sadder and more maudlin as the night wore on, until they were crooning "The Patriot Game."

From the windows you could see the jets tiptoeing into Kennedy Airport across Jamaica Bay, and boats, like celestial stars, bobbing in the water. Jack sat at the end of the bar, where he had sat when he first saw Nora, drawing curious looks from the regulars. She had been a barmaid then, and bristling with wit and spit. And the way she'd walked: she'd had lift and grace in her step almost four years ago, and he'd taken pleasure just watching her cross the room. It was only later, when she'd told him that she had always wanted to be a dancer, that he understood. A dancer!

Yes, he could see that. Life might have cheated her of the

chance to become a professional dancer, but it couldn't stop her from moving like a dancer.

In Ireland, he recognized now with a sinking sensation, the dance had gone out of her step. She now walked flat and uncertainly, as if the accumulating guilt of living off stolen money (even if it was stolen from criminals) had cost her some crucial balance. That, and the burden of the children and the books and the running of the house. It had aged her and weighed down her step.

"You sit here all night drinking that piss?!" declared a fair-sized customer. He was half-bald, and like a lot of men whose hair is falling out, had devised his own technique for dealing with it. He wore short-sleeved shirts in the dead of winter and his great arms bulged and throbbed as he moved the ale from the bar to his lips. He raised and lowered his glass so often that the movement was almost like flexing a muscle, and it distracted attention from his glistening head.

Jack smiled at him. No telling how big he was, slumped on the stool that way. His speech was slurred and his eyes were half-lidded and he had a chip in his voice.

"Whyn't you take your fucking business to a damn tea shop?" He began to unfold from the stool, and Jack could see that he was an oversized man, with a wide chest and knobby fists. He was turning and leaning closer so that Jack could smell his sour breath. Jack brought his bandaged hand up and put it on the bar so the man would not start a fight.

"I'll fight you with one hand, you faggotty-assed pisshead," slurred the oversized man.

If I had my gun now, if I was still a cop, I'd shoot him, thought Jack. This is not one you take a chance with. And one shot wouldn't bring him down. Probably take all five. If I had a chance to get them off.

"You're really starting to make me mad," said the half-bald brute.

So far, Jack had not said a word. He turned away from the man and was checking for a stray bottle of beer to grab and break over his head. He'd lose, he was certain, but he'd put a dent in him all the same. Maybe he'd have time to daze him a little and bring the stool down on his head.

"Fuckin' ignore me, you little crippled weasel!"

"Eddie! How the hell are you?"

Jack looked bewildered. The man who'd come up behind him was calling *him* "Eddie."

It was Callan, the owner, who had come to Jack's rescue. He clapped Jack on the shoulder and turned to introduce him to the brute.

"O'Doyle, you crazy bastard, I'd like you to meet one of the great heroes of the Gulf, just back from the war where he was wounded by the heathen Turks, Eddie McManus."

O'Doyle's eyes rolled around and he was blushing red, looking to see how many of the regulars noticed that he had made an ass out of himself.

"Callan, you moron, we weren't fighting the Turks," shouted one elbow-bender from the middle of the bar. "It was the Iranians."

"Whatever," Callan called out, leading Jack away from the bar. "Eddie, here, did himself proud anyway. Saved a whole platoon, didn't you, Eddie?"

Before Jack could answer, Callan called to the bartender that it was on the house—no Gulf War hero was going to spend a nickel in his bar. When he got Jack alone in his private office behind the bar, Callan smiled and shook his head.

"O'Doyle is a nice man when he's sober," he said. "It's the liquor brings out the beast in him."

"Well, you saved me," said Jack, collapsing in a chair. His hand throbbed.

"How's Nora?" Callan asked, smiling.

"How did you know?"

"Oh, I was around when you first had the trouble two years ago," Callan said. "You didn't notice me, but I ran some errands for Michael. I was going to be a fireman, but I bought the bar instead."

"That explains it."

"So, has Nora found Michael yet?"

Jack became cautious. "Not yet."

Callan laughed. Brought out a cigarette. "Michael won't be found unless he wants to be found."

"That's for sure."

"Is she still at the bookshop?"

"That's the problem," said Jack, conspiratorially. "I've lost track of her." He held up his arm. "She told me to look you up if I had to find her."

Callan was hesitant. But then he smiled, as if he had made up his mind that he could trust Jack. "The last I heard she was in that bookshop on the Upper West Side, near Columbia. What's the name? Broadway Books. That's it. I don't know if she's still there. I haven't heard a word for weeks."

As Jack came out of the office, the big man stopped him. He put one great paw on Jack's sore shoulder and Jack winced.

"Sorry!" said O'Doyle timidly. "I just wanted to say how proud we all are of the thing you did. I hope you killed a couple of those ragheads before you got hit."

Jack smiled modestly, put his head down and made for the door.

"Can I buy you a drink?" O'Doyle called.

Jack shook his head.

"A diet cola?"

And Jack was gone.

He didn't notice the two men, one with almost no chin, who got up quickly from a dark table and followed him out the door.

14

It was too cold outside the Waldorf, so Nora waited for him behind a column in the lobby—as if a shadow could protect her against her brother's powers of destruction. When she saw him coming across the lobby, she stepped out into the open, so he wouldn't think that she was hiding or afraid. Like a mean dog, Michael could sense fear.

They walked out into the night without speaking. Michael pulled her along with him like a tide. It was brisk on Park Avenue as they marched north. At the intersections he didn't look down or sideways, acting as if he were walking alone. She noticed that she was almost as tall as he was. It was nothing that she hadn't known, but his small size somehow became significant. And now when she looked she saw gray in his hair. She felt it like a sob, all of her brother's immunity of youth and strength coming undone at once.

She touched the Davis P-32 pistol in her pocket and thought for one insane instant, I could shoot him. I, alone, could bring down the legendary Michael who had eluded and confounded all the professional assassins in the elite sections of British and American intelligence agencies. Me. By myself. On this street. It was not really a temptation—merely a passing notion, like a hot wind, or an intoxicating possibility. She forced the thought out of her mind.

They passed Fifty-seventh Street and started into the high-rent residential district. He slowed a little and moved towards the gutter so that he could not be overheard by the doormen. No, she thought, he was not vulnerable if he was alert to such latent threats. He turned his back on his sister because he gauged human temperament, weighed all risk, and knew he was in no danger from his own sister. And when he looked over at her, Nora saw some softening in his eyes, as if there might be some agenda other than his own in the world. He nodded and they headed west, striking Central Park at Fifth Avenue. He sat on a stone bench and she took the seat on his right. There was a good eighteen inches between them. A beggar came up, and Michael fished a dollar out of his coat pocket and handed it to the man just to keep him moving.

"When I was in H-block we smelled like that," he said, nodding at the beggar who stank like an unflushed toilet.

Nora nodded. He was facing the front, but she knew that he could see her nodding. She thought: He remembered the smell of Long Kesh, but did he remember Seamus? Did he remember her son and his sour-sweet kisses? Did he remember the ticklish spot on his belly? She could see Seamus rolling helplessly with laughter when she buried her face in his rubbery midsection. Did Michael remember the baby smells of spoiled diapers and mother's milk? Did he remember the dimple in Seamus's chin or the red hair growing wild on his head like a scratchy garden? She could remember. She could feel it now, on the tips of her fingers.

What did he feel? Did he have any sense-memory of the lives he so dramatically changed? Did he remember at all the women he found and seduced and used for cover when he went into hiding? Did he even care? Was there any true feeling, or was it all fake emotions that he donned like disguises? Were the only things that endured the stench of bombs and gunpowder and fresh blood? The truth was that she had no idea what boiled inside the volcano of her brother's life.

"Was Da a brave man?" she asked.

Michael was jolted. "He was," he said quickly. "He was brave and he was unusual."

"What do you mean, unusual?"

"He had a gift—a kind of second sight—so that he knew when trouble was coming."

"A mystic. So we know where you got that from."

"He was better liked than I am," admitted Michael. "The people who knew him, they spoke of him with affection." He snorted. "No one speaks of me with affection. Fear, I'm sure, and I'd guess some respect, but I'm not famous for my winning ways." He smiled at her, then turned away as if he were ashamed.

"Where are you living now?" she asked, then bit her lip. It wasn't a question that one asked Michael. He made his living arrangements according to the requirements of the mission. He went from woman to woman. They were convenient and willing. There was always a thrill-seeker who recognized the white-water rapids in his eyes. Not that he ever talked about it. He didn't tell anyone. She remembered seeing him once in Ballymurphy in Belfast. Him and some dark beauty. He'd walked past her, never giving a sign. She was certain in her heart that if he had just planted a rebel bomb and his own sister had been walking into the killing zone, he wouldn't have given it away. He was security-minded.

He didn't bother to answer her question.

"You know, Da was in there with me," he said. He meant the H-block, where the hard cases shit in their blankets and starved themselves to death just to demonstrate their limitless pride. Trouble was, nobody cared. Michael laughed softly. "A family kind of place, it was. He was there for something, Da, and I was there for something else, and we didn't talk about it because for all I knew, he was working the other side."

"Da?"

He looked at her with a penetrating tolerance. "They told me, when they let me join up, don't trust a soul. Not your mother. Not your wife. Not your fucking priest. Not a soul. I was very young and very impressionable. I believed them."

"Of course you believed them." She said it as a kind of terrible judgment.

"Over the years I have found it to be true," he said wistfully. "Almost the only truth. As far as man and flesh is concerned." Then, almost apologetically, he added: "Not that I didn't have my weak moments. A man always has his weak moments." His voice came to attention. "But, yes, I believe that the rule was a good one. If you don't know who will betray you, best not to trust anyone."

"Michael," she said softly, almost whispering, "do you actually believe that? That I would betray you? After what I have done, after what I've gone through on your behalf?"

She meant Seamus—she always meant Seamus now—but there was a long history of loyalty beforehand.

He looked at her briefly, then turned back again to watch the splendid building across Fifth Avenue with the awning and uniformed, deterrent doorman huddling inside the door, keeping track of all the homeless and sorry souls who might camp near the entrance for the heat.

"I believe that anyone is capable of anything," said Michael with an almost weary resignation. "There's always something that someone wants—some glory, some heroic cause. If they said to me right this minute that I could have a free and united Ireland and all I'd have to do would be to give up the people I work with, the people I love, I couldn't answer for myself. I don't know that I could stop myself—not now, not after everything. If you give yourself up to a cause, never mind what cause, there's no stopping. If they told some mother that she could save her child, well . . ."

"My child is dead," she uttered with all the bitterness of lost hope and icy despair.

He nodded. "No one wanted that," he said.

Her eyes flashed and she felt a clutch of something beyond sorrow. It almost sounded as if Michael was acknowledging that he bore some responsibility, some moral weight for what had happened to Seamus. A hint of guilt. Well, she thought, we're not Catholic for nothing.

"Your damn rules!" she muttered, turning fiercely away.

His head moved in a tentative nod. "Da understood it," he said. "He never spoke a word to me that couldn't be overheard by a jailer. He knew the rules."

"I suppose you get that from him. A certain reliable tenacity."

"A man has to hold on to something."

She heard something wild and desperate in his voice. Maybe it was the cold, maybe the wind, maybe it was her imagination. But she thought that he sounded as if he were clinging to something by his fingernails.

They sat for a while and watched the dog-walkers and security patrols and furtive nightcrawlers passing by. The cabs raced down the avenue, heading for the meatier traffic of midtown where the couples would be spilling out of fancy restaurants or shows by now. And on Fifth Avenue in the shadows of the great plane trees no one paid attention to them. They were one more unfathomable couple sitting out in the cold in the bitter grip of early March. No one was actively curious or wanted to know their story; New Yorkers knew too many scary stories already.

She noticed now, when the lights of a car caught him full, that his face was cracked with too many lines. Too many shadows from too many secrets. Once he had been a grey-hound and the girls of the rebellion had held him in their hearts like a rock star. But now the skin stretched like old parchment and the eyes were weary and sore. She could see that the great rage of his youth had turned into something heavy and hard to lift. A burden. She'd always thought that her brother was an exciting, dangerous man, until this night on the bench outside of Central Park. Now he looked like some political prisoner held too long, unaccustomed to the outside world.

"You followed me," he began. Nora started to say something, but he held up his hand. He didn't want to hear any lies. Then he turned to face her and smiled more broadly than she had ever seen him smile before. "So you're not too far off the rule yourself," he said.

"I get it from Da," she replied coldly.

He nodded. "It's fine. Don't trust me. You shouldn't. But there's something I want from you."

"And what's that?"

"A pledge."

It struck her that he didn't use her name. She remembered that he seldom used her name in public. He was always on guard against being overheard. God, she thought, what a strain and effort his life must be: to remain on guard forever.

"I made a pledge and I need one from you," he continued.

"What have I to do with your pledge?" she asked.

He looked up at the sky, clapped his hands together, as if he might be feeling the cold for the first time. "Listen to me. I am here on a mission. It might seem a trifle to you now, all things considered. It's certainly not significant to you. But to me . . . it's . . . a mission. Once, not too long ago, these things were important to you, too. Worth your life."

"Not worth Seamus. Nothing's worth that. If I ever felt that way, it was long before I lost my son. Do you remember him, Michael? Do you remember him at all? His face? The little hands. The laugh. My God, the laugh. Did you ever hear such a laugh?"

It was a long time before Michael answered. "I remember. Nothing can help him now. Nothing. It's hard, but true."

She flared. "That's right!" She thought: Tell me he was a soldier who died in battle. Tell me again how many mothers and widows have consoled themselves with that cold comfort! But she held her tongue.

He got up. Held up his hand so that she should remain seated. "I'm sorry about the boy. Truly. He was . . . the nicest . . . He's gone. You have to give me time . . ."

"Time? You want time? How much time?" she asked quickly.

"Two weeks," he replied.

She thought about it. Well, she had her own timetable. She could play his game. "I'm not to do a thing until a week from next Monday?" she asked.

He nodded. "You'll gum it up for us," he said. He didn't have to say that he could not tolerate that.

"You couldn't tell me what this vital mission concerns?" she asked.

"You know better," he said.

"Fine," she replied. "Two weeks."

He blinked and his hand reached out, almost as if to touch her, but he pulled it back. He might burn himself on the flame of family emotion, thought Nora bitterly. Then he whirled and went east.

She watched him walk away and wondered, why did she have to lie low for two weeks? And what, for Christ's sake, was the Mafia to him? Why couldn't she just murder the man who was responsible for the death of her child?

She didn't know, but she knew that she would break her promise to her brother before he was out of sight. There was even some advantage in assuring him that she would cooperate with his mission. Now his guard would be lowered and she could act without worrying about him.

"You should have remembered the rule," she whispered when he had gone.

The unmarked car was parked on Cross Bay Boulevard. Sergeant Vinnie Manero was in the driver's seat, staring straight ahead, but checking out the traffic in the rearview mirror. He had the motor running so that he could make a quick move when the bus came. His partner, Detective Rocco Valone, was watching the bus stop, which was one block away. There was only one passenger waiting for the bus. Jack Mann. He was heading to a subway which would take him back to Manhattan.

"I probably got time to get us some coffee," Rocco Valone said.

Sergeant Manero looked to make certain that his partner was joking.

"That poor bastard might freeze his nuts before the fucking bus comes," said Rocco.

Manero turned up the heat.

"You know, I didn't think he'd make it," Rocco said, looking at Jack in the cold.

Manero turned to see what he meant.

"I thought we put one in his chest, you know back there in Ireland . . ."

"I remember."

"He was bleeding pretty bad; I thought we did him good."

"Obviously not," Sergeant Manero noted.

"Actually, he looks pretty good, considering he took a couple of good slugs," Rocco said with admiration.

"Probably got a good medical plan."

They waited quietly.

"You know," Detective Valone said, breaking the silence, "we could whack him now. There's no one out there. He's alone. Just drive by and put two in his belly."

"No," Manero said, pulling rank.

"It would sure make the don happy. Did you see how excited he got when we told him that this guy's here?"

Vinnie Manero considered it, then shook his head.

"Why not? I got an extra gun, we toss it in the bay when we cross the bridge. We're not even signed out to Queens. Bing! Bing! Ba-da-bing! And we're out of the doghouse."

Vinnie Manero's face had the long-suffering expression of a

man who had spent too much time being partnered with a man who could read his thoughts. Not for the first time, he wished the guy in the passenger's seat had a brain.

"The don wants the money. The money, get it? He don't care about this guy. In fact, we don't give a shit about the don," he said.

"We don't?"

Vinnie shook his head.

"I thought we did," said Rocco.

"Look, if anybody tries to hurt that man standing at the bus stop, we take them out. Like that asshole back at the bar. I was ready to put one between his eyes if he kept at him."

Valone was puzzled. He turned away to see if Vinnie was pulling his leg again.

"Watch the bus stop, you cucumber."

Rocco didn't like being called a cucumber. He didn't know why, because it wasn't like being called a meathead, which is what Vinnie Manero used to call him until he put his foot down and said he wouldn't stand for it anymore. But there was something undignified and insulting about being called a cucumber. He just didn't know why. Besides, he didn't even like cucumbers.

Sullenly, he turned back to watch the bus stop, just in time to see Jack board the bus that would take him to the subway station. "Here we go," he said.

Vinnie let out the handbrake and put the car in a smooth U-turn and dropped into traffic behind the bus.

There was a staccato cackle from the police radio, with its steady chain of coded domestic calls, burglary runs, and time checks. Sergeant Manero didn't feel comfortable driving unless he had the official chatter of a police radio rasping in the background. Even when he was off duty and driving his own car, he kept tuned into the active channel over the objections of his children, who would have preferred music. His wife came to his defense, assigning importance and virtue to his never-ending attention to duty. In fact, the thing that Vinnie Manero was always listening for was his own name on a be-on-the-lookout call. It was the Catholic curse—a moral bruise of guilt. Sooner or later he fully expected to pay for his many sins.

"Tell me, Vin, why do we wanna protect this bozo?" asked Rocco-the-cucumber as they trailed the bus.

Occupied as he was with the driving as well as the need to remain a hundred yards behind and in the blind right lane, Sergeant Manero took a moment to collect himself, then decided that he could not bring this thing off unless he included his partner in the scheme.

"The guy in that bus is not here to lock up Joey Sharks," said Sergeant Manero.

Rocco laughed. "Some chance! He's not even a cop anymore."

"You know why he's here? I mean, in America?"

Rocco thought about it. "Well, he could be out for our ass. I mean, after all, that Moe Berger was his partner. Somebody takes me out, you'd go after them, right?"

"Of course, Rock."

"I know I would for you."

Vinnie often thought of taking Rocco Valone out himself. He certainly could not imagine setting off on a vendetta to avenge his partner.

Vinnie shook his head. "He's not here in America looking for us," he said. "First of all, I don't think he even knows who we are. Second, even if he did, I don't think he's that kind of guy—coming after us, I mean."

"So, what's he doing here?"

"Nora."

It still did not penetrate Rocco Valone's mind. He couldn't make the connection. "So, he's after Nora. So what? The don wants him dead. Why'n't we just whack him out when we had the chance? I never saw a better spot than that bus stop; it's late at night, there's nobody around, no lights, the sound gets eaten up by the water. I'm tellin' you, Vin, we're never gonna get a better shot at the guy."

"That guy," Vinnie said, jutting his head at the bus pulling ahead on the boulevard, "is sitting on our pension money."

"What the fuck are you talking about?"

"I am talking about three million bucks."

The car became silent as the weight of his partner's words sank into Rocco Valone's head. Finally, he piped up. "But he didn't have the money. She had the money. Nora. Isn't that why the don asked us to go to Ireland in the first place? So we could grab her kid and she would pay back the money to get back the kid?"

"He is gonna lead us to the money," said Sergeant Manero stepping on the gas, pulling closer to the bus so that he wouldn't lose it. "First he's gonna lead us to Nora, and she is gonna lead us to the money. Remember Watergate? Follow the money."

"What's this got to do with Watergate?"

"Cucumber. You're a fucking cucumber."

Vallone was hurt. "Explain it to me, Vinnie."

"She's gonna give us the money."

"Why? Why would she give us three million bucks?"

"Because we'll convince her."

Finally Rocco smiled. He knew all the ways of convincing people. Rough, painful ways.

"Maybe we can do it easy; we tell her that we can take her to the people who killed her kid," Vinnie said breezily.

"But that's us!"

Manero looked at his partner with utter despair. "She doesn't know that, you cucumber!"

15

Friday, March 15, 1991

He found her address, after convincing the bookstore owner that he had nothing but friendly intentions. Nora was not surprised to see Jack Mann waiting for her on the street. She came out of her building early that Friday morning and there was Jack, leaning against a lamppost. He smiled and she couldn't help smiling back.

She didn't ignore him, but began walking south on Broadway at her usual quick clip, and Jack exerted himself to keep up. They walked side by side, like any other couple in the unsettled stage of a fight. She didn't move with the smooth glide that he remembered. She marched like a soldier with a purpose. He struggled to stay in step.

He was astonished at her spirit. She looked unbent, alive, vivid, like someone who had taken a high dive into the water and was coming up for air with her mouth open and her face flushed. As if life had dealt her only smiles. Not like a grieving mother. When you went looking for Nora, you never knew what to expect.

"You're well," she said with some satisfaction. She looked at him and nodded. "You've even put on a pound or two."

"I haven't got all my wind back," he said, and she turned and smiled at him. It was a tolerant smile—a grown-up who forgets that her legs are longer and stronger than her less able companion's. Jack didn't have her grit.

"That's why I had to leave you behind," she said finally, though not unkindly. "I knew that you couldn't keep up with me. Or would want to."

It was then—at that precise instant, hearing the sharp, decisive voice—that he knew she had come to America to wreak havoc. In her voice was the sound of her brother, Michael, and her father, too, no doubt. Something that would send chills down any bystander's spine. The woman clearly had explosive plans.

"The wounds," she said clinically, indicating his shoulder and hand. "You healed well."

"Not all the feeling's back," he said, trying to flex his fingers. "The doctors say I'll get back the best of it." He shrugged. "The shoulder's fine, except for a twinge now and then. Nothing I can't tolerate."

"Then you're fine." She nodded. "I was worried."

He also heard the absence of emotion. Not affection, because she still liked him, he could hear that, too, but the deeper emotions were gone, if they had ever existed. She was in the grip of something stronger.

"Could we stop someplace and have a cup of coffee?" he asked.

She looked at her watch. It was nine in the morning and she had time. She noticed the two men in the unmarked car, leapfrogging like fools from parking spot to parking spot, following them down Broadway. Christ, she thought, such amateurs! An insult to an alert professional. Which is what she now was. The touchy IRA soldiers would have dragged them out of their car and broken all their limbs as a lesson in respect—as well as simple tactics.

"Why not?" she said, and they went into a Greek coffee shop where she was a known stranger, which was the way most New Yorkers conducted business. She had tea and he had coffee and they had nothing to say to each other for a while.

"I went to see Seamus quite a few times," he began, not looking up from his cup.

"Jack, I appreciate the fact that I am not alone in my grief," she said in a voice that was much too steady. Her hand, he noticed, trembled. "I know that there are others who suffer, too. Dee Dee, if no one else. And I know that you have feelings for my son, my Seamus," and here her voice almost broke, but she called it back to attention. "But I tell you now that I cannot hear it. Not one word! You are a dear man and I hold you high in my regard. But I cannot hear a single word about my dead child."

She looked him in the face and her eyes were on fire. "You and I . . . well. I'm not even going to try to tell you what has happened. I think you know. We both know."

She could see that it was wounding, no matter if they both knew that it was true—had been true for a long time. It had nothing to do with Seamus, although what happened to him had quickened matters. But all the same, hearing it spoken aloud was wounding.

She looked outside and could see through the coffee shop window the two policemen—they couldn't be anything but policemen, being that clumsy and that brazen—sitting clearly in their plain unmarked car, as if they had a right to spy on anyone.

"I am not talking about us," he said.

She smiled a sorrowful smile. "We've nothing to talk about, dear Jack. You've found me, God knows why . . ."

"Because I know that you intend to do something drastic," he said.

The indifferent waiter came by and poured fresh coffee in Nora's teacup. She didn't even try to stop him.

She shook her head. "I'm not worth the candle," she said.

"Truly. Go away. Reassemble your life. You're a good man. You can do that. I've put some money aside for you, it'll show up in your account. There's nothing else we can do for each other. Not anymore. Trust me to settle things. Do what I have to do. There's nothing else to do, dontcha see that? I must have a last word with my child's killers."

"This is a huge mistake," he said. He was a cop. Maybe a former cop, but still ingrained with the belief that it was his duty, if it came to shooting, to take the bullet. He preferred a civilized alternative, and she was declaring her uncivilized alternative. "Nora, there's got to be some better way of handling this. This is crazy."

She held up her hand and shook her head. "You're making a mistake, you're making the wrong assumptions," she said. "I'm just here on a shopping trip, then I'm going home. For the time being, I'd prefer to be alone. It's a natural enough thing, considering one thing and another."

She showed him a wintry smile without a hint of hope.

He was wasting his time. He could see the determination in her face. He got up, kissed Nora on the forehead and left. She watched him go, followed by the unmarked car with the two policemen in the front.

They moved out of the hotel when the expenses mounted. Officer Mattie Nolan and Inspector Tim McCormick found reasonable sublets a block away from each other on Clark Street in Brooklyn Heights. It was a short walk across the bridge from police headquarters.

Tim McCormick couldn't hear the bell with the shower running, so Officer Mattie Nolan just used her own key on the door. She had bread and eggs and bacon in her arms and as soon as she got her coat off, she started rattling around the kitchen, making breakfast. He heard the pans as soon as he turned off the water and his mood brightened with every clash of metal. He took some extra time with his hair, covering the sparse areas with the longer strands. The smell of frying bacon struck him cozily as he emerged from the bathroom. He saw Mattie in the kitchen, her back turned, humming a happy tune as she juggled plates and food, and the sight of her like that—so content and preoccupied—made him feel settled and domestic.

He was not a very expressive man and, like many of her Irish ancestors, she was content to let matters speak for themselves. And so they drifted together wordlessly during their American sojourn. It was a romance of homebodies and habits, an adjustment of routines rather than wild passion. Still, he followed the line of her body with his eyes and was moved by the contours. He brushed against her in the narrow spaces of his kitchen and he could hear her gasp gently and felt his own stirrings and closed his eyes; he would wait until the night when they could perform their naked, uninhibited romps in the dark, when he could picture her face raw and wide with lust and hear her screaming at the moon, like some unleashed creature.

"Have you seen the scandal sheets?" she asked, without turning around, for she had her own deferred dreams.

"No," he said, taking his first sip of scalding tea, flapping the napkin over his knee. "Is there something to see?"

"Well," she said, turning away from the stove, placing before him a hot plate of eggs and toast and bacon, "they mention that we're to march in the parade. Honored guests."

"Do they?"

"Read the thing," she said, putting down her own plate across the table from Tim McCormick, then seating herself. He read the article about the parade, which was taking place a day earlier than the true St. Patrick's Day. Down at the bottom of the story, after the news about whether or not gay contingents had a right to march, after the well-leaked warning of the cardinal's planned snub because of his aversion to homosexuals and lesbians, and the mayor's waffling intervention on behalf of the gays, was the detail about a contingent from Ireland—namely Officer Mattie Nolan and Detective

Inspector Timothy McCormick—who would march down Fifth Avenue. Mattie sipped her whitened tea. She had almost put some milk in Tim's tea, but he was trying out the American style, using lemon. Mattie didn't approve. She thought it a bad sign—that he gave up on things too easily. He made quicker adjustments, and it wasn't always for the best.

"Well, I suppose we can't get out of it now," he said, smiling at her. He knew that it was the American way of keeping them busy, making it seem as if there was a purpose to the wild-goose chase. Tim and Mattie were being patronized.

They hadn't brought uniforms, but they both had badges and green streamers that said "Irish Garda" that they would wear slashed across their chests when they marched tomorrow.

Tim looked at his watch and said they should hurry. It was almost nine-thirty and they were to meet the liaison cops at ten-thirty. He gulped down his eggs and his toast and left the bacon. He was worried about the extra pounds. And the poor nutrition. You couldn't listen to the news or read the papers in this country and not start counting your cholesterol and having your blood pressure checked and giving up tasty food. Every paper had a daily scare item about one more of life's pleasures that was bound to be fatal. But he'd almost forgotten about his digestive problems—a cure he ascribed to Mattie's soothing influence.

"You left the bacon," said Mattie, who thought that a man should go out into the world with a full belly and that God put bacon and ham on the earth to fill hungry bellies. It was no use with Tim, who read the food articles, which gave him something to feel bad about. So Mattie ate the bacon, rather than let it go to waste, which was all too common here and one of the reasons she'd be glad to get him back to Ireland where people worried about the right things.

She straightened her suit and checked herself in the mirror. Maybe a bit of powder and some color on the lips, to offset the freckles that had broken out on her face when she was born. And as she drew the line on her lips, Tim McCormick watched from the bedroom door. She's pretty, he thought. At home she'd run a comb through her hair and that was all the makeup she'd tolerate. Maybe it was time to get her back to Galway. And he sprayed his mouth with mint.

Nora didn't notice the man dressed in layers, the uniform of the homeless, who lagged behind her and the unmarked car. He seemed to move slowly because of the heavy-duty garbage bag that he had in tow and because no one expected speed from one of the tribe of the downtrodden who had taken up a permanent place in the heart of New York.

She was up to something, the ragged man thought. He recognized that purposeful, resolute gait. She would not keep the promise. At least, he couldn't trust her to keep it.

At Columbus Circle, Michael removed one of the layers of his clothing and became a different homeless wanderer. That was the beauty of the disguise—you could shed the layers like skins and remain undetected. Nora went into a dress shop and Michael stopped, bent low, and held out an empty half-crushed container of coffee. He was a good actor and got quarters and dollar bills from his pathetic pose.

In half an hour, she was out again, carrying a dress box. The unmarked car moved off, leaving only Michael on the trail of his sister. She kept moving south and stopped at a costume shop near Fifty-first Street.

A policeman came along and told Michael to move out of the area. Michael didn't hesitate. The cop had the look of someone who was passing along an argument he had lost with his sergeant. Michael took up another position, out of sight, and saw Nora emerge from the costume shop with another bundle.

He was standing near a subway stop, and the late-arriving executives were on their way to work. They were less free with their money than the underlings. Well, thought Michael, they didn't get to be executives by being generous.

Nora had turned around and was headed back north. Whatever she had to do was done. He'd seen enough. Michael stopped in a deli and ordered a tea from the man behind the counter.

"Let's see your money," said the counterman.

Michael reached into the container in his hand and counted out seventy-five cents. He took out another dollar and flung it across the counter. "Keep the change," he said.

Outside, the cop was waiting for him. "I thought I told you to move on," he said. He was young, Michael noticed. Too young to be this nasty. Bad marriage. Bad career choice. Hard to tell what made them so bitter at this stage of the game.

"I just stopped for some tea, Officer," he said meekly.

The cop opened the door of the deli and leaned into the store. "Did this bum pay you for that tea?"

The counterman paused, then said, "No, Officer, he just grabbed it and ran." No one else in the store said a word.

"Here, I'll pay for it again," said Michael, on the receiving end of the counterman's spite. He reached into his cup and took out another dollar bill.

"Let's see some identification," said the patrolman, after handing the counterman the dollar bill.

Michael had a choice. He could let himself be rousted by the cop, maybe even arrested on some vagrancy charge, thus risking the mission. Or he could make a run for it. The street was relatively crowded and the risk of the cop shooting into such pedestrian traffic was slim.

He ran. It was hard with the burden of rags, but he was still in good condition. Better than the policeman. He'd put a block between himself and the policeman when some construction worker on Forty-seventh Street decided to play hero and put himself in front of Michael. He was a big man and had a shovel in his hand. Michael kicked the shovel out of his hand, then, out of frustration and anger, laid him out with a stroke across his throat. The other members of the construction crew were paralyzed by the speed and dexterity coming from a homeless vagrant. The cop, who was winded, stopped chasing Michael and bent to help the choking construction worker.

At Fortieth Street, Michael slipped into a garage bathroom and removed the next two layers of rags. Under the shreds and the knit hat was a well dressed, middle-class citizen who bore no resemblance to the bum on Forty-seventh Street. He cleaned his face with a trickle of water in the sink, buried the homeless disguise in the bottom of the wastebasket and left the garage as if he had just parked his Audi. The attendant even saluted as he went into the street.

He walked east, heading for his room near the hotel. And he began to think about what could be done. His plan was in peril. Well, he should have known when Nora tracked him down that she was in it too deep to be ignored. The genes would always tell. She wasn't even afraid of him anymore. He laughed. One of the few. She was not tongue-tied in his presence. She had the spit and courage of a soldier going straight for the guns. Not an ounce of fear. He couldn't help but be proud of her.

He knew that feeling. What was there to be afraid of when you already counted yourself dead? You kill a woman's child, even if it was an accident, and you might as well be prepared to kill the mother. Any mother. Even your sister.

16

Sergeant Vinnie Manero was aggressively smoking a cigarette—something he knew annoyed Inspector Tim McCormick. It got so far under the inspector's skin that he blinked—not from the smoke but from the effort to control his emotions. The resentment was especially bad when they were bunched together in an enclosed space. And Tim McCormick's office, built as a storage area, had one small window that didn't open.

It gave Manero a rare pleasure to display his feelings for the Irish policeman by literally, as well as figuratively, blowing smoke in his direction. He puffed hard, and turned maliciously when he spoke to the Irish inspector. Mattie stood in the background, forming hard opinions about the American cop.

"Yeah, so we tried to pick up her trail," said the sergeant boastfully. "We didn't get her—yet! But it can't be that hard. Even though she is some piece of work! We're gonna stay on it. If she's here, we're gonna find her. Of course she may have gone back to Ireland. Especially if she knows that we're after her. You never know."

"I suppose you're aware of the fact that she's done nothing illegal," said McCormick.

"So far," Manero said.

Manero noticed that there was something different about the two Irish police officers today, something soaked with hidden meaning. A kind of smug secret. Sex, he guessed correctly. All that pent-up lust had been expressed. It made them both easier to deal with, less brittle on the surface. He was grateful for the change. They'd fed him Jack like some piece of candy and now Manero was establishing—in advance—his legitimate interest in Nora's potentially illegal activities.

Inspector McCormick cleared his throat, took a sip from a glass of water, and folded his hands on his desk. "When you say, 'some piece of work,' exactly what does that mean?" he asked as if he were pursuing some subtle but important clue. "Does it mean that Nora is impressive?"

The New York sergeant looked over at Rocco Valone. Valone was tilted back in his chair and giggled at the signal from Manero, who turned back to McCormick now that he was confident someone was listening and appreciating his performance. "Yeah," said Manero sarcastically. "Like we really admire her."

Mattie Nolan did not like these two detectives. They had shown up suddenly, volunteers from the Internal Affairs Division offering to help with legwork when Deputy Inspector Bob Reymond had gone on leave. At once she suspected their motives and loathed their attitudes. "I think you'll find that the term has derisive and definite negative connotations," she said, addressing Tim McCormick. " 'Some piece of work' translates roughly to 'Some bitch!' "

McCormick nodded. "Thank you, Officer Nolan." Then, turning back to Manero, who was lighting another cigarette from the burning end of the last, he added: "She has a good ear for these things, but then again men are so crude when it comes to insulting women."

It was almost noon. The small Irish inspector suggested that they go to lunch. His treat. To celebrate, so he said, the fact that now they had proper manpower to hunt down Nora Burns. If the two American detectives stayed on the trail of Jack Mann, eventually they'd find Nora. And Nora would lead them to the killer of Seamus and his baby-sitter. That, after all, was the Garda's reason for sending Tim McCormick to New York—to hunt for the killers.

It was a very delicate matter. Nora was a tourist. He tried to impress this upon the two American detectives, but they seemed to have an agenda of their own.

"You know, here's something to kick around: she might even have done her kid," suggested Manero.

McCormick paused, as if to consider such a ridiculous possibility, but really to frame a good reply. "Why would she ever do such a thing?" he asked.

Manero shrugged. "Maybe the kid was a pest. Mothers do it all the time."

"I don't think so," said McCormick with ill-concealed contempt.

"I'm not saying she did it, but, Christ, women here stuff their kids in garbage cans. You wouldn't believe the things that mothers do. You got crack mothers who toss 'em out in alleys. Nothing sacred about motherhood anymore."

"There is in Ireland," said Mattie. Inspector McCormick shot her a restraining look, as if to say this was not the time or the place to begin this.

"We'll talk about it over lunch," he said.

"I could eat," said Detective Valone.

"Yes," said Mattie Nolan, smiling.

"We all need a break," said the inspector.

She's pretty when she smiles, thought Manero, who was feeling happy and expansive now that they had a real prospect of getting at the money. All he had to do was figure out how to extract it before killing Nora. Maybe a simple thing, like extortion. Tell her that we'll let her go in exchange for seven zeros. Of course, you hadda be careful with these IRA types. Blow themselves up and take you with them. Kamikaze killers. Not like regular hit men. On the other hand, no one gives away three million bucks without putting up some kind of struggle.

"How about Chinatown," said Manero cheerfully. He had found out what he had come to find out—namely, that the Irish cops didn't have a clue about who killed Seamus and Pat, or where the money was, for that matter.

"Chinatown, fine," said McCormick, who knew far more than he was willing to let on. "But we have to make a stop first. Near the docks. I have to meet someone."

"Fine, fine," said Manero.

Before they left the office, Inspector McCormick looked around. There was something undone, but he couldn't remember what it was. Manero had rattled him, with his smoke and bullshit. "Let's get on with it," he said, giving up.

"You know, Harvey, I just need a few more days of vacation," Bonnie Hudson said into the phone.

Harvey Levy's patience was gone. He had made excuses, apologized and used up his expense budget trying to placate the suits and the on-air talent at Channel 9. He told everyone that she had had a death in the family and was suffering privately. No one believed him. They wanted her in the office so that they could confront her, make her squirm with remorse.

"You gotta come in," said the managing editor of the news program. "I am holding off lions without a chair or a whip."

Bonnie had not been into the station since her last encounter with Childers. She knew what awaited her. "Harvey, you're the best man with an excuse I know. Tell them I have a slight drug problem. Or that I'm hormonally impaired. Anything."

She heard the key in the lock. "Oh, gotta go. Listen, I'll call you later ..." She hung up the phone, then took it off the hook, dropped it on the table.

"So?" she asked Jack, who had collapsed into a chair without taking his coat off.

"I wish I was still drinking," he said.

"What happened?"

"I spoke to her."

Bonnie said nothing. She was terrified that a single word would be a gust of wind that would kick up the old flame between Jack and Nora.

"I found her, I spoke to her." He smiled half-heartedly and shrugged.

"And?"

Jack looked at her. She saw how tired he was. How weary, and how wracked with guilt.

"And . . . and. And I am convinced that she is every bit as dangerous as her brother."

"What are you talking about?"

He shook his head. "I don't know." Then he looked up. "She's up to something bad. She wouldn't tell me. She is wrapped up in her own shit. This is a woman who has a will of iron. She's gonna do something very bad. I gotta talk to McCormick."

"Wouldn't that be like a betrayal? I mean, giving her up to the cops?"

Jack looked around. "Is there any coffee? Tea? Whiskey?"

"Coffee," said Bonnie, and went into the kitchen.

Jack took the coffee Bonnie handed to him. "McCormick's a good guy. Besides, it's not a real betrayal. He's not after Nora. She's the victim in his eyes. If she's out to blow up somebody, that's in the future. They'd have to wait until after the fact. That's how cops are. Remember? I used to be one. You can't arrest someone for thinking bad thoughts. Dreaming of revenge. Christ, I dream of revenge."

Bonnie sat on the dining room table—a habit she had developed that Jack found cute and slightly daffy. His reaction encouraged her to do it whenever she wanted his attention.

"I gotta go see McCormick," said Jack.

"You can use the phone; I'll put it back on the hook."

"No. I wanna see him."

"I'll get dressed," said Bonnie, standing up.

"You stay here."

She explained patiently from the bedroom. "You can't get into headquarters without me. I have an excuse. A member of the press. Maybe I don't have a press card, but they know me down there. They'll assume I have a good 'weather' reason for visiting. McCormick's office is on the pressroom floor. If I go, you won't have a problem."

She was right. He was nodding in an empty room. Why do I even bother questioning her, he thought.

When they got to police headquarters, Jack leaped behind a pillar and pulled Bonnie after him. His heart turned over in his chest and he felt light-headed and terrified at the same time. For just as he was approaching the building, he saw Inspector McCormick, Officer Nolan, Detective Sergeant Vincent Manero, and Detective Rocco Valone. They were deep in conversation and hadn't noticed him. He hoped.

"What is it?" asked Bonnie, seeing the sweat suddenly break out on his face.

"It's them," he said in a voice that quivered.

"Who?"

"The guys who killed Seamus and Pat," he said, nodding at the four officers.

Bonnie looked again.

"Wait a minute. That's McCormick and his sidekick, what's-her-face."

He nodded. "I know. Those two guys with him. They shot Seamus and Pat and me."

Bonnie and Jack watched the four enter the unmarked car parked in the reserved spot and drive off.

"You sure?" asked Bonnie.

She looked at his face, and he didn't have to answer. For the first time since she'd known him she saw active fear under his confusion.

Manero drove because he liked to control things and because it gave him a chance to show off his reckless streak. Valone was in the passenger seat, as always. Inspector McCormick sat behind Manero, watching him in the rearview mirror. Beside McCormick, Officer Nolan pretended to watch the scenery.

"Head up to the piers on west Thirtieth Street," said Inspector McCormick.

"You got a boat coming in?" Valone asked.

"Or going out?" piped in Manero, smiling.

"Someone to meet," McCormick said.

They swirled in and out of traffic on the Avenue of the Americas, torn up because of repairs. Manero managed to squeak through tight spots.

"I could never get accustomed to your American traffic," said McCormick.

"Why's that?" asked Valone.

"Opposite side of the road. That sort of thing. And the cowboys on bicycles. Heaven help us."

"Oh, yeah," said Valone.

"You know about driving on the left?"

"Sure. We was shaving trees when we was there."

"Really? You've been to Ireland?"

Valone realized he had spoken out of turn and looked at Manero, who tried to retrieve the situation. "We were in England. Same thing, am I right?"

"Same thing," McCormick agreed.

After missing a turn, Manero went west on Forty-second Street, then headed south again along the West Side Drive. The trucks and cabs were honking nonstop and it jangled the nerves.

"So, you wanna let me pick the joint?" asked Manero. "They know me at the Golden Bowl, and you won't even have to put it on the voucher. Fact, they give us all a voucher and don't charge a dime."

"Sounds good," said McCormick. They were approaching the pier he indicated, pulling through the metal gates and parking in the empty lot. The great liners had long since stopped calling here, and the French Line signs on the roof and the front were fading fast. The windows were broken and the parking lot was strewn with empty beer cans, discarded crack vials, and used condoms from the midnight hookers and truckers.

The front doors were bent out enough to allow entry.

They sat in the car for a moment.

"This person we're meeting, he's got some information about the murders," McCormick said.

Manero turned in his seat.

"What kind of information?"

"Don't know. He called this morning. Said he could put his finger on the villains," McCormick said. "Probably another feather in the wind, but we have to look into every one, don't we?"

"Why don't you come with us?" suggested Officer Nolan.

"Good idea," Manero said. He didn't want to take any chances that some witness might actually be there who could name them as the villains. He wouldn't let such a witness walk out alive.

"Yeah," Vallone agreed.

Both men touched the weapons on their hips as they emerged from the car. Old habits. Reassurance. McCormick and Nolan got out after them. They all squeezed through the broken door. McCormick was last, making certain that they were not being observed. The pier was empty and cold. Their breath blew like smoke.

There was the rustle of rats scurrying to hide as they advanced into the dark chamber. The only light came from the holes in the ceiling and the broken windows. The wind blew in as if there were no walls at all.

"God, it's cold," said Valone.

"This shouldn't take long," said McCormick. "Then we'll stuff ourselves with Peking Duck."

They kept walking, the Americans on the flanks and the two Irish cops in the center. Bad training, thought Manero. Leaving themselves exposed like that. Without us on the flanks, watching their backs, they'd both be easy targets.

Accidentally, Valone kicked a bottle, and the sound made both Americans drop to their knees and reach for their weapons.

"There was a famous Irish labor leader," began McCormick, ruminating quietly, almost like someone whistling. "Big Jim Larkin. He sailed to America during one of the economic calamities on one of the famous liners, traveled first-class, smoked a big, expensive cigar. And when he got back to Ireland, the reporters came on deck to interview him and there he was, looking grand in his cashmere coat. Well, one of the reporters says to him, 'Jim, how can you justify the first-class travel and the cashmere coat when the times are so hard?' Big Jim Larkin did not blink an eye. He looks the reporter straight in the face and says, 'Nothin's too good for the working man.' "

Mattie had heard the story before, but she laughed all the same.

"It's the pier brings it to mind," explained McCormick.

Manero and Valone were puffing, nearing the end of the pier, and there was no sign of an informant.

The Americans stood up straight when they reached the end, holstered their guns and wiped away the sweat. McCormick and Nolan kept their weapons out.

"There's no one here," declared Manero.

"Ah, but there is," said McCormick. He raised his gun and aimed it at Manero's heart.

Valone saw that Nolan had hers pointed at him. She moved

around quickly and disarmed them both while McCormick kept them covered. She stayed behind them so they couldn't use her as a shield.

Not so badly trained, thought Manero. "You wanna tell us what's going on here?" he asked.

Nolan had put their guns in her purse. She patted them down and took an extra gun from an ankle holster on Manero.

"Let's not trouble the poor men wasting time," McCormick said.

It was the killings, Manero thought. Somehow, these two had learned something. But they couldn't prove anything. He wasn't worried. And even if they had some evidence, they weren't going to extradite them. If they kept their mouths shut, there was no proof. His only worry had been that Jack would be here and name them both as the killers. Why else bring them to the pier?

"You killed them," McCormick declared.

"What the fuck are you talking about?" Vallone shouted, as if he were trying to call for help.

"Who said we killed anybody?" asked Manero.

"Michael," replied McCormick, and Manero's face turned white.

"Listen, we were on an assignment," begged Valone. Suddenly, he understood the danger. They were not just rube Irish cops on a lark. They were working with Michael. They knew it all.

"We can get the money from Nora," suggested Manero.

"On your knees," said McCormick in a voice that neither of them had ever heard before.

Mattie Nolan handcuffed them both and when they were down on their knees begging for their lives, she put a bullet from his own gun through the head of Officer Rocco Valone. She executed Detective Sergeant Vincent Manero with his gun.

They left them there dead, their brains and blood splattered across the cement floor of the pier.

They collected the shells and left the pier, careful that they weren't seen. Then they walked slowly east to Fifth Avenue where they caught a downtown bus. They didn't speak, but they were holding hands.

17

Elio Siracusa maneuvered his pushcart into a blocking position in front of the entrance to the Channel 9 Newscenter on west Sixty-ninth Street. For ten years the small, compact man had run the choicest dining spot on that particular sidewalk. Now no one could go in or out of the building.

A small crowd of employees and delivery personnel gathered on both sides of the steaming barricade. The spectators were all annoyed by this, the latest in New York City's endless permutations of cutting-edge urban hardships. Something new to worry about: crazed pushcart peddlars! Elio's lumber-thick arms were locked on the handlebars of his pushcart, holding it in place, and his foot was crushing down on the brakes so it was clear that it would take a lot of force to remove him. He was staring straight ahead, looking east towards the park and beyond, and there was an odd fire in his eyes.

"Why are you doing this?" cried Harvey Levy from a second-floor window over Elio's head. The pushcart man didn't answer, merely kept his mouth clamped shut and his eyes fixed in the distance. Nothing was able to shatter his concentration.

Inside the glass doors, five private security guards who had been summoned from all parts of the building stood in an urgent swoon. Their arms were folded across their chests in a clear and open declaration of their neutrality. They had already held a small caucus and decided that their authority stopped at the glass doors. Technically, they were helpless to prevent Elio Siracusa from sealing the entrance with his cart of frankfurters and pungent sauerkraut and salty pretzels. They had looked out and seen his expression. From the look on his face, this was trouble and every one of the guards could sense the earth rumbling under Elio's feet.

"Why?" cried Harvey Levy, who had been a steady customer, almost a friend, of Elio Siracusa. Once a month the managing editor of the television news show splurged on a single boiled hot dog, breaking every dietary and health rule by which he lived. However, there were some days when he faced such an onslaught of sour duties that the thought of a hot dog was all that brought him to work.

On such days, the feast was accompanied by a song, with Harvey Levy cooing his delight about the uncommon tastes running riot in his mouth. The two men—Harvey and Elio— found themselves delving from indulgence into philosophy, with Harvey confiding that even a man with a nervous stomach is obliged on occasion to face the wild hot dog, if only to remind himself that life still has zest and tang. Elio took an opposite view, that he, as the keeper of the flame, so to speak, that kept the water boiling, had to remain frankfurter-pure, in a constant state of denial lest he succumb and be lost to hot dog consumption forever.

Theirs was one of those exotic intellectual relationships that break out from time to time between people of unlikely backgrounds in New York City. Usually, it happened in taxi cabs when wizened drivers in working-class caps start out the day with a long soliloquy of bitter complaints and educated comments about the state of the universe, the evidence of decline, as well as the end of civilization as we know it. Such arias would often turn into a duet. In the case of Harvey and Elio, a dedicated stoic hot dog vendor and a relativist binge executive met over mustard in unguarded speculation about the nature of things, this and that.

Once, on one of those afternoons when Levy was in a full state of gustatory bliss, Elio delivered a credible version of how he came to be a pushcart Thoreau. It was, he said, the sweet simplicity of his life: his cart, his virtuous supply of hot dogs and fresh rolls—these were nature's unspoiled bounty and he was the uncomplicated provider. And he wallowed in added benefits: the haze of the park on summer evenings when the softball players kicked up dust; the glow of the lights blazing like a man-made aurora in the winter when New Yorkers were either approaching or retreating from Christmas. As for himself, he was unencumbered by family, debt, or the chains of corporate obligations. He owned his cart and his own soul. He was a man at peace.

On one thing, however, Elio was troubled and passionate. The weather. His life, his simple business, his very being—if he were to speculate and carry it that far—depended on the raw forces of nature. The life he led was guided by unfathomable air currents and mystifying jet streams and moving pressure troughs and complicated weather systems. In other words, he liked to know the night before what he was in for when he went to work the next day. The weather. Not until Bonnie Hudson came to work for Channel 9 did he have anything but grief from the infuriatingly evasive and self-absorbed weather forecasters. As far as style went, he was equally passionate: not until Bonnie's plain, straight-from-the-shoulder delivery did any weatherperson speak to him as a grown-up. The others had toyed with him.

"You know how it is, Mister Levy?" he said one day when he was in the flush of his first rapture with Bonnie. "I have to get to sleep early because I get up at three-thirty to get my cart and get to work. This is not an easy job. But I can't go to sleep until I have the latest weather. Before this girl, the weather bastards were all like stripteasers. They come on the television and they make it like a game, you know? They wear silly grins and say silly things and then they say, well, could be good news tomorrow, or could be bad. Stay tuned and coming up next, we'll tell you. Like they can't tell you now it's gonna rain. It's against the law. Then they come back ten minutes later and they say there are storms in Texas and floods someplace in the midwest, there are lows and highs pushing up from the Gulf. But do they tell you if you should buy more hot dogs because it's gonna be a nice day? Do they say, you should wear an extra sweater or else you're gonna freeze? Do they say hot, cold, whatever? No. They say, you should tune in later, then maybe we'll give a complete weather report. So I'm up all night waiting for these bastards to tell me what's what. You see what I'm getting at?"

"No," Harvey said back then, only half listening because he was still enchanted with the hot dog's aftertaste and Elio was just Elio, not a pushcart terrorist blocking the front door.

"This girl, she does not play games," said Elio then. "She says it's gonna rain, that's it. Bring an umbrella. I go to sleep. Or, it's gonna be cold, wear a sweater. 'Hey, it's only weather!' I like that, too. People say that to me, 'Hey, it's only weather.' I say it, too, so they should know that her, I like. Her, I watch."

That was when Harvey Levy knew that Bonnie Hudson was a born weather star. No matter what she wanted, regardless of his fake promises to pay attention to her burning desire to be a real journalist, he would keep her strapped to the weather map (if he could ever get her to use one), because that was where she belonged. When Elio told him he could go to sleep without grinding his teeth because she didn't beat around the bush, Harvey knew that he had struck rare video gold.

But now she was off the air, and Elio was out front with his locked pushcart and that glint in his eyes.

"Call the cops!" screamed Leslie Beth, one of the new Channel 9 reporters, caught outside with some footage of an oil slick in the Narrows which she thought should lead the newscast. "Have the little jerk arrested!"

"Wait a minute," said her cameraman, Frankie Maldonado, a Staten Island native who had three dogs for lunch every day and didn't want to switch to pizza. "Let's see what he wants. What gives, Elio?"

"I want her back!" Elio said through clenched teeth.

"Who?" cried Leslie Beth, dizzy with impatience.

From his window, Harvey Levy remembered Elio's passion and groaned. "He wants Bonnie. That's who he wants back."

"Call the cops," shrieked Chuck Childers from a third-floor window.

Suddenly, they all heard a rustle against the brick and turned to see a basket being lowered from the third-floor window next to Childers. The basket was held by an extension cable and the cable was held by Max Gross, the soundman. Chuck Childer's empty "in" basket was being guided down by the soundman. The basket landed between Elio's arms. Elio looked up.

"Two, with," called Max Gross, smiling.

Elio didn't smile back. He stood for a moment, thinking. Then he said, in a voice that carried up the three floors to Max: "I'm not giving you sauerkraut."

"Okay," Max said, "but heavy on the mustard."

"To drink?"

"Cream."

Others hung from windows in fascination or stood back, agape.

"I want you to get this on film!" Chuck Childers cried to the cameraman, Maldonado.

But Frankie Maldonado had something else in mind. "I'll

take the usual," the cameraman said to Elio, shifting his camera so he could handle his lunch.

"I want this on film!" Childers kept crying.

Maldonado gave him a surly look and said, "Hey, Mister Childers, hold your water. Okay? I'm on a break."

"Did you hear that?" Childers screamed down at Levy, who lowered his head as if water were being dumped on it. "Harvey, you tell him: I want this on film, this is a breaking story."

"Right, it's breaking and I'm breaking; my lunch break," called Maldonado. Then in a slightly lower but still audible voice: "So don't break my balls."

"He's entitled to his meal," said Levy, looking up, trying to mollify his anchorman.

Just then a cab pulled up in front of the building and out stepped Jack Mann and Bonnie Hudson. Childers began screaming incoherently as Jack and Bonnie paused, took in the scene, then shared one with mustard. Elio unlocked the brakes of his cart and pushed it out of the way to let Bonnie in the building.

"Looks cold for tomorrow, Elio," she said, gazing back at the sky, then plunging into the newscenter.

"You see what I mean?" said Elio, looking up as Harvey Levy ducked back inside to head Bonnie off before she collided with the unmollified Childers.

The lieutenant from the NYPD's public relations office called Inspector McCormick at home and asked him to come down to headquarters. Something bad had just gone down, he said. Two cops had been found dead on a pier and they were signed out on the duty sheet as working liaison with the two visiting Irish cops. The lieutenant was preparing for the press conference at which the police commissioner would announce the deaths in the line of duty of two highly decorated "hero" detectives, and he needed some background filler.

"Yes, well, this is really terrible," said McCormick when he and Mattie arrived at the overheated headquarters. The lieutenant who called them in was a weary old hack on the verge of retirement and just looking to satisfy the technical requirements. "We saw them just this morning," McCormick said. "Hard to believe. Jesus!"

Mattie lowered her head, as if she might be on the verge of tears.

"We're trying to nail down what they were doing on the pier," the lieutenant said. "They signed out the duty book to you, but from what I understand, their main assignment was in Internal Affairs."

"Right, right," McCormick said.

"So were they working with you?"

"Not today."

"You said you saw them today."

"They were helping us out on the search for one of our nationals, who, as you may or may not know, may or may not be in this country. Just routine things. We're strangers and they would brief us about how to go about things."

"So, what was today?"

"Liaison, Lieutenant. Checking over some notes. We had a tip from an informer who said we might find our person in Manhattan."

"And what were Sergeant Manero and Detective Vallone doing?"

"They were pointing us to the Upper West Side of Manhattan. Nothing more. Then they left for something of their own." McCormick smiled ruefully.

"So you did see them today?"

"Just for some directions. They had something else to do, something of their own. They didn't tell us what it was."

The lieutenant nodded, taking notes.

"They did mention something about narcotics," interjected Officer Mattie Nolan.

McCormick looked confused. Then he brightened. "Yes, well, I think that they did, now that you mention it, Officer Nolan." Then he turned to the lieutenant. "Frankly, I wasn't paying too much attention—getting ready for the parade to-morrow. Our own case is not going famously."

The lieutenant, caught in the middle of something far above his level of competence—international intrigue, not to mention two dead cops—was trying to take notes on a large, legal-sized yellow pad and nodding fiercely. "So you don't know anything about what they were doing on a pier?"

"Not at all," Mattie Nolan said. "They had their own duties to perform and they made it quite clear that they were only helping us out part-time."

The lieutenant understood politics and rivalry and the resulting bitterness of the two Irish cops who had been kept at arm's length, as would have been the custom.

They were in a wood-paneled conference room on the main floor at headquarters. The building was alive with grim police officers and reporters milling about, walking fast, back and forth, between nowhere, just to burn off the rage. They always assemble like that, thought McCormick. When a cop dies in Belfast, they all turn out in just that same, flat, furious way. As if they will be available to make the cavalry charge when the bugle sounds. Displaying their energy. Must be some very primitive urge, he thought. Cops all cluster like this for warmth and comfort and to see for themselves just how grief-stricken and vengeful they all are.

The door burst open and the commissioner marched in, trailed by a platoon of chiefs and deputy chiefs. A black man promoted to command for political reasons, as well as his own ability, the commissioner was a former patrolman who'd once walked a beat in Harlem. He was a huge man, and his open palm felt like a fist when he took McCormick's hand in his own and shook it gravely.

"You have my sympathy," said the commissioner, as if McCormick and Nolan were blood relatives of the dead cops.

"I didn't know they were working on your case," said one of the chiefs—a familiar face, head of the detective division.

"Strictly informal," Inspector McCormick replied.

"Christ, on the eve of St. Patrick's Day," muttered one of the deputy chiefs awkwardly.

"What the fuck were they doing on that pier?" asked the commissioner. He made a full circle of the room and no one had any answer.

"We'll have a full investigation," said the head of the detective division. "These guys were not amateurs."

"Excuse me, but Inspector McCormick heard them mention drugs," said the lieutenant from public relations.

"And Officer Nolan heard it as well," said McCormick. "Just this morning when they were going out. When we split up."

The detective chief shook his head. "They wouldn't go on a drug buy with their own unmarked car," he said. "Every street dealer knows an unmarked car when he sees one. Besides, they weren't working narcotics."

The head of the detective command was more restrained than the others in the room. He knew that the two "hero" cops were, in fact, employees of Don Iennello and had probably been paid back for some offense of greed. "No, I don't believe the drug thing," he said.

"But if they were trying to nail some bad cops?" suggested the head of Manhattan South.

"Well, we'll see," the commissioner said, recognizing the rising emotion and clashing interests between his chiefs. "Right now, we can tell the sharks outside that they died in the line of duty, murdered execution-style."

Which is how the story ran on the wires: *Two veteran New York City detectives—Sergeant Vincent Manero and Detective Rocco Valone—were killed today in the line of duty. They were found shot execution-style . . .*

Photographs of the two slain detectives were distributed to newspapers and television stations, along with a special telephone number to report leads. The two Irish police officers were not mentioned, as the connection with the active case was not considered vital.

Tim and Mattie were relieved on their walk home across

the Brooklyn Bridge. The way the New York police handled
the deaths proved that they dismissed the significance of the
Irish end. They would now be able to operate freely under
Michael's orders without the snooping detectives breathing
down their necks.

"It's a pretty sight," Mattie said as they paused on the
pedestrian walk, looking at New York Harbor. The Statue of
Liberty glowed in the distance.

"It is," agreed Tim, looking around them to see if they had
been followed. Paranoia came with the territory.

"It doesn't stop here, does it?" Mattie continued, noting
Tim's caution.

He shook his head. "It can't stop until Michael completes
his job," he said.

She sighed. "I'll be happy to get Irish soil under my feet
again."

"Let's just make certain we don't get planted under six feet
of the old sod."

The way was clear—even the muggers were put off by the
wind—and they hurried back to Tim's room on Clark Street
for a night of honeymoon bliss.

Bonnie was in makeup, sitting in the barber chair, waiting
her turn. Next to her was a rough man with a two-day-old
beard. He reached over and held out his hand. "Bruno," he
said, smiling engagingly. "I'm the hit man."

For a second Bonnie didn't get it, then realized he was
telling her that he was a guest for Chuck Childer's segment,
"Movers and Shakers." He was a professional assassin.

"Which one are you?" she asked. "A mover or a shaker?"

Bruno leaned back in the chair, the protective napkin
pinned around his collar like a dental guard, and puffed on his
cigar. "Both," he said. "First I shake 'em, then I move." He
laughed at his own wit.

After a minute, while the makeup woman played around

with his forehead to take off some of the glisten, he turned to
Bonnie again. "I know you from someplace, am I right?"

"I'm the weather moll," she said.

He leaned on his elbow for a better look, rudely pushing
away the makeup woman, who didn't want to touch his beard
because it gave him a sinister look, and said, "Right. The
weathergirl. I knew I knew you. You're the one . . . what's that
thing? Oh, yeah: 'Hey! It's only the weather!' "

He laughed and Bonnie was obliged to issue her own small
laugh. Bruno did not seem like a guy who tolerated modesty
or rejection.

"So," she said by way of making conversation, "how come
you're going public? I mean, I'd think that appearing on a
television show and being named as a known hit man, admit-
ting it even, would put you in some danger, maybe even make
some people angry. Your employers, not to mention the cops."

He leaned over, to speak in confidence. "This is bullshit,"
he said. "I never whacked nobody. Well, nobody big. I'm
strictly a legman."

"What?"

"I break legs. Guy doesn't pay the vig—that's the interest—I break his legs. Or maybe an arm, if his legs are
already broken. I even do fingers, which can be a very painful
thing. You'd be surprised. Somebody thinks you're coming
after their fingers, they get very generous."

Then he leaned back and spoke in normal voice. "Besides,
this guy, what's-his-name, he says he's not gonna put my face
on the camera. Makes for better TV, he says. Nobody will
recognize me with the electronic gizmo disguise. And he'll
change my voice. Nobody will be able to tell it's me talkin'. No
sweat."

"Why bother, though? I mean, why even go on a program
like this?"

He looked bewildered. He held up his arms. "Are you
kiddin'? Hey, I never been on TV," he said, getting up and

heading for the studio, accompanied by the member of the public relations staff assigned to guide him around and fetch him coffee. "My wife's gonna tape it, are you kiddin' me?"

Bonnie let the makeup woman dust her face lightly; it had a soothing effect. Her lecture from Harvey moments ago was still irritating, but she knew that she had to endure some reprimand, make some pledge to behave within the norms of television protocol. She had sworn to Harvey Levy when he pulled her into his office and shook his finger in her face that she would not mention Childer's hair again. She would not ridicule him on the air, she would not explode when he acted stupid, and she would make some attempt to use the maps.

"Isn't that something," the makeup girl said, making certain that the facial softener hadn't gotten onto Bonnie's blouse.

"What?"

"A hit man. In my chair. Can you imagine?"

"But he said he wasn't a hit man," said Bonnie.

The makeup girl smirked knowingly. "You think he's gonna tell you?"

Jack was waiting on the rim of the set when Bonnie hurried through to her station by the weather map. Chuck Childers was reading a breaking story on the teleprompter about two hero cops who had been brutally murdered, execution-style, on a Manhattan pier. They were victims of an important drug sting "gone bad."

Childers continued, "Later on, during my nightly 'Movers and Shakers' segment, we'll be talking to a mob hit man who may be able to shed some light on this horrible crime. Meanwhile, police have just released the names and pictures of the two slain detectives."

Bonnie finished straightening her suit jacket, then looked up and saw the photographs of Sergeant Vincent Manero and Detective Rocco Valone.

Childers turned in her direction, his smiling face beaming with the victory of Bonnie's humiliation. "Now to Bonnie

Hudson, our own weathergirl, who's back with us after a short vacation. What's the good word for the outlook, Bonnie?"

"Holy shit!" said Bonnie. The dead cops were the two detectives she had seen in the morning leaving headquarters with Inspector McCormick and Officer Nolan.

18

The don was getting very tired of the girl he called "Staten Island." She kept pulling at what she called his "gweat big sausage monster," trying, in her baby-talk voice, to summon it back to life after four marathon sessions of every conceivable sex variation. They had undergone oral, anal, genital, and masturbatory sequences—each culminating in thrashing, screaming climaxes.

Staten Island had never been with a man who could keep up with her enormous appetite. Not one could even come close. She could not believe that this old man had the endurance and power of a bull and almost matched her lust.

But now he had collapsed in the soft bed of the Pierre Hotel, convinced that he had injured himself in some important way during their naked acrobatics. Even Staten Island's ample "front porch" and the combined efforts of her mouth and her hand failed to arouse the exhausted beast into a fifth round of action.

"Listen, listen," he said, still unable to catch his breath. "Gimme a minute, will ya?"

But as Cecilia, the sensuous woman/child whom he called Staten Island, stopped working on his limp monster, she went into a baby-girl pout, her lower lip protruding as if she had been denied her promised candy. The don't wind settled down and in the sudden quiet he smelled the moisture from the sweat and his own semen and her unabated arousal emanating like summer scents from the dark, swampy patch of her pubic region. Her nipples were still hard and she brushed back her hair with her little hand—the same little hand that had just been whacking away at him in a shamelessly lustful manner—and out of the crypt of his groin, the slain monster rose again.

Her face, when she glanced down and saw the stirring, was glowing with anticipation and ancient with pride. She pretended to ignore him, turning away to display her breasts in outthrust profile, letting them sway in seductive slow-motion, stretching, as if a yawn was what she really intended in that languid move. Wantonly, she threw her long, dark hair back, and the little don was now growling and half-wild with desire. He grabbed her breasts roughly and she squeaked, "Oh, no!" acting as if she were the innocent maiden and had not invited the beast back into her life. And then she groaned as he turned her and licked and nibbled at her.

Throwing her back on the bed, the don held her arms over her head. She wet her lips, as if they were dry from fear rather than moist with greed. "What are you going to do to me?" she whispered in that same high, teenaged voice.

"I'm going to fuck you," he snarled, looming above her, letting her see the full extent of his arousal.

"With that?" she asked, staring at it, her eyes widening as he stuck his knees between her legs and forced them open. "Oh, it won't fit!" she cried, her eyes still glued to the throbbing thing.

"We'll make it fit," he said, pushing her legs out and up and then entering her as she growled in aching, arching pleasure.

Afterward, as she lay in the puddle of her contentment, she reached over and stroked the don's cheek. He let her rub her hand across his face, but he was angry at himself. She was getting too familiar. She was getting to know too many tricks and ways of putting him in her power. He had spent his whole life refusing to submit to anyone, and now this little piece of ass was encroaching on his territory, occupying his thoughts, casting a spell over him.

"I'm hungry," she said in that weak little voice that was so potent with the don.

"What?" he asked, although he knew what she wanted.

"I'm soooo hungry," she said, rolling over and embracing his arm, letting him feel the texture of her smooth skin, down to her rough pubic hair, knowing the fierce voice he used was there because she put it there with her seductive ways. She understood her strength in a very primitive way. He could slap her—and he probably would—but it would be a sign of his weakness. A show of her strength. This, she understood, although she would not be able to explain it.

"I'm hungry, too," he said in a husky voice, thinking, even as he said it, that he was growing old and soft and that it was all the fault of this little bitch.

"Can we get some room service, hon?" she asked, rubbing up and down on his arm.

"No!" he said, pulling away. "Go take a shower. You smell. Then we'll go downtown and eat."

She knew that he meant Scargulio's and it was not an unpleasant thought. She'd have the veal scaloppini, she thought as she grabbed a towel and her shampoo and the hair dryer she carried in her huge shoulder bag.

"Don't take all night," yelled the don, deciding that he was not yet completely tired of her. He crept into the shower where she was singing and grabbed her from behind. She screamed and he laughed, and then she looked down and saw that he had brought the monster into the shower with them.

* * *

Nora tried the wigs. First the black curly wig, then the long red one. They both fit nicely. She put on the dress that was a size too big, and stuffed rubber falsies down the front. They gave her an awkward, unbalanced look, which is what she was after. Then she applied the heavy eye shadow and lipstick and rouge. She studied herself in the mirror. She looked—with her red wig and thick lips and heavy-lidded eyes—seductive. Then Nora had an inspiration. She took the eyebrow pencil and drew a faint line on her upper lip and a small spot on her chin. She studied herself in the mirror again and was happy. She still looked glamorous, but there was a hint of some indefinable shadow in her face.

She studied the outfit. It flattered her new lush figure. Her purse matched the coat and the dress, and she made certain that the Davis P-32 with two extra clips fit into it safely under a small kerchief, a book of matches and a pair of gloves, which were three sizes too big.

She worried that someone would see her coming out of the apartment on Ninety-eighth Street. And she was right. Pat Duggan, the landlord, was waiting for her on the landing. He had never seen her dressed up.

"You look good enough to eat," he said hungrily. "Date?"

She smiled.

He stood blocking the door.

"Listen, I'm going to need the room," he said.

She thought it was a trick to jack up the rent or force some tenant concession. She wasn't in the market at the moment. Not at this late stage of her plans. "When?" she asked.

"We could work something out tonight. Maybe even lower the rent, if you play your cards right."

"I'm late," she said, trying to keep her face away from the light. She pushed past him and he felt the strength in her arms.

"I'll be needing the room," he shouted after her.

It was cold on Columbus Avenue and she walked quickly until she found a cab on Broadway and took it south down to Sheridan Square. The cabdriver kept his radio blaring on an

Indian station that whanged in her head. She would have said something, but not tonight. She could not call attention to herself. Through the bulletproof Plexiglas with the air holes she could see the driver watching her in the rearview mirror. His name was Bandar, according to the hack license in the front. He wore a colorful sweater and a headband and sang along with the Indian music. On the top of his meter was a shamrock, indicating his solidarity with the Irish holiday. Christ, she thought, this culture is so overwhelming and absorbing that if they were American the Queen of England and the Prime Minister and the Archbishop of Canterbury would wear green on St. Patrick's Day. Because of the party. Because of the politics of being a good sport. Because it is America and every maniac wing of every lunatic fringe group had an equal right to celebrate.

She got out on Seventh Avenue and paid the $9.75 fare; she handed the driver twelve dollars, told him to keep the change. Bandar pulled away without a thank-you. Gratitude was not part of the deal. Greenwich Village was busy with pre–St. Patrick's Day celebrations. The bars all had shamrocks in the windows and green derbies out front. It was almost eight o'clock and the residents and tourists already had a few under their belts and made their way down the streets with an unsteady if gay kind of dance step. There were more than a few who sang out at her to join them, then, sensing some dark, sad agenda, let her go.

At Eleventh Street, she stopped in the White Horse Tavern, where Dylan Thomas drank his last drink before dying. A corner table where he wrote was set aside as a permanent memorial. A plaque overhead commemorated the great immoderate Welsh poet. At the bar she ordered a beer and then a plain whiskey and drank them both quickly, shuddering as the fire of the liquor struck her belly. A man sidled up to her and offered to buy her a drink. He was in his thirties and wore expensive clothing, and he smelled of cologne. But Nora was repelled in some deep fashion, as if he should know that he was raising a trivial issue while she was on an important mission.

"Mission." Funny. The first time she'd thought of it that way. A mission. Not something cursed, like a crime or a sin. A patriotic mission whose grandeur raised the sordid act above human condemnation. She would not allow herself to consider the moral implications of what she was about to do.

She left the bar and walked along Seventh Avenue, unnoticed among the Friday-night parade of eccentrics. The gay couples walked hand-in-hand, as free and unremarkable as strolling teenagers in any American city. Transvestites slithered in their overdressed spangles, batting false lashes at the world. Bikers with tattoos, and longshoremen with chips on their shoulders stalked the Greenwich Village streets looking for action or trouble.

Nora, in her Bensonhurst best, attracted no attention. The kids in jeans outside the public theaters were more interested in the gaudier show. The middle-class restaurant trade off West Fourth Street had hunger on their minds, and the street show was mere atmosphere.

Down past the Holland Tunnel, a more desperate street life made itself felt. There were the crack hookers, wearing hotpants despite the weather, soliciting truckers on their way out to Jersey and the heartland. They did not welcome the competition and glared at Nora. She turned east on Canal Street and headed deep into Chinatown and Little Italy. A couple of boys followed her for two blocks. They were obviously suburbanites trying to make up their minds whether or not she was a working girl. She picked up the pace, making it clear that she was uninterested, and they dropped away.

The streets of Chinatown and lower Broadway were aglitter with Friday-night traffic. Couples meeting after work, and families chugging through the congestion worked their way towards the brilliant restaurants that were sprinkled along Mott Street or east Broadway. Nora was choked by a sudden clutch of grief as she walked past a family of three, a young boy of Seamus's age hand-in-hand between the two parents. She'd held his hand like that in Cork. Jack on one side, she on the other. He wanted to run across a bridge, but she wouldn't let him. Too much traffic, too dangerous. She saw his face, with that disappointed scowl, because his mother was overprotective. Not protective enough, she thought now, as she felt him swing from the lifted arms of Jack and herself. "Getting heavy," she'd said then, laughing. "Soon we won't be able to get you off the ground." But she'd been wrong. He'd never grow heavy enough now. He was forever five.

Put it out of your mind, Nora, she told herself in New York City's Chinatown. There's work to do.

Every once in a while she stopped in a jade and china gift shop, pretending to study the porcelain junk while watching the street for a tracker. The shop owners were accustomed to Caucasian tourists, who were always in some state of indecision. They never knew the value of things, or even which restaurants were good. They usually entered the ones with the biggest lines, which, it turned out, was a pretty good index to the quality of the food.

The streets were patrolled by teams of police from the nearby Elizabeth Street station house, but the cops seemed indifferent to the street vendors trying to cheat the tourists or the open sale of fireworks. The police were a blind presence, meant to deter more flagrant crimes or spring into action when open violence could not be ignored. Young toughs fresh from Hong Kong roamed the avenues in defiant clusters, breaking only for the police teams. They had long hair and cigarettes tucked behind their ears and they spoke in loud, pushy voices—a distinctly different presence than the earlier, modest immigrants from Taiwan or the mainland. These were the gang members who dealt in drugs and carried high-caliber weapons and occasionally marched into restaurants and sprayed everyone with automatic fire.

But Nora was enchanted by the exotic atmosphere. Even if the streets were slippery with lettuce and rotting garbage, they smelled of garlic and onion and the spices that seasoned the ducks and chickens hanging in long lines in the shop windows. And the singing dialects rang in her ears.

She turned down Chambers Street, and disappeared into the crowds.

"Some salad to start," said Aldo, the maitre d', who had seated the don at his usual far table with his back to the wall.

"How are ya tonight, Aldo?" said Staten Island; she had grown familiar and possessive in the afterglow of the session at the Pierre. It was a bad signal for the don, who decided to rid himself of her clinging presence after tonight. It would be painful, because she was a wildcat when it came to sex. But that, in itself, was a dangerous thing. He had to keep moving, even in his infatuations.

The don did not suffer over his loss. He had, over the years, built up a complicated series of defenses against sentimental inhibitions. The first thought he conjured up was a mental picture—in complete clarity—of how she would look in twenty years, with the heavy jowls and the mountain range of rolls on her stomach and the shapely legs grown into trees. The second was self-pity. He was being denied a tasty morsel. He was the victim.

It didn't occur to him that it was he, himself, who was the instrument of the deprivation. He leaped to the conclusion she had to go. Let them get too comfortable, too close, and they would start to get ideas. He knew because, when he thought about it, if he were in their spot, he would get ideas. Ambition. Greed. His motto was: Better to keep changing the girls on the sheets than let one get too close.

Benny-the-Blinker and a young gunman sat at a nearby table, keeping a protective eye on the don, at a respectful but safe distance.

"Aldo is fine, now shut up," said the don. Then, turning to the maitre d', he added. "Not too quick."

"Certainly, Mister Iennello. You just let us know when you're ready."

Then he backed away.

The idea of dumping Staten Island had excited him, made him think of one last moment, one last opportunity. He had an urge for her ripe body. And so he took her hand and placed it on the stiffening bulge in his lap. She blushed and looked around, then worked the zipper slowly, as if it might be overheard.

She took it out, there in the back of Scargulio's, the monster, and sighed and oohed, and worked her hand up and down the shaft. The don looked away, looked around the room, saw that no one was watching. He took her by the neck and pushed her head down and she was face-to-face with his desire. The don moved the tablecloth so that her head was not visible, bobbing up and down. Still, it excited him even more that there were people in the restaurant who knew exactly what was going on.

At the entrance to the restaurant a glittering redhead made her way to the front of the line waiting for tables.

"I'm meeting someone," she said. "Pat Duggan." It was the name she had used when making the reservation.

"I'm afraid he's not here yet," said Aldo.

Nora smiled.

"Do you mind if I use the ladies' room?" she asked.

The ladies' room was near the back, just in front of the back room in which Benny-the-Blinker and his sidekick kept guard. Nora walked back slowly, scanning around as if she were lost, although she had made two previous visits to the restaurant.

At the spot where she was supposed to turn right for the ladies' room, she kept going straight through the arch that separated the front from the rear, heading for the table where the cloth was moving up and down almost imperceptibly. She slipped on a pair of gloves big enough for the hands of a man as she walked through the restaurant.

Benny started to rise, but then decided that she was just lost and would soon catch on; maybe the don would get a little thrill out of being caught. Besides, a woman was no threat.

In front of the don's table, Nora reached into her purse, and the don, whose radar was turned to high alert, sensed trouble. He tried to pull away from Staten Island, but she had locked herself onto his shaft. Now Nora had the gun out of her purse and was bending her knees to keep steady as she fired off four rounds into the don's face and chest. After each shot she whispered:

"Seamus! Seamus! Seamus! Seamus!"

She turned and fired one in Benny's face and another in the sidekick's face, then she dropped the gun and the oversized gloves and walked slowly out of the restaurant, the eyeliner running down her face with her tears.

The shots had thrown Scargulio's into an uproar. The first reaction was shock and then everyone ducked while Nora made good her escape. No one thought to stop her, a woman. The rush was headed the other way. Cops, DAs, reporters— they were all running for the back room where Staten Island was emerging from below the table, covered with blood, screaming, but otherwise unhurt.

Outside, Nora dropped the red wig and the rubber falsies into a trash can, then turned the coat inside out. The first cops on the scene quickly found all the clues. They sent out an alarm for a man dressed as a woman.

19

Saturday, March 16, 1991

The parade was high-stepping its way up Fifth Avenue, puffed up by the proud Irish pipes and twinkling with the polished brass and uncertain notes of borough-bred Catholic high school bands. The flushed, budding young twirlers were spinning their batons in the cold sun of the bright late March morning as they ignored the goose bumps on their bare legs and pranced along the spine of Manhattan.

Inspector McCormick was surprised to find himself moved at the sight of such a powerful mass of enthusiastic marchers; he was accustomed to the softer, foot-dragging participants of Galway, with their spiritual tone and grudging rituals. They didn't have black and gay and lesbian contingents marching alongside to honor an Irish saint in Galway. The Americans, no matter what else you said about them, exploded with energy and variety and a drive that was irresistible. They marched along Fifth Avenue and past the reviewing stand as if they were on their way to war.

"Will you look at them!" he said, half whispering to Officer Mattie Nolan marching beside him in their place of honor near the front—the authentic Irish contingent.

"Yes," she said, equally struck by the parade's brawn.

They were both choking back something, realizing for the first time what the great famines and migrations had driven from their homeland and saved here in America. These husky and lighthearted Americans might be Sunday Irish and they might have tavern and whiskey sentiments for the old country, but the berets were worn like jaunty victory wreaths and the sound of the pipes was an ancient reminder of unbroken roots. They were still Irish, for all their narrow pride and potbellied complacency.

The sergeants and lieutenants and Veterans of Foreign Wars came up to shake hands—for this was not like their own Galway parades, where lines of march were inviolable. The people here came in and out with great, informal freedom. They whispered "God bless!" or just stared with eyes wet with emotion.

"I wish this was done," said Mattie between St. Patrick's Cathedral and the park.

"Not much more," replied McCormick.

"I don't mean the march," she said. She kept her eyes in front and her head steady like a step dancer.

"Well." He sighed, smiling to the crowds. "It won't be long now." He noticed now that the crowds were changing slightly. There were roving bands of drunken youths—high school kids taking this holiday as permission to load up on green beer.

"Do you know something or is that a guess?" she asked, turning her head to look at him.

He knew something. Michael's job was coming to its conclusion. He knew that much. Their assignment—to provide tactical backup, and whatever else was required—would end at the same time. And there were other signs in the air. He had seen the newspapers and knew about the murder of the don in the downtown restaurant. He could guess who had committed that one. And he didn't think that it was a man dressed up as a woman, although the high thinkers of the special Mafia task forces were committed to that peculiar view. They even told their pet reporters that it was a favorite mob tactic—to dress up an assassin as a woman—which was an outright lie. Mafia killers were terrified of being thought in any way feminine. They'd rather get gunned down during an escape than be caught in a dress.

No, he'd swear that Nora had taken her revenge. Or, at least, had taken a great chunk of it. Not that he blamed her. But was she done? He couldn't answer that. Not until he spoke to his superior. Not until he spoke to Michael.

"We'll find out soon enough," he said, and Mattie took that as a sign that they were halfway home.

Michael was hungry. He hadn't eaten breakfast and it was almost lunchtime when he pulled off of the expressway at Castleton Corners and found an open restaurant. It was a neighborhood spot in the heart of Staten Island and he drew long native stares from the regulars. Somewhere between assessment and deterrence. He returned a friendly nod and took a table in the corner, and when the owner who doubled as a waiter came up, Michael asked for toast and tea.

The newspapers were full of last night's slaughter, and he could see the tabloid picture in the rack near the door from where he sat. The don's face was flung back and his chest was torn open by bullets. His arms were flung out by his sides, giving his body a Christlike appearance. Michael could hear the regulars commenting knowingly on what they called "the rubout."

"They all end up like that; no matter how big or how powerful, that's how they end up!"

"Still, did you see the girlfriend? She's a local girl. A kid, a pretty kid, from Annadale. With that old man! Can you believe it? Really disgusting!"

"Well, he was a powerful guy and girls are attracted to all that . . ."

"All that what?"

"You know, the limousines and the fancy restaurants . . ."

"Yeah, well, that's how he ended up—in some fancy restaurant with four fancy bullets in his fancy chest."

"I wonder how they missed her?"

"Professionals. These guys are good."

This last comment came from an ex-cop, one of those spreaders of the Mafia myth. Michael finished his tea and toast and got ready to leave.

"How much?" he asked the owner, keeping the accent out of his voice.

"Lessee, that's one tea and one order of toast, is, lemme just write it down. That's one dollar, fifteen."

Michael laid out a dollar and a half and the owner/waiter rang it up as he left.

He inhaled the crisp air, and almost choked on the sulphur drifting in from the marshes. He got into the rented car, started it up and sat there for a moment, trying to think ahead. Trying to assess how he stood, now that leadership and authority had been rearranged. The don was well murdered. A planned, professional deed. It could have been one of those mob paybacks. One Mafia family taking revenge for some unforgiven offense. A grudge being laid to rest. It was possible.

But Michael didn't believe that. It was Nora. She had promised to wait and she didn't. She had taken her revenge, and from the descriptions, she'd done it seamlessly. He should be angry, Michael thought. She didn't wait. He had to think, but his head was swimming. A soldier under orders would have waited. There's a penalty for that kind of indiscipline, he thought. But then he remembered her sitting on a bench outside the park, keening with sharp memories over Seamus, and how could he blame her? Well, he could. Because he had to blame her. If she had killed the don—and he had no doubt

that it had been she—she'd violated the pledge she had made
to him. She was unreliable. She could topple his plan. The
woman had to be restrained. He called himself to attention,
shook off the wave of pity, and cleared his head.

He looked at his watch. It was ten past noon. According to
the arrangements made in their phone calls, he was right on
time. He drove along the service road on Old Place and, near
an abandoned truck terminal, found the dirt road that led to
Waldo's secret lab. The old man was standing out in front,
waiting for him. He was wearing his white smock and under
it a clean shirt and a bow tie. Michael couldn't help but smile
at the tender habits of old men.

"I wasn't sure you could make it," Waldo said. Michael got
out of the car and looked around. Michael was always checking for the trap that he was certain would one day spring up
in his face. It wasn't his fate that bothered him. He knew what
that would be. It was how he conducted himself until that last,
lethal moment that concerned him. He wanted to face his own
death on his feet, with dignity.

"Well, my friend," he said, looking for fresh tire marks in
the mud even as he slapped Waldo happily on the back, "it was
such a nice day for a drive, what with the sunshine and the nip
in the air. It reminded me of a fine day in Derry. Have you
ever been to Derry?"

"Not even in Londonderry," answered Waldo, accustomed
to such chitchat before getting down to business. He dealt with
people who always took their time, looking for God-knows-
what. Like dogs circling a blanket before they lay down, he
told his wife.

"Well, you should come," said Michael, circling the blanket.
"It's beautiful country, and then you go down to Sligo and
Yeats country with its terrible beauty. The Irish are chiseled
out of those marble and granite hills, those deep lakes in
between."

"As long as they don't try to chisel me," quipped Waldo,
and Michael laughed.

"Good, very good."

They walked around the shed, and now Michael had Waldo looking for traps and signs and ambushes. Waldo had seen cautious men, but this one was at war. He walked a distance into a field, the mud sucking at his shoes, and he didn't seem to mind. Waldo, who was wearing galoshes, followed him.

"Any trouble?" asked Michael, certain now that they were not being overheard.

"Some," answered Waldo.

Michael looked a little alarmed.

"Technical difficulties," said Waldo, waving them off. He was a scientist who had solved the problems. "You had this American La France Model PCW, which has a two-and-a-half-gallon capacity." He had adopted the lecturing tone of a professor. "Naturally, you couldn't load a two-and-a-half-gallon charge of our material in there, so I had to first install a dummy charge above and below the lethal dose of a quart. Which is all you would need. The Serin would be released after a small safety charge of CO_2, less than a gallon, but you have to be very careful."

Michael took it in, nodded. "Both cylinders?" he asked.

"Both," replied Waldo.

"Any trouble getting your hands on the Serin?"

Waldo shook his head. "We can get anything in America," he said.

They headed back to the shack and loaded the two cylinders into the trunk of the car. They surrounded it with bubble packaging to guard against bumps. They stuffed the protective suits in the trunk on top of the cylinders.

"You would have to have a pretty bad accident to break those two cylinders open," said Waldo.

Michael said he would be careful anyway.

"This thing last night," began Waldo. "I don't know what it means to you."

"At this stage, nothing."

Waldo nodded. "Of course, it was the don's people who put us in touch, so I wasn't certain."

"My relationship with the don was strictly business," said Michael.

"Just as well. Just as well. Mine, also."

"Then it's good that you'll be getting away," said Michael.

"You can't know how good," laughed the chemist. "My wife thinks that I am at the end of my rope. Not that she has any idea why. She thinks I work too hard."

"You do."

"In a way. I've been very bothered. This business in Kuwait."

"What?"

"The burning oil fields. No one realizes how bad that is. No one appreciates the toxic effects, the deadly particles that will rain down on that whole region. People will get cancer for a hundred years from those fires."

Michael looked across the Arthur Kill river where the smoke from burning dumps in Port Reading were like fingers pointing at the sky. "We're not doing ourselves proud here, either," he said.

"No," said Waldo. "The people who run Perth Amboy and Port Mobil have more immediate concerns than the environment."

Michael handed him the attaché case with its contents of $100,000.

Waldo paused, looked down at the ground, almost as if he were ashamed of what he said when he lifted his head. "I thought you might kill me," said Waldo, smiling at Michael, his voice trembling.

Michael had considered it. Years earlier it would have been essential. He would not have left someone behind who could identify him. But now, with all things running out, with the sorrows coming in battalions, he'd decided against it. In his life he had left behind a trail of so many bodies that this one was his penance, his token act of contrition. Waldo was his gift back to the gods.

Michael smiled wanly. "I like the way you speak of the environment," he said. "The earth. We've got to have people like you around who tend to the earth." He looked around. "So much of it's dying."

The old man laughed nervously, recognizing how close a shave he had had.

"Well," said Waldo afterward, as Michael was about to leave, "I should warn you that the killing of the don has created great turmoil."

"What do you mean?"

"I had a call. Not here. Not at home. At a phone that is safely untapped. It was an intermediary. And he was frantic. A man of solid grounding, a reliable man, yet he was half-crazed, asking me who I thought shot his leader, screaming that he would take revenge if it took a thousand years or more, telling me to look for signs in you. Though why you should kill that fellow I have no idea."

Michael could think of one good reason. He thanked the chemist and drove off, avoiding the bumps. He had to sneak the cylinders back into the hotel, set them up before anyone noticed, make certain that the inspection dates were fresh, then make an appointment with his backup team. He could not take a chance that the mission would unravel because of Nora's impatience.

The mission, he told himself, as he had told himself a hundred times before, nothing must interfere with the mission. Of course, no mission was ever just another mission to Michael. This one was the act that would set his nation free. This bomb, or that ambush, or the other kidnapping was the final act in the long drama of Ireland's tragedy. It was an old calculation he had made as a boy when he joined the IRA; there was always a price. If someone was killed—if many were killed—well, that was the price of a United Ireland. And a

United Ireland was worth a few casualties. He believed that. He had to believe that. Otherwise he could never set off the cylinders of nerve gas bundled up like babies in the back of his car. But now, as he drove across the Verrazano-Narrows Bridge, doubts encroached on his concentration. The traffic slowed as it neared the old toll plaza, in spite of the fact that there were no tolls to pay going into the city. And in his turmoil and confusion, Michael slammed his hand against the horn and screamed at the driver ahead.

The other motorists saw only one more man driven mad with frustration behind the wheel of his car.

There were dark and numerous bars in the Inwood section of Manhattan, near enough to Gaelic Park where they played gaelic football. One bar in particular, called Paddy's, off St. Nicholas Avenue, retained the feel of a pub. The bar girls were green card immigrants accustomed to the rude touch of strangers, and their customers were off-the-books construction workers who knew better than to ask too many questions. Three people of average looks would not be noticed in such a spot.

Michael arrived early, as was his custom, to ensure the safety of the territory. He secured a dim booth in the rear of the bar and set up three beers. His backup team arrived, separately, members of the Provisional Irish Republican Army assigned to assist him. First came the woman, drawing off attention as the men in Paddy's turned to take her measure. Then the male member of the team, a short man you wouldn't notice unless you were on the lookout.

There was a grave and sober look to them both. Mattie Nolan and Timothy McCormick were both soldiers and knew the importance of obedience; still, it was unusual for Michael to put up a rocket for an emergency meeting. They both knew that something important—crucial to the mission—must be at stake. Each had an inkling, but neither wanted to consider the possibility.

Mattie spotted Michael first and showed no sign, just slipped into the padded seat across from him. Inspector McCormick circled the bar once, seeming to look for the men's room but really counting the house, measuring the possible threats. Then he slid next to Michael so that they both had their backs to the wall.

"King Billy," said Michael, holding up his glass.

"May he rot in hell," replied McCormick and Mattie.

They emptied their beers, refilled their glasses, and then ordered another pitcher.

"How was the march?" asked Michael.

McCormick was ecstatic. "Oh, grand. You should have seen them wobbling down the street. Hundreds. Thousands. My feet are sore, but there'll be some sore heads in the morning."

"Green beer," Michael said, shaking his head. "Can you imagine?"

"Well, I don't see the harm of it," said Mattie.

The two men nodded. "Not a great deal," said Michael.

Up at the bar, they were singing about the rebel Roddy McCorley's hanging at the bridge of Toomb. It was a wobbly sound, made unsteadier by the number of beers the patrons had taken in. The men held each other around the shoulders and swayed, and Michael could see the danger of a collapse.

"I have to get back," Michael said.

McCormick nodded. "Let's have it, then."

"It's Nora," Michael said.

"What about her?" McCormick asked.

"Well," said Michael, "little more than a week to go. Things can't be stopped. Not from my end. It's a desperate thing."

Mattie and Tim nodded. Michael went on, his head low. "There's some people who can stop us."

"That's what we're here for—to watch your back," Tim said.

Michael shook his head. He looked around. Then, in a voice so low it drew them closer, he said: "She did that man last night."

"He was a criminal," Mattie offered.

Michael nodded.

"Well, she did, knowing her," McCormick said.

Michael leaned across the table, holding his voice down, but its intensity was like a switchblade. The old Michael spoke: "The problem is that the Italian people take these things badly. They even take them personally. They got it into their heads that Nora put four bullets into their chief, then cut down his bodyguards. They know she's my sister. Since they are vital—vital—to my assignment, I cannot afford to have them as my enemy. Not now. Not with eight days left to go before the Academy Awards."

"I don't get it," McCormick said. "What in God's name are you getting at?"

Michael's voice was flat. "Nora promised me that she would stay out of it. She swore that she would let me complete the assignment before going after that man."

"She broke her word," Mattie said.

"I don't give a damn about that. You think I give a tinker's damn about her word?"

McCormick was still a little thick. "And so you have a solution."

"I do."

"And what would that be?" Mattie asked brazenly.

There was a pause and all three parties at the table filled their glasses and swallowed their beer.

Michael's voice emerged from some pitch-black hole of unbending duty:

"There's no other way; she's got to be killed."

20

Monday, March 18, 1991

The subways changed tone and pace at seven on workday nights. It happened suddenly and with uncanny regularity. One minute to the next. Before seven, during the evening rush hour, riding the subway had a dizzying, roller-coaster feel, with its headlong plunge of office workers frantic to get home, their faces tight with battlefield urgency. And then, at the stroke of seven, everything changed, as if the system had reached its crest and begun an ominous descent, with that mood of slow, sour menace and suggestion of uncontrolled free-fall.

When the business-types were gone, they left behind the desperados. Afterward the subways belonged to the panhandlers, the strung-out outlaws, the prowling predators, the urine-soaked homeless, and the hard-core subway gypsies who scrounged food and spare change, and found a makeshift home in the tunnels and caves of the underground. During the day, they withdrew into the shadows, and came out like hunted things in the dark.

There were still some workers coming home late or going out early, the tourists who didn't know the timetable and the kids who didn't know better. But there came a time when the balance of power within the system was turned over to the outcasts.

Jack and Bonnie boarded the Number One Broadway local heading uptown at 7:35 P.M. They had been unable to connect with Inspector McCormick or Officer Nolan, and Jack had decided that they should find Nora. If she was on a rampage, he had a duty to try and stop her. If she was innocent, he'd help her evade the authorities. After what she'd been through, someone owed her some kind of assistance.

There were thirty or more people already on the train. A couple heading for Lincoln Center in pumps and evening wear, talking together at the end of the car, their eyes rolling in fear. Another couple—a young pair with unwashed hair and filthy rags, heads leaning against each other as they slouched in their drugged sleep, drooling down the sides of their gaunt, doomed faces. Single, furtive figures leaned against the doors, as if they were closer to safety near an exit. Lone travelers read fiercely, as if a book's fictional locale could change the dire setting of the subway at night.

Two men sat directly across from Jack and Bonnie, and they seemed to be in the midst of a hot argument. They were middle-aged men, ordinary types, carrying bundles and over-night bags and wearing warm coats. Almost normal, in the first, glancing impression.

"You know," Jack started to say ... and Bonnie leaned over and whispered, "Shhhhh! Listen."

Jack sat up straighter and saw that she was looking at the two men across the aisle.

"So, I says to him, 'Look, you can't talk to me like that,' an' he says, 'Why not?' Can you believe that? 'Why not?!' "

The first angry man was short and stocky, in his thirties, and wore a hunter's cap with ear flaps that bounced as the train jostled past Fourteenth Street. He was jumping in his seat, excited by the memory of indignation and insult. At the same time, the second angry man spoke.

"You know what she does? She's got a doll and she keeps it in the closet and when she takes it out, she puts things in it, little pins; like knives, you can't believe the pain!"

The second angry man was larger, with broad, thick features. He was wearing a sheepskin coat and carrying a bag from Henri Bendel. He was about fifty, and he clutched his hands together, wringing them continuously. He had scabs from old sores on the hands, he had washed them white with his unsettled emotions.

"I'm not gonna take that," the first angry man said. "What am I, a schmuck? He's gonna tell me that I have a problem when he has to move out to Scarsdale? No, sir! No, sir! *No, sir!*"

"It's not the pain. Just that the bitch has everybody on her side. Nobody wants to hear about the closet and the doll, like she's so pure and untouchable! The bitch! The fucking bitch! The miserable, cunt, fucking bitch!!"

Bonnie turned and put her face against Jack's coat so that the two men would not notice her whisper. "They're not talking to each other," she said.

He looked across and saw that she was right. He had assumed, since they were sitting side by side that way, in a train in which there were a lot of empty seats, that they were together.

"No sir!" the first man cried. "I got a problem and he lives in Scarsdale! Does that make any sense?"

"This woman is a cunt, a bitch, a shithead, and an *asshole!*" enunciated the second. "And she puts things in my food. I know it. I know it. I know it! I haven't seen her yet, but I'll catch her at it. Then the police'll believe me. They don't believe me now, but they'll believe me when I catch her at it."

Again Bonnie whispered into Jack's coat: "They're talking to themselves."

"What are the chances of that?" asked Jack, who knew that the two men were not concerned about being noticed. They were lost in their long psychotic monologues. "Really a long-shot: two psychos with the same functional disorder finding each other on the subway. Betcha it's a million to one."

As they sat there, Bonnie took Jack's hand in hers and examined it.

"What are you looking for?" he asked.

She shrugged.

"Tell me," he insisted.

She became almost kittenish and started to tell him about her friend. Funny, he thought, how easily you slip in and out of the public presence on the subway. One minute they were caught up in the drama of the two crazy men, now he and Bonnie were absorbed in their own conversation.

"When I covered the cops, I had a lawyer friend who called me in," she began. "He said that his client was being held for resisting arrest and assaulting a woman in one of those sleazy Times Square porno theaters. Well, this lawyer, he was an 18-B lawyer. You know the type—only takes cases that are assigned by the courts. Makes fifteen hundred for a lot of work and resents it. A kind of minimum-wage lawyer. A McDonald's counsel. So he's not particularly friendly to his clients."

"Hard life those guys lead," said Jack knowingly. "The other lawyers hate you because you're taking away potential clients, the court hates you because they think of you as the dregs—without ambition or talent, bringing down the profession, like an ambulance-chaser . . ."

"Which is more often true than not," said Bonnie.

"And, maybe worst of all, the clients hate you because they don't have to pay a fee. You're free and you know what that's worth. I've seen guys talked into pleas and when they went in front of the judge, they denounce their 18-B lawyers as scum."

"A hard life," agreed Bonnie. "But my guy's no different; he's one of those bitter pills. A true nonbeliever. Takes all the cases because he needs the money. He thinks everyone is guilty. Everyone. Especially if they're black. Except, one day he calls me up and takes me to dinner and he's buying, which is like a sighting of Halley's Comet."

"He's a friend?" Jack said.

At that moment, as the subway rolled and shuddered into Fourteenth Street, a woman of late middle age, in a prim coat and with a pinched face, who was sitting nearby the two ranting men, had enough. She bolted out of her seat and backed away from the two men. "You shut up!" she shouted to the second man, who was cursing and nodding his head. "You shut up! You . . . you . . . pervert!"

The second man didn't seem to notice. "The fucking, bitch, ratshit asshole!" he went on. "Pins in my side and in my back. And I don't know what she puts in my food."

"I'm going to call the police on you, you crazy man," said the woman.

"He thinks I don't know anyone. He thinks I'm helpless and that he can just talk to me that way," said the first angry man.

And Jack's heart sank. He could imagine the lockup ward at Bellevue—each of them lost in his own unappeased grievance. Each of them running out of medication.

"Friend?" Bonnie said, a little bewildered by Jack's question. "He's a professional friend. A guy who uses me to plant stories and a guy I get stories from."

Jack understood, but had a cynical version. "By those standards, Hitler could qualify as a friend."

"Not a bad news source," said Bonnie. "Anyway, my 18-B guy tells me about his client, who was in a movie theater with his cousin one night. They were sitting behind these two women. According to the DD 5 report, the cousin reaches over and fondles the woman's tit. She screams cop and there are, like, ten undercovers in the place because this is Forty-second Street, heavy drug traffic. They take the cousin to the basement of the theater and he's not cooperating. Then they bring my 18-B friend's client down, so maybe he can talk the cousin into confessing. Well, for some reason, and it's not clear why, they claim that my friend's client—the innocent guy—starts a fight and they have to subdue him."

"Happens," said Jack. "Guys get nuts around cops."

"So, I ask my friend, what's the big deal, because I know he hates black people and all the people in this are black. And he tells me that when he goes to see his client at Riker's Island, the guy's face is all puffed up and distorted. He's got a broken arm and gashes in his scalp. He's a mess. The cops, meanwhile, who are charging him with assaulting them, also have injuries."

"Yeah? So?"

"All the injuries to the cops are to their fingers and their knuckles."

"So they beat the shit out of him and charged him with assault."

She held up her hands. "Happens."

"And now you look at my hands to see if I have any damage to my knuckles and fingers. If I was one of those brutal cops in the basement of that theater."

She hugged his arm, but he had stiffened. "You never did that. Not you. I know that."

"Well, you're wrong."

She looked at his face. His expression had turned to stone. He faced her.

"I have taken some pieces off of some people," he said. "Bad people. But people." He saw the look on her face. Somewhere between disbelief and disgust. "Ah, you don't know what it's like," he went on. "You're not out there on the street where some asshole is selling crack and he's laughing in your face because there's not a fucking thing you can do about it. He knows it and you know it and he knows we all know it. He doesn't keep his stash on him. He's got a nine-year-old cousin who holds it. A nine-year-old cousin who is trained to say that he found this bag in the street. Who is trained to hate you."

From the outside, they looked like any other couple in an

intense conversation. Manhattan burns with wild, fiery conversations.

Just then, the train stalled between Penn Station and Times Square. The far uptown door of the car opened and a pair of well-dressed men appeared. "Pardon me, ladies and gentlemen," began the taller of the two men, a freshly shaven black man with a fur cap. The smaller of the two carried a can with a long slit in the top and a batch of literature. "We are sorry to disturb your evening, but we represent the Municipal Coalition for Aiding the Homeless." He spoke slowly, carefully, a rehearsed speech delivered with dignity. "As you know, we publish a newsletter, with some very famous contributors, and we try to find homes for those unfortunates who cannot help themselves. My friend and I were once homeless, but the coalition has helped us."

The smaller friend had blinking eyes and his hands twitched. He stood very close to his taller, more poised colleague. Jack could see the telltale signs of drugs on his nerves, cut raw.

"We are not out robbing or stealing," continued the taller man. "We are trying to set up small industries so that we can get back on our feet."

At that moment, the downtown door opened and a man with one leg hobbled in. He carried a bucket and a crutch in one hand.

"Sorry to bother you folks!" His voice overwhelmed the two at the uptown end of the car. "As you can see, I am disabled and I represent the Municipal Coalition for Aiding the Homeless . . ."

Several people in the downtown end of the car reached out and tossed coins and bills into the bucket of the legless man—clearly a man who didn't have to prove his worthiness for charity.

Jack and Bonnie were sitting near the uptown end. The

taller one of the first pair of men threw his head back and muttered, "That fucking Shabazz!" The little one nodded.

The train started up, landed at Times Square, and the two well-dressed men left. Bonnie deposited a dollar in Shabazz's bucket. One of the two mad talkers also left. He was followed by the irate woman, who was looking around for a cop so that she could report him.

Jack was watchful, but he kept talking. "One day, me and my dead partner, Moe Berger, grab Jose and we take him to an empty basement. And he is clean because Jose is smart, and he is smug, because Jose is stupid, and Moe cannot help himself, he puts a knee in Jose's groin. And while this smart-stupid dealer is down on the ground writhing from Moe's street justice, I get in some licks of my own. I take out a few ribs and I crack a few fingers and I tell him, as he drifts in and out of consciousness, that the only reason we are not leaving him dead with some planted dope and an untraceable gun on his body is because some part of us—me and Moe—has a conscience. But that with his open and flagrant dealing of drugs he is reaching that outer limit of our tolerance which will permit us to perform a summary execution and sleep well at night. In other words, he is fucking with us in a very fundamental way."

"My God! What happened?"

Jack softened and smiled. "Later, when he recovered, Jose sold some deadly smack to someone's sister. Turned out to be the wrong someone—someone who left him stone dead in a cold basement. He should have taken the hint."

He seemed almost happy about the outcome. A life, and he was content. Not that Bonnie expected something different. Jack had been a cop, with all that that implied. It was a world of identifiable good guys and unqualified bad guys. There was always a certain uncompromising streak of hard opinion about cops. The ethical grid had to be maintained. Therefore, disrespect for authority was bound to be unbearable. Even among the best of them. And he was the very best.

And yet she found when she covered them that even the decent ones, the cops with a heart, always found themselves fighting a moral undertow.

"You think I did something wrong?" he asked.

She thought about it for a moment. "I think you think you did something wrong."

He laughed. "I think you're right, but life isn't all that clear-cut, is it? In any case, I can live with it."

Up past Columbus Circle, where the Lincoln Center couple got off, they were silent. At Eighty-sixth Street, their stop, they ran for the door. As they walked up the stairs, she took his hand and ran her palms across the knuckles, as if she were wiping something away.

When Nora looked out of her window she saw nothing unusual in the street and only the normal nighttime clientele in the pizza parlor across the street. She didn't notice the couple sitting at the second table along the wall with a view of her doors. Bonnie had her back to the door and Jack was shielded by her back.

Nora was marching fast when she left the building. The pace put some quick distance between herself and the apartment and allowed her to pause after two blocks, stare in some store windows, and see if anyone was rushing to catch up. Jack knew the routine, and when he saw her getting ready to make her check, he pulled Bonnie into a doorway. Nora didn't spot them.

In that stammering fashion, Nora made her way down Broadway, stopped finally and boarded a bus. Jack and Bonnie got into a cab.

"See that bus?"

"Don't tell me," the cabdriver said.

"We don't wanna lose that bus," Jack said in his official voice.

"I ast you not to tell me that. You a cop?"

"We're not allowed to say."

"You're a cop. I always know a cop. There's something. I wisht I knew what it was. Not the shoes or the cheap pants. Something you can never put your finger on."

He jabbered a lot, but the cabdriver got into the chase, changing lanes so that he wouldn't be detected, making the traffic lights, running ahead of the bus, following from the front. All that erratic, rubber-squealing pursuit seemed like normal taxicab behavior. Bonnie laughed at the driver's yen to get into the middle of their movie.

The driver looked into his rearview mirror.

"Hey! You know something? You're the . . . What's that, you know what I mean? The, uh, uh! C'mon!"

She didn't help. They were waiting at a light.

"You know what I mean. Hey! I got it. You know who you are?"

"Who?"

"You're the weather lady!"

"I thought I looked familiar."

" 'Hey, it's only weather!' Am I right, or what?"

"You're right. When you're right you're right. I gotta hand it to you."

"You'd be surprised how many times I hafta use that. People get in the cab and they're all pissy because the traffic is bad and I say, 'Hey, it's only weather!' "

"Great," Jack said, "but could you keep one eye on the bus? I think it's getting ahead of us."

"Relax, pal; 'Hey, it's only weather!' "

They said it in unison, all three.

Nora got off the bus at Fourteenth Street and they went ahead to Twelfth before they got out. She was looking behind, but Jack was an old cop and knew a few tricks of his own.

She made her way to the White Horse Tavern and went in. There was a restaurant across the street, and Jack got a table near the window while Bonnie went into the bar after Nora.

"Spritzer!" Bonnie said to the bartender, taking a place at the bar.

Nora, farther down the bar, was absorbed in conversation with a woman on her left. A woman of about her own size and coloring. The other woman clearly had sexual designs and Nora was encouraging her, laughing at her jokes, touching her on the arm—sending off signals that were unmistakably welcome.

They left together, and headed back uptown. It wasn't so hard to follow, because Jack knew where they were going.

"Is she?" asked Bonnie in the cab as they headed up Eighth Avenue.

Jack was facing front, watching the cab ahead, as if he could detect something from the distance. See into the heart of the matter.

"I mean . . ." Bonnie continued.

Odd, Jack thought as they followed Nora's cab, that he should take offense, as if Nora's deviation from the heterosexual person he knew was something personal. But he couldn't take it any other way. Not being the person that he was. Not after the Catholicism of his youth and the blunt cop culture of his later years. Even his enlightened maturity didn't take the sting out of it. He felt rejected in the most primitive sense.

"I know what you mean," Jack replied crisply, watching Nora and the woman get out of their own cab near her room on Columbus Avenue. Nora had her arm around the woman. Then he saw that he was mistaken—it was the other woman who had her arm around Nora.

"I'm sorry I asked." Bonnie had complicated feelings of her own—somewhere between jealousy and vindication.

He paid the driver and they got out of the cab and stood on the sidewalk. He shivered, although it wasn't that cold. "No," he said, "I didn't know. I don't know. I never saw that side of her. In fact, I don't believe it now."

He stared at the window where the light went on, refusing to believe his own eyes.

21

Timothy McCormick and Mattie Nolan had slipped the lock and snuck into the house when it was empty. They knew that they'd be undisturbed because they'd overheard the landlord complain as he passed them in the street about the long ordeal of taking his family to visit relatives in Brooklyn.

They now sat in the dark of Nora's room, absorbing her things—the books, the quilt, the ceramic pot for tea—not making a sound. There was a strangely erotic tension in the dark room, which each of them felt and neither would ever admit aloud. They saved their expressions of lust for their dark, deniable encounters in the Brooklyn rooms when they were safely alone. But now, in Nora's forbidden room, the excitement was strong and connected to the fact that they were off together in a far country on a desperate mission with everything hanging in the balance. That fact, in itself, stirred something.

They had been sitting there for an hour in a disciplined hush when they heard the key in the lock. As soon as Nora opened the door, McCormick was on her, grabbing her from behind while Mattie Nolan frisked her from the front. They hadn't counted on the other woman, and Mattie finished quickly to handle the surprise guest.

They put Nora in a chair, roughing her up a bit, just to throw her off balance, then McCormick leveled a gun at her belly. Mattie threw the other woman against the wall, making certain that her arms and legs were spread out and that she leaned at a steep angle against the torn wallpaper. The attitude was deliberately harsh to intimidate and soften up the two women. It was a tactic used by all police and paramilitary forces—overwhelm and thus demoralize a prisoner.

"Who's she?" McCormick asked, nodding toward the spare woman.

Nora remained smolderingly silent and turned her head away as a sign of contempt. Not that McCormick expected cooperation. She knows how it works, he thought. She's a hard case. The kind you don't break. Well, it's to be expected, considering the family line she comes from.

The other woman, who was in her late twenties, trembled with fear. She was clearly a civilian, decided McCormick, although you never knew. When they're beautifully trained, when they're the best, they can act like babies, then turn into efficient killers once your guard is down. Mattie searched her quickly and professionally.

"Not a thing," she reported to McCormick.

"This some secret vice?" McCormick asked, again nodding his head at the woman. "The priest will fall down dead at that, Nora."

"Go stuff yourself," she said.

A mistake. She spoke. She gave up that little bit of sullen mystery about herself. Now they knew that they were bothering her, that they could get through to her, that she hadn't gone dangerously catatonic on them. Bad to let them see that you're human, they said during the training. Let them guess at what's going on inside. Let them worry themselves sick.

McCormick took a seat on the bed opposite Nora. Mattie kept an eye on the civilian, who was sweating and breathing hard.

"I am going to have to get tough," McCormick said softly, as if getting tough was the last thing that he wanted to do, as if asking her help in avoiding that odious tactic.

Nora bristled. Her red hair was tightly curled and it slapped against her neck when she turned her head to face him. She didn't want to display herself, show all of her feelings—after all, she had been sworn to silence, if only to drive British captors mad; they were expected to be gallantly reticent. They would be thrown off by a stoic enemy, seeing a mirror-image of themselves. But Nora had been alone too long and these captors were Irish. Her emotions boiled over in sharp, bitter barbs. "Oh? Whose idea is that, may I ask? Getting tough, I mean. Breaking kneecaps, I suppose. Putting sticks under my fingernails. A field telephone and seventy volts on my tits. Then taking me for a ride. You're working for the Mafia now?"

"You know very well who I work for," he said sadly. "Once, there was a time when we all had the same employer."

"Not lately," she replied. A dancer, she thought. I'm a dancer and this is some bad dream during the intermission. A dancer with a dancer's concentration. Never mind the feet bleeding through the slippers. Of course, it could be the spiritual thing, too. She was not blind to that possibility. She was a Catholic, or, rather, had been a Catholic at one time, and she believed, in spite of the falling away, that God existed and that this was not the end of time. Otherwise, how could she be a dancer in her next life? What was the point of losing Seamus if he couldn't come back again and be her darling angel boy? All this effort and sacrifice had to have another end.

"You know, Nora, they used to say at the Maze prison that Bobby Sands didn't really starve himself to death," said

McCormick gently, as if trying to include her in his thoughts. As if this were merely a conversation taking place in some cozy pub.

"Oh, really? Then what happened to the poor bastard? Did he die of an improper dental plan?"

"No," replied McCormick, chuckling at the feisty wit. "He starved himself into a coma. If he'd've known that death was the true outcome, he'd've gobbled up a pig. That's what they say, anyway."

Nora shook her head. "You're one of them, now, are you? One of the pigs?"

He leaned forward. "You cannot say that, Nora Burns. Not you, not anyone. I'm doing my duty."

She looked at him. He was bothered by this accusation of treachery. Now that she had suffered the slaughter of her child, she understood a little better. "The Troubles." Killing babies. That's what it came down to in the end. You were killing someone's baby. That's what she did when she helped Michael. She carried his kit and he planted the bombs, but it made no real difference who did what. She was guilty of murdering infants. That's why it could never end, this fight. When you killed someone's child, they were going to come after you. Just as she was coming after the killers of Seamus. All the killers. The ones who fired the guns and the ones who told them to fire the guns. The ones who carried the kit, God help us!

At the bottom of her broken heart, she knew that none of them understood the inconsolable pain of a dead child. None of them—neither Ulstermen or Republicans—stayed awake at night listening for his breathing, the way she had listened when he was an infant, and hung for dear life on those sighs and sounds coming from Seamus's crib. And now in the night she'd prayed to her lost God, well, maybe it was a dream after all, and I'll hear him again and he'll be asleep in the next room. But the only thing she heard was the wail of sirens in the night.

The tragedy was inevitable, when you had both sides

spiritually inflamed: mothers like herself wound up burying their innocent children. And good men like McCormick wound up committing heartfelt atrocities.

She looked at McCormick and the fire of her hatred made him turn away. "I don't give a shit for your duty," she said through clenched teeth.

The momentary silence was broken by the sudden whimper and cry of the other woman. Nora remembered that her name was Alice. "Listen," Alice said in a voice that trilled with terror, "I have no idea what's going on here."

"Not that complicated," McCormick said lightly.

"I don't want to know," Alice said, gaining a little strength. "I would just like to leave. I am a copywriter in an advertising agency, and I met this woman for the first time tonight." She indicated Nora with her head.

"Well, that's the God's truth," Nora said.

"I would just like to leave here and go home because I can see that you people have business to discuss and I would not like to interfere. This is none of my concern—I have a whole different life . . ."

She started to move away from the wall, slowly, so as not to alarm anyone with a quick, threatening action.

"Stay still," Mattie said harshly.

"I'm afraid you're going to have to cooperate with us a bit more," said McCormick. "Just be quiet there and you won't get hurt."

He never took his eyes off Nora. Mattie never took her eyes off of Alice.

"Can I make some tea?" asked Nora.

"No," McCormick said in a voice that held no hope.

"You know, my brother will not tolerate this," she said.

As a reply, McCormick got off the couch and handed the gun to Mattie who turned to guard Nora. He went to the wall where Alice was spread out like a pinned butterfly. He took her head in his hands and in one swift and ruthless motion twisted it quicker than her body could accommodate.

Nora could hear the bones and cartilage crack under McCormick's hand. It was something he'd learned in the martial arts school—no great trick. Just the breaking of the spine, the murder of a complete stranger. The usual battle drill for an IRA master killer.

Alice's dead eyes rolled back in her head. She fell to the floor and twitched for a second, some bile and blood spilled out of her mouth, and then she was still. A sigh was the last sound she made. It almost sounded like a sigh of relief.

Well, Nora thought coldly, that saves me the trouble.

"Do you take my meaning?" asked McCormick, retrieving his gun and resuming his seat on the couch. Mattie took a chair and sat on Nora's opposite flank.

"It means that you're going to murder me," she said calmly.

He smiled sadly. "Well, it doesn't look good for your future," he said.

She was still confused. "Why?" she asked.

"You know better than to ask that," he said. "We follow orders."

"And you know my brother's here on a mission?"

He slapped his thigh. "Of course we know that, you damned idiot. Who do you think we're working for?"

"What?" It was not true surprise—not in the sense that she hadn't glimpsed the possibility. It was simply a hard thing to accept the fact that her own brother had sent killers after her. He wasn't incapable of it, but she thought that she'd seen something soft and vulnerable when they walked near the park. She thought then that he was done as a maniac terrorist. He couldn't keep that up when he had human qualms. Well, she was wrong, and here was the proof. She was, nevertheless, calm.

"This is because of the Mafia thing?" she asked.

McCormick knew her back in the days when the uprising was clean and chaste and still possible. He'd never been out on a job with her, but he'd seen her and knew her underground tale. She was a bright thing, a reliable courier, fetching messages and supplies, dodging checkpoints and fearless under army questioning. Once, when he was a young gunman he thought, though he couldn't be certain, she was his guide for an hour when he slipped the border. It was a dark night and she was an obedient soldier and so he never got close enough to tell for sure. But he thought it was Nora. He was too scared himself to pay much attention. After all, she was Michael's sister and everyone knew better than to trouble him.

"Some tea," he said to Mattie, who went fishing in the kitchenette, knowing from the long stakeout just about where everything was stored.

"You've interfered with the mission," he said facing Nora squarely.

"And how's that?"

"Michael asked you to leave the old man alone. You promised that you'd keep a distance."

"What's that to do with Michael?"

He ran his free hand through his thin hair. The job was clearly troubling him. "He can't be bothered now," said McCormick. "He's got everything on him, the whole mission . . ."

"The thing at the hotel," she guessed.

"For Christ's sake! We've only got a week and you go throwing a monkey wrench into everything. This is a very important mission. You think they'd send me and Mattie if it weren't something of the highest importance? Christ Almighty, you can be a difficult woman. Why couldn't you just leave the old man alone? Oh, never mind, never mind, what's the difference."

"But it's Michael's job; what's the old man got to do with it?"

"Ahhhh! But you're dense! Are you daft or are you playing me for time? Is that it? Because it won't do you any good at all."

Then she knew. It had been apparent, something she should have known, but then, she was not a pragmatist and didn't understand the ways of power politics—that sometimes you bargain with an enemy because, as the saying from the Middle East goes, "The enemy of my enemy is my friend." So Michael had made some fiendish pact in order to pull off his mission. Knowing Michael, it made sense. She couldn't even hate him. Or, at least no more than she could hate everyone and everything that served the deadly cause.

In the dim light Mattie knocked over a cup. It was just enough noise to cause McCormick to flinch. Nora, the dancer, with her fine dancer's reactions, saw it coming and kicked the gun out of his hand. One flick of her foot. The gun landed close to her chair and she fell on it. McCormick wasn't slow, just a little slower than she was. He leaped for the gun but she was already there and by the time he was on the floor next to her she had the barrel aimed at his face. The shot was soft, almost delicate, but the bullet broke up going through his skull and spread all through his brain. He was dead by the time she put the second bullet in his face.

Mattie, though highly trained, held a pot in one hand and a saucer in the other. Her gun was on the kitchen counter. She dropped both the pot and the saucer, heading for the gun, but Nora was already on her feet, crouched in a combat stance and squeezing off one round into Mattie's chest and another into her belly as she slid to the floor.

Mattie Nolan was dead before she took in the fact that something had gone wrong.

There were extra clips of ammunition in McCormick's suit pocket and Nora put them in her purse, along with Mattie's extra gun. Then she plucked the identification from Alice's purse and put the gun she had used to kill the two Garda in Alice's hand.

She made certain that Alice's features were obliterated by bashing her face with a heavy pan. Some blood splattered on her dress. She left her own purse and identification near the body. From the closet she took a bag she had ready for emergencies. In the bottom it had cash and a passport and prepaid

open airplane tickets to four different countries. There
were also some credit cards. In the top were three changes of
clothing.

Nora turned on the oven. She let the room fill up with gas
while she waited outside in the hall. Then she started a fire in
the hallway, with the door still open, making certain to remove the battery from the hall fire alarm. She had less than a
minute, she figured, as the fire ate towards the gas-filled room.
She ran out of the building just as the flames reached the room.
First the windows blew out; then fingers of flame clawed out
of the top-floor apartment into the night.

"Oh, Lord!" said Bonnie, when she saw the flames and then
the explosion. She and Jack had just seen a figure huddled in
a winter coat and carrying an overnight bag leave the building,
then walk south at a fast but not noticeable pace. Jack knew
who it was from the silhouette alone. Only Nora had that fluid
gait and light motion.

Jack took Bonnie's arm and they fell in behind Nora, who
was not expecting them. Maybe Michael, but certainly not
Jack and Bonnie. Nora was still tingling with the excitement
of the killings. She had not known that she was that capable,
but neither was she surprised. She was capable of all sorts of
things, now that she didn't care what happened to her.

"It's her," Bonnie said. They crossed to the west side of the
street and kept pace with Nora.

"Yes," Jack replied.

"Where's the other one? The one she brought home."

They looked back at the burning building and the spectators gathering in nightclothes in the street.

The streets farther downtown were almost empty near midnight on this Monday night and it was difficult to follow Nora
as she hurried along. The thing that made it easier was the fact
that Nora didn't look back. She kept going, head down, as if
convinced that she could outdistance anyone following her.

In the fifties, on Ninth Avenue, she entered a Howard

Johnson's Hotel. Through the window Jack watched her register. After she had gone up to her room, Jack came in and asked
if they had a spare room.

The clerk still had Nora's registration card in his hand when
he turned to look at the keys in the empty boxes, Jack read that
"Alice Cohen" was registered in Room 505. When the clerk
faced front again, Jack was on his way outside.

22

Friday, March 22, 1991

Michael had a bad dream. He couldn't remember all the details, but he knew that his dream was violent and disturbing—filled with explosions and gunfire and pieces of human flesh and shards of bone flying past his frozen face. He sat up in bed, trembling with the aftermath of the dream. It was a dream, but it was also the blurred replay of a vivid portion of his life.

No one understood about his work. People had romantic notions about shootouts. They didn't appreciate the fact that the human body was soft and vulnerable—easily torn apart by exploding bullets. Michael had huddled in the smoke of battle, in air filled with the pink mist of blood and the debris of bones and the soft tissue of wet flesh.

You can anticipate serious mutilations and traumatic amputations with a bomb. After all, that's what explosions do—rip open the human body. Arms and legs fly. But bullets take slices and shreds of people with them, too.

That wasn't the worst part of his dream. The nightmare was dim and only suggested something he couldn't quite face. It was Nora. She was his blood sister and he could remember wheeling her in her carriage when she was a baby. He had seen her smile at him—baby recognition of his face. And a little later, when he was hanging out with his teenage friends, he could still recall a moment when she came down the block clutching her little rag doll. These memories came back as he sat in bed, trying to shake off the dream. Instead, he remembered something that wasn't a dream: Nora had asked if he remembered Seamus. He remembered Nora. She was the baby to him. The sour-sweet smell of milk was on her breath as a child. And he remembered, too, that out of his mouth had come the order to kill her.

"What else could I do?" he said out loud.

Then he looked around the empty bedroom. He had other problems, he told himself fiercely. He conjured up the old discipline, like a scarred and battered boxer summoning the last drop of courage for one more round. Think of the operation. Do not dwell on useless, morbid thoughts. Think of what you are here to do. Only this could get him through the next few days.

He concentrated on technical questions. What would the gas do? What use were the suits? Could the plan he'd devised go wrong and the gas not be released?

The academic questions served to calm him down. His breath was still quick and shallow. When he'd first woken up, he couldn't place whose bed he was in. That was always an open question to a man who never had a bed he could call his own. He looked around the room and there were dolls and doilies and other touches of a sentimental feminine presence: notes stuck to the refrigerator with cuddly-bear magnets, a sign on the bathroom door saying, WC. Frills and lace that strained to declare the gender of the occupant.

He looked over and saw that the table was set for breakfast.

There were fresh flowers in the vase and a plate of food covered by another plate to keep it warm. There was a note in an elaborate and large script:

> You had a bad night, dearest. Had to go to work
> but didn't want to wake you. Not after the night-
> mares. Found some fresh sausage.
>   Hope the eggs are still warm. You know how
> I feel about you.
>
> S.

The sheet was soaked from his sweat.

Slowly, he became oriented. He had met Samantha two weeks earlier, when he had decided to slip deeper under cover. She was a guest at one of the uptown museum soirees he had crashed. Samantha was an investment counselor at a bank. That, and a writer. She said she spent hours every night at the word processor, but, of course, he knew that she was deceiving herself. He never saw her suffering over a story. He couldn't detect the writer's dense concentration, canny insights about human nature, or clever assessments of character. She was a writer in name only. Michael recognized the type. The city was overrun with dewy, self-proclaimed writers who didn't write.

Samantha had the word processor and a thesaurus and a dictionary and a thousand schemes to weave in and out of books, but he knew that it took more than that. She was like the pub singers who declared their loyalty to the rebellion and acted on it by singing a rude song and having another pint.

Not that he held it against her. In fact, he depended upon her active guilt and credulity. When he met Samantha, he was looking for just such a blind romantic. She was dark and attractive in a safe sort of way. A little too plump to be beautiful. Therefore no one would take a blood oath for her hand. He wouldn't have to watch his back for old lovers.

She was past thirty, but not quite thirty-five, an age that put most single women at the mercy of that relentless biological clock. That, and that other thing. They glimpsed a long loom- ing loneliness ahead and it put the fear of spinsterhood even into the most ardent feminists. Friends dropped off, one by one, gratefully settling for compromised or damaged men whom they would have spurned a few years earlier; they became couples, involved with real estate and families and a whole range of domestic concerns that shut out the singles. They were almost gleeful in their secret obsession of becom- ing a couple. Meanwhile, a hard edge of suspicion and envy crept into the voices of the holdouts.

But there was an enduring sweetness to Samantha, and it was to that kindly nature that Michael made his appeal. He'd managed to smile at her over some leafy hors d'oeuvres, and he was, after all, unattached, and therefore a catch. They'd gone to dinner and then had a few drinks and it wasn't long before he had her enchanted with his mysterious evasions and gift of charm. He didn't drink too much, he wasn't saddled with alimony or visitation rights, he had impeccable table manners, and, the answer to a prayer, he cleaved to her in the night when she craved affection.

"And what is it you do?" she'd asked that first night, when they were probing each other like doctors staging top-to- bottom examinations.

"I cannot say." He smiled and her heart dipped and bounded into her throat.

In no time at all she was head over heels in love with Michael.

She would learn, after she took him home to her precious apartment on Jane Street, that he had no need of money and that he was not an adventurer, at least of that variety. He went somewhere in the evening, although he would never say where, and when he came home, he would not speak of it. Of course she devised elaborate fantasies about his secret life. He was a CIA agent. No. He was an antiterrorist operative work- ing Interpol (there were such people and it made sense that they did not speak of it). He was a merchant prince fed up with the material demands of his greedy stockholders. He was in hiding from bandit conspiracies. He was a poet in retreat who walked the city in the dark because his soul required solitary nourishment.

Whatever he was, she always associated it with good. It never occurred to her that he might be someone with blood on his hands. Someone actively evil. Two Sundays ago, they'd strolled along the waterfront and he'd pointed out the pier on Twelfth Street where the survivors of the Titanic had been brought in seventy-nine years earlier. They were going to tear it down now, because Pier 52 had become a waterfront hag, a haven for crack addicts and prostitutes and transvestites and homosexual predators. And he said it with such sad resignation that she knew instinctively that he had a good heart filled with layers of regret.

That day they'd bought a schefflera plant from an outdoor merchant and Michael had thought for a moment that he could vanish into domestic bliss. He could enjoy the sheer pleasure this woman took in his physical presence—the sex and the cooking and the bumping together in the bathroom and the brushing of hands on the street and the comfortable silences. She understood the way that the city worked, the strategy for getting around, the tricks of shopping and buying crisp vegetables and fresh meat and unusual bread. He could have a few years of peace, until they found him. A few years wasn't a bad future. Not for a man like Michael.

But, of course, he couldn't. He was already promised. To the cause. His life wasn't his own, and those sentimental lapses into domestic daydreams, which were coming more and more frequently, had to be suppressed, pushed out of his mind ruthlessly. He was a soldier on a mission. He had gone too far, done too much, spilled too much blood to get away clean. Even a year or two was asking too much. His life was forfeit and he knew it. He even thought that he deserved it.

He looked over at the clock. It was noon. Time to get going.

He shaved his face, brushed his teeth, did his pushups and his kneebends and his ten martial arts exercises, then showered and ate his cold breakfast. He knew that he had mentally cleansed himself of human yearnings because he could taste nothing when he ate. Not the sausage for which she had scoured the markets, not the eggs she had tried to keep warm, nor the soda bread she had found in an obscure bakery because she knew that he liked it. His mouth was filled with nutrients, not the offerings of a good woman.

It was almost one. Time to meet his contact.

Earlier, Jack Mann had been waiting for his appointment on the third floor of police headquarters at One Police Plaza. The bench was hard and cold and the uniformed policemen and policewomen walking by had that brisk show of official business that let Jack know he was an interloper, a civilian. Finally, a uniformed woman said that Deputy Inspector Bob Reymond would see him now. The office was behind a frosty glass and Reymond was tucked behind an important-looking desk, his hands folded on top of a pile of folders. His body language spoke of limited time.

"How's retirement?" Inspector Reymond said, letting Jack know that he was up-to-date on his visitor.

"Not all that it's cracked up to be," Jack said, one cop to another.

"Oh? Why's that?"

Jack shrugged. "Well, for one thing, I lost my partner."

Reymond paused, then nodded. "Moe Berger," he said, looking off at another folder. "Supposedly a very good cop, but, you know, he had some problems, a little dirty laundry in his closet."

"What? Bullshit! Moe was the straightest cop I ever knew."

Reymond unclasped his hands and picked up the top folder. He put on a pair of half glasses and opened the file. "Did you know that he fought in the Israeli Army? The Israeli Defense Forces, did you know that?"

Jack didn't say anything.

"Of course you knew that. You helped him get his shield back. You smoothed his way back into the department. You took oaths—false oaths, I should point out—that he was hurt in a car accident in Italy, not killing Syrians on the Golan Heights in the Six-Day War."

"What kind of asshole are you?" Jack asked. Reymond sat up straight, his nostrils flaring. "Moe Berger was a great cop, and if you're trying to spoil his reputation on some half-assed technicality, you can stick it up your ass, Inspector! You wanna come after me, fine. I'm alive. I can take you on. I still got a pension, and I don't give a shit about technicalities. But lay off Moe Berger."

"Get the fuck outta here, Mann!"

Jack just sat there. He returned Reymond's glare.

"You know, Mann, just for fun I'm gonna have you arrested, taken out of here in handcuffs, printed, charged with assault—because I will swear that you took a punch at me—and see that you spend at least one night in the Tombs. That's just for fucking starters . . ."

"No you're not. You're not gonna do one single thing. The reason you aren't gonna do shit is because I'm working with a reporter who will back up my testimony that you came gunning for me like you came gunning for Moe Berger. I will swear that you are in the pocket of the mob and that you let our two guests from Ireland, who were under your care, get murdered. Even if it's all bullshit, it will stir up so much shit that everything—I mean every fucking thing—will hit the fan. I'm not gonna tell you the name of the reporter, but trust me, it's someone you can't fuck with. Second, I'm here to talk serious shit about the murders of two hero cops—Sergeant Vincent Manero and Detective Rocco Valone—not to mention the two cops from Ireland."

Inspector Reymond took a long time considering Jack's outburst, measuring his intent, then pushed the key on his intercom. "Two coffees," he said when the officer outside asked what he wanted.

When they were settled in with their coffees and alone again, Reymond spoke confidentially. "Look, Jack, you know what I wanna do in about a year? I wanna move to Ireland and live in a mansion and drink ale in a pub all day. I wanna put the gun away forever and gaze out at the ocean."

"Not too many African-Americans in Ireland," Jack said. He took a sip of coffee.

"You tellin' me that I won't be welcome?"

Jack shook his head, his tongue momentarily numbed by the blistering coffee. "No," he said, regaining his voice. "I am just trying to acquaint you with the quaint Irish customs."

"Good. Because I'm not an African-American, to begin with. I'm a native of Jamaica, an island boy, so if I go to Ireland, they'll think it's a spelling error. I'll just be returning home."

They both laughed. Jack raised his plastic cup. "To the Emerald Isle."

"Jamaica!" said Reymond.

Reymond took Jack for a walk on the street, up along east Broadway, touching him enough to make certain that he wasn't wired. Reymond seemed like a decent cop, but he made it clear that the investigation into the deaths of Manero and Valone was out of his hands.

"McCormick and Nolan's deaths have been officially declared an accident," Reymond said. "They were visiting a citizen of the Irish Republic at her apartment on the Upper West Side when a fire broke out and all three were killed. No one else in the building was home."

Jack nodded, impatient to tell the inspector what he knew. "The Irish citizen, it was a woman," he said.

"Nora Burns," said Reymond. "Not wanted, not a fugitive. Lost her son in some terrorist political act. The inspector had apparently tracked her down. They were visiting."

He didn't mention the fact that McCormick and Nolan had

been shot. The bodies were so badly burned in the fire that it was possible to overlook the bullet wounds, attribute all the horrible injuries to the explosion. To end the matter once and for all, high police officials had asked the coroner to list them as fire victims. Period. Anything else would be a can of worms.

"I don't think it was Nora Burns," said Jack, and that stopped the inspector in his tracks. He gazed at Jack to see if he was speculating or talking from direct knowledge.

"You know something?"

Jack sensed something. Nothing he could name. Something vague, but still powerful. Conspiracies and treachery popped into his head. He had been to all his old cronies with his suspicions—never mentioning the fact that he'd followed Nora after the fire, because he still didn't know who he could trust. They had all sent him to Reymond, who was, technically, in charge of the investigation. And now Reymond had hidden emotions about this case.

"I don't know anything solid," Jack said.

They continued walking toward Chinatown, the civilians making a wide path for a uniformed member of the New York City Police Department. The Hong Kong gang members walked up to them in defiance, then moved aside.

"The case is closed," Reymond said, sounding almost relieved. "The Irish cops were killed in a fire, and the Internal Affairs cops were shot in a bad drug buy. End of the story. Go back to Ireland. Live off the fat of the land. That's what I intend to do in three hundred and seventy-two days."

As he watched Jack walk away, fighting the traffic along the Bowery, Deputy Inspector Robert Reymond recognized a familiar type: an old-style cop. Someone who would not walk away and let his partner face it alone. A bulldog. He knew that Jack Mann would not go away. He would not return to Ireland; he would stick it out until it was settled, one way or another.

Reymond looked around until he found a pagoda-style

telephone booth. Then he set in motion the arrangements to alert Michael to a possible complication.

The contact was not someone Michael would recognize. He was just another go-between in the intricate weave of cutouts that protected the leadership of the Mafia. He was a short man, in his late twenties and nervous, though he had undoubtedly earned some trust, thought Michael as they sat back-to-back in a restaurant on Second Avenue. The message, which had reached Michael through his own blur of cutouts, said that the meeting was crucial.

"You the guy with the hammer?" asked the contact as Michael spotted his identifying green necktie and blue shirt. Michael carried a copy of Le Carré's novel, *The Little Drummer Girl.*

"And if this is a waste of my time, you're the nail," Michael said.

The man's hands began to twitch. "Okay, okay," Michael said. "But no more coffee for you."

The waitress approached. "Tea," Michael said. She looked disappointed. "And a bagel."

"With a smear?" she asked.

"Yes," he said quickly. "With cream cheese."

The man in the booth behind him had an uneaten hamburger and a plate of french fries and a cup of coffee, refilled for the third time.

"The word is," he whispered sideways, when they were alone again, "that this guy, Jack, and I don't know any other name but that—just Jack . . ."

"I know who it is," said Michael.

"The word is that this here guy Jack is going around and starting some trouble."

"So?"

"So, some people thought maybe you wanted to put off your vacation, you know, until things cooled down."

Michael understood the message. The mob was telling him to postpone the mission. Not that he would. Not after the full cost had been already paid, with his sister and his nephew and a few good colleagues. He might be getting soft and a little slow, but his determination was still there. He was not going to back off.

"You tell them that's it's a package deal. Prepaid. I can't postpone. Have you got that?"

"There's one other thing," the contact said.

"What's that?"

"Nora."

Michael flared. He almost leaped out of his seat, but the waitress reappeared and left his tea and his bagel and his cream cheese.

"What's she got to do with it?" he hissed when the waitress left.

"Listen, I don't know what any of this means. I'm just a parrot, repeatin' things."

"So, repeat what they said."

"They said she may still be around."

The contact left, dropping his check on Michael's bagel. Michael sat there for a while, not knowing how he felt. Could she be alive? Was it possible?

And then he thought: how much did she know?

23

Monday, March 25, 1991

On the day of the action, Michael cleansed himself of all other earthly concerns. That was his habit when embarking on a mission. He awoke in a state of high alert, his mind clicking like a machine as he checked and rechecked his agenda and his state of readiness.

He had breakfast with Samantha, who was pleased to see him awake at eight in the morning. She didn't even mind that he didn't touch the eggs she had prepared. He only sipped orange juice and coffee—combat rations. She was chatting about business and the economic climate, her outlook typically sunny, and didn't notice the faraway look in Michael's eyes, which was the closest he could come to saying good-bye.

"So, I was thinking," Samantha was saying, "that for anyone looking to buy an apartment in Manhattan, what with the state of the real estate market, now would be a perfect time."

Michael heard the hint, and ignored it. He was busy testing the muscle tone of his arms and legs and stomach. He was a gladiator with a thin coat of sweat from his morning exercises.

He wondered about the sweat. The shower should have eliminated it. This was another kind of sweat.

"So, what do you think?" Samantha said, breaking into his self-absorbed inventory of target and weapon.

"What about?" he asked.

"The apartment, silly," she said, her expression too intense for the lightness of her tone.

"What apartment?"

She rolled her eyes. "The one on Hudson Street. I told you. Two bedrooms, working fireplace, twenty-four-hour doorman."

"How much?" he asked, telling himself that he was humoring her, though he thought that the apartment sounded nice, if impossible.

"Five hundred and twenty-five thousand," she said, "but I know I could get it for five."

She almost said "we." He could hear the effort it took to bring it back to "I" and he experienced one more wave of guilt and sorrow. No time for this, he thought. Not on the day of a mission. In the past, on such a day he was always given over to total concentration, complete dedication. He was unswervingly correct in his moves. It was what kept him alive.

"Let's talk about it tomorrow," he said, and she quickly agreed.

From her point of view, it was a long step towards a concession from Michael. Of course she knew that it was only two weeks, but she could name couples who had formed on shorter acquaintance. She only knew that she liked waking up next to Michael in the morning, she liked shopping for two, finding his brand of tea on the shelf; she was overcome by the hundreds of gestures of surrender and mutual deferral that had to be made by two; she was enthralled by the consideration of consequences required by living with another person.

She got up from the table, wiped her mouth, kissed him on the forehead, and hurried off to work, feeling happy and married.

Michael cleaned off the table, washed the dishes, and began packing his bag. He would not be here when she returned. Or ever again. The realization was unusually painful. Good that this was his last job, he thought. He didn't know why he knew that it was his last job, but he did. He had no plans for afterward. He did another round of pushups, but it didn't stop the singing in his ears. He took a shower, but that didn't stop the sweat. Then he went for a walk.

Greenwich Village was quiet on a Monday morning—moving slowly, as if the weekend revelries had bruised the whole community with rude tourists and rough trade. A few mothers were out with carriages, walking in groups for protection as much as for company. At Sheridan Square off Christopher Street, a homeless community had taken root on the benches. All the plazas and parks of the city had been occupied by the growing colonies of homeless with their makeshift spigots and cardboard shelters.

Like everyone else who had closed their eyes to the plight of the homeless, Michael was becoming blind to their presence. But he was brought up short by something he noticed in Sheridan Square. Amidst the usual clutter of drugged-out, boozy, smelly squatters, with their dazed eyes and rag wardrobes and plastic bags, was a man sitting quietly on a bench reading a book. A book! Michael couldn't see what book the man was reading, but so powerful was that image, so suggestive of thought and culture and an interior life, that suddenly the entire world of the homeless was no longer an unsightly horde of mad, jibbering, doomed creatures. One of them sat on a bench and read a book. This one man had conferred upon them all a touch of humanity and dignity that had been taken away from these pathetic vagrants, along with their homes.

It was exalting to see a thin pulse of intellectual life, yet deeply depressing to realize how easily it would be crushed. In the end, Michael was glad to be done with America. It was too big and too contradictory for a single-minded man such as

himself. Best to get back to Ireland where he had a clear-cut
view of the world and his place in it.

He glanced at his watch and saw that it was eleven. He had
time, but he hurried anyway. He found a bookstore on Seventh Avenue and bought a copy of Ibsen's *A Doll's House*. He
had it gift-wrapped and went back to the apartment on Jane
Street where he left the pretty package on the pillow of
Samantha's bed, next to her stuffed bear.

"Believe me, you wouldn't want the assignment," said Harvey Levy. This feud between Bonnie and Chuck had almost
driven him back to smoking cigarettes. He clenched a pipe
between his teeth to fend off the inevitable.

"It's only the dumb Academy Awards!" Bonnie said furi-
ously, leaning forward, half across his Mission desk, as if she
were going to get at him; Harvey leaned as far back in his chair
as he could without showing outright fear. "What could be
more like the weather report than the Academy Awards East
Coast Ceremony?" she half screamed. "I'll even bring the
fucking maps!"

Harvey smiled and slipped an antacid tablet between the
pipe and his lips. "Well, actually, Bon, it would mean a dupli-
cation. As you know, Chuck will be at the Waldorf doing a
color piece." He smiled. "Listen, call it a budget thing. You
know, going on location—two people, same location. I know!
I know! It really sounds stupid . . ."

"Lame, Harv. We've left stupid in the dust. We're way past
stupid. I don't even mind stupid anymore. I kinda like it. It's
familiar. Especially around here. Lame, however, has a certain
insulting quality. You know? It has the ring of dissembling.
That's lying. As if you were treating me like a child and not
telling me the truth behind why you are preventing me from
attending the ceremonies tonight at the Waldorf-Astoria
Hotel."

"Okay, okay, I'll level with you." A little drool came out of
the side of his mouth as he had trouble clenching the pipe and

lying at the same time. "The truth, God help us, is that the new owners of our station, International Computer Conglomerate, like Chuck. Did I mention that? I must've mentioned it. They did a bunch of focus groups with their own sales managers and department chiefs and they all said that he had a high Q rating. They like him. Their wives like him. Even their kids like him."

"Christ! That's why this country's going into the dumper," she replied. "We've got digital computer sales reps making programming choices for a local news show! Guys who understand megabytes! If that's not a constitutional crisis I don't know what is."

"Bonnie, Bonnie, Bonnie!" He was smiling, but she knew that volcanoes were churning in his belly. His teeth were grinding that pipestem into pulp. His hair, what little was left, was turning gray right before her eyes. She took a certain satisfaction in his suffering. He deserved it. He knew better. And, after all, no matter how nice a guy he was, he was still management. He still went behind those locked doors and cursed the day Bonnie Hudson had come into his life. He still believed, deep down, in his heart of hearts, that simple Chucky Childers—that intellectually impaired lip-syncher of the news—was easier to handle, therefore a better buy. She was trouble, always questioning things. High maintenance.

"Wait a minute. Let me see if I got this straight. You're telling me that I can't go to the Waldorf-Astoria tonight?"

"That's right. I couldn't have put it better myself. Brilliant. God, why don't I have your gift for seeing through to the heart of things?"

"Because you're a weasel, Harv. A weasel with a heart the size of a pea and shrinking." She got up and stormed out the door. "Not that I hold it against you. It comes with the job. In fact, I'm sure that there are worse weasels with smaller hearts. You just happen to be my weasel."

"Bonnie, Bon-Bon!"

She stopped with her hand on the doorknob. "One more

thing, weasel. I do not, under any circumstances, intend to use a weather map tonight."

Then she spun on her heels and was gone.

"But they like the maps!" he called after her. "They did focus groups on it."

The door swung open again and Bonnie's bright face peered in. "Hey!" she said, "it's only weather!"

In the dressing area, where Chuck Childers had the largest room, he sat on the couch holding a bag with a change of shirt and some extra makeup in case there was an emergency. He was staring at the motto above his mirror:

And that's the way it is . . .—Walter Cronkite.

Chuck had on his game face, and a clerk was holding his tuxedo in a garment bag. The silence was broken by a buzz of the phone.

"The car is here," his assistant said.

He got up, his face set with determination. "Let's do it," he said to his entourage.

As he marched down the hall, heading for the limousine that would carry him to the plush suite reserved for him at the Waldorf-Astoria Hotel, he passed Bonnie coming the other way.

"Asshole!" she said, loud enough for all to hear.

Chuck stopped. "Did you hear that? You heard what she called me?"

"I didn't hear anything," said the clerk holding the tuxedo.

"You had to hear that. You couldn't miss."

"No, see, I was holding your tux and it was between me and her and it blocked out all sound . . ."

"Sound travels through a laundry bag! You must've heard. What about you?" he asked his executive assistant.

"Huh?" she said. "Sorry, I was filling out the trip ticket. I missed it."

Childers groaned and went on, heading for the Waldorf. Bonnie prepared for an afternoon weather update and a call from Jack.

*   *   *

The dinner was scheduled to start at eight, but the orders for the staff had been to come in no later than five. The management didn't want trouble with security and complaints from the stars and celebrities and politicians.

Michael, who was a captain now and had six tables under his supervision, started for work at three. The cabdriver who brought him up from Jane Street talked about nothing else but the awards when he heard the destination.

"Everybody's gonna be there, ya know that?" the driver said merrily, as if he were one of the invited guests. He was a man who read gossip columns and passed along the rumors as if they were personal secrets. "Who they got? They got Streep. They got the mayor. I hear De Niro may even make an appearance an' you know he don't go nowhere. He's 'sposed to be on the West Coast, but they figure he'll stay close to home."

"I wouldn't know," Michael said.

"Yeah, well, I'll tell ya, I'm turning in early because, first of all, you won't be able to move because of the traffic, and second, none of these people take a cab. They come in limos the size of aircraft carriers. 'Sides, I wanna watch. The wife likes to see who's wearing what."

The cabdriver didn't stop talking about the movies he'd seen and the movies he hadn't. He admired Jeremy Irons, but he didn't think the role was sympathetic enough for an Academy Award—that should go to a part of distinction.

"Hey, get me some autographs," the driver yelled as he dropped Michael at the service entrance.

Michael changed into his captain's uniform in the locker room where Carmine Paolo, the shop steward, was waiting for him.

"How are you?" Carmine asked the man who was known in the hotel as Michael Miller.

"Big night," said Michael.

Carmine laughed. "You handled New Year's Eve like you

been doing it all your life." He shook his head. "Nah! You ain't shook by this stuff."

"So, what's the problem?"

The shop steward shrugged. "I swear, you're the best thing to come down the pike, as far as the job is concerned." He looked around the locker room to make certain that they were not overheard. "But as far as the other thing is concerned—you know, how you got the job; all that muscle to get one guy into the union. It don't make much sense. Especially a guy like you, one in a million."

"I still don't get it; what's the problem?" said Michael, beginning to tense. "Is there something wrong?"

Paolo moved a little closer. "Guys have been coming around," he said softly. "Very tough guys. Asking about you. They wanna know if you still work here."

Michael nodded. Began to glimpse what Paolo was trying to tell him. "And you told them I did."

"Yeah. They wanted me to take you off the floor tonight. I told them you was a captain and I counted on you—at least Dunlap counted on you."

"Did that calm them down?"

He shook his head. "They wanted you off the floor. Period. Said that it was important as far as my own health was concerned."

Paolo was a tough man, even if he was in debt to the mob. There were lines of honor he would not cross, and over the months he had grown fond of Michael Miller, in a distant but powerful sort of way. The man's word was good and he put in an honest day's work, not like so many of them. These were important signs of character and Carmine felt obliged to honor them.

"I told them to handle it themselves," he said.

Michael ran a cloth across his shoes. Then he looked up. "Think they're gonna?"

Paolo held his hands out, palms up. "Personally, knowing

these people, they don't make idle chatter, if you know what I mean. I think they're comin' back."

"That's what I think," Michael said.

"So, if you gotta split because it could be dangerous, I would understand."

Michael closed his locker and patted Carmine's arm. "Big night," he said. "I really don't wanna miss it. I got a bet on *Dances With Wolves.*"

"Just givin' you the word," said Carmine, walking with Michael, who was heading out to the floor. They passed the first fire extinguisher, which was on the wall behind a pillar near the pantry where Michael had replaced it. It was an inconspicuous yet handy spot. The second was at the other end of the room, behind sealed glass that had to be broken. Michael never seriously considered using Waldo's chemical suit. It didn't fit into his plan, which was to be far away when the gas was released, and even if that failed and he had to do it himself, he wasn't sure he wanted to walk away from this one.

"I appreciate it," said Michael who noted with some satisfaction that the tags and labels on the lethal fire extinguisher were intact, that no one had noticed the switch he had made.

By six o'clock, the hotel was vibrating with the electric jolt of an important event. Security forces had scoured the guest list. Metal detectors had been set up outside the main entry. Managers and submanagers were rising to high levels of importance and intolerance. They shared the frustration and suspicion of the security forces who had to contend with a hundred-odd phone requests from people who claimed special privilege. They were running out of patience with the persistent public as well.

In Suite 624, Nora Burns checked her pistol and her ammunition. She had been living in the suite for two days under the name of Alice Cohen, taking most of her meals through room service, checking the schedules in the ballroom, memorizing the lay of the land. She had spent one thousand dollars on a second-hand Armani gown, which was long and black and off-the-shoulder, exposing a little too much muscle for a glamourpuss.

The ticket for the awards ceremony in the Grand Ballroom was on the dresser and she went over and opened the envelope to check it once again. That had been expensive, but well worth it. She had been particularly clever about getting it, too. She had found a hungry documentary cinematographer in the phone book. His name was Fred Hollings and he had once won an award for a film about seals. Since then, he had spent his time living off development money and promising ideas. Over an expensive lunch at The Four Seasons, Nora told him she was a British producer who was planning to make a BBC series about the nature of the American movie industry. It was an ambitious project, but she had time and money. When she handed over the cashier's check for five thousand dollars, as a sign of good faith, he was more than eager to take her to the awards dinner in place of his wife.

She went to the phone and asked for the kitchen of the main ballroom. At first the headwaiter, John Dunlap, didn't want to connect her to Table Captain Michael Miller. She said, "Just tell him it's Nora."

They met in the cocktail lounge. It was a little unusual, a captain from the ballroom having a conversation with a guest. Nora was still in her business suit.

"I thought you were dead," he said when he saw her.

She looked dead. Or, at least, beyond hope. He had seen such looks before. Usually, they were on the faces of men who didn't come back from action.

She smiled a frosty, lifeless smile. "You should have come yourself rather than send those two after me."

He didn't deny it. He just stared at her. She had her hand inside her purse and he had his hand inside his coat pocket.

They were leveling guns at each other. The mission hung by a thread.

"You can just walk away," he said. "As far as everyone knows you're dead. You can start life all over again. Completely clean. Rebuild the orphanage."

Then she asked the one question that he couldn't answer, the question that he feared most: "And what about Seamus?"

He looked away. There was no answer for that one. They were at the far end of a cocktail lounge. He held his hand up and asked for a beer. She asked the waitress to bring her a whiskey. A few tables away sat some plainclothes city cops and federal agents. They were laughing too loud to be listening to anything but their own jokes.

Nora didn't notice Jack, who was hidden in the darkest corner of the lounge. He had tracked her to the hotel when she moved out of the Howard Johnson's Hotel. He was not close enough to eavesdrop, but when he poked his head up, he saw that she was having an unpleasant conversation.

"Nora, we can talk later; this is not the time or the place to discuss this," Michael said.

"No," she said. "We can't talk later."

He knew that all she had to do was to scream or yell or simply call attention to them. Almost anything could upset his plan. But he could see, too, that she wanted something.

The waitress brought their drinks. Nora leaned over and emptied her whiskey and held it up. They remained silent until the waitress brought a refill.

"What's the scheme, Michael?"

She knew that he couldn't tell her the plan.

"It's not something that can be altered," he said.

"Isn't it?" she asked.

He didn't answer.

"Tell me, Michael, did you send your gunmen after me because of the Mafia thing? Was it the old man? Did you think that I killed him?"

He sipped his beer. "Didn't you?"

She looked away. A few more people had drifted into the lounge, killing time before the ceremony.

"And if I did? What's it to you?"

He shrugged.

"Because you are tied to them. I haven't figured it all out yet. I'm not that clever. But, somehow, they made this possible, whatever it is, am I right?" she asked.

"Look, Nora, I can't debate this now. We can kill each other or walk away. But we cannot discuss it."

She was half-drunk, and wild with something. A dangerous thing, he thought. He was trying not to arouse her, trying to pacify her, but he wasn't sure it was possible. So far, all she had revealed about Seamus was her grief. She hadn't mentioned his death—or rather, who was to blame for his death. Only indirectly, referring to the Mafia.

"Just tell me that, and I swear by Jesus I'll walk away," she said. "I'll not bother you, I'll not interfere with whatever scummy work you have planned. I will stagger away and you will never see me again."

"Tell you what?"

"If that's it. The reason you sent McCormick and Nolan after me. To appease them. The mob. Because they made your work here possible. All you have to do is to tell me that, let my mind rest."

He blew a long breath out. "First of all, I didn't send them after you. If they came after you, it was on their own. And they weren't supposed to kill you. Just take you home, get you out of the way."

"How did you know that, Michael?"

"What?"

"That they weren't supposed to kill me. If you didn't send them, how did you know that they were supposed to gently take me back to my beloved home? Can you answer me that?"

"Nora, I'm your brother. Listen to me. I know a few things because it's my job to know. I had no part of any of it."

He got up and walked away and she let him because she was stunned. It was at that moment that the full scope of her brother's betrayal became clear. He was lying about McCormick and Nolan. And he was lying about the mob making it possible for him to work in the hotel where his vital mission was to take place.

And his lie confirmed the worst: that he had had a hand in the death of her son. It was Michael who had led the Mafia to her in Galway. It was Michael who had engineered the job. It was for money. The mob wanted their money back and he wanted help from the mob. She should have guessed sooner. They always wanted their money back. She knew that. They tried every way to get it.

But the one way that had had a chance of working was through Michael. It was her own brother who was responsible for murdering his own nephew. In exchange for giving her up to the Mafia, they had cooperated with him in his American operation.

He would pay for it. Through all the years of hell and beyond, she would make certain to extract a terrible price. Michael, you poor, stupid son-of-a-bitch, she said silently, you are doomed and gone.

24

There was no one near the bank of house phones, but Jack cupped his hand over the receiver all the same. "Nine-six-two-four," he said softly. He had waited for ten minutes—time enough for her to get back to her room from the cocktail lounge—before he called.

"Yes?" she said after the second ring, and he felt a cold recognition when he heard her voice.

"Is this Alice Cohen?" he asked, and the phone fell silent because Nora recognized the voice on the other end just as quickly. There was a long pause.

"Where are you?" she asked suddenly, in that slashing, razor tone.

"In the lobby," he replied.

There was another long pause and in the silence he knew that whatever had been between them had dissolved into a thin ghost of sentiment. There was nothing left that he could call on, even for old time's sake; he couldn't make her do what he wanted, which was to expose Michael and surrender herself to the police. To do the right thing, which was what he always wanted.

"Why?" she asked. Every word she spoke was an icy wind in his face.

"I wanted to talk to you," he said quietly, gently, as if he could remind her that they had a history, things in common, a past. They had been friends, if not lovers. He had crossed an ocean for her. These were things that couldn't be entirely ignored or dismissed.

The ice cracked a little bit and there was a sound of regret in her voice. "Jack, we have nothing to say to each other anymore. We can't. I can't. Please."

"We do."

"Go away, Jack. For my sake."

He became firm. "It's not like that, Nora. I'm not going away. Not without talking."

"Good Christ, you Americans and your damned talk! That's all you want to do is talk. And share. And display out in public every single private emotion until there's nothing left but shame. Gibberish! Enough talk, for Christ's sake! Leave me in peace."

"Well, I would, but you haven't talked me into it," he said.

"Ah," she half groaned, stifling a laugh, because he could do that to her—make her laugh in the middle of a crisis. That was another cop gift that he had: making people see the soft, human side of rage. "You're an ass, you know that?"

"A horse's ass," he agreed. "And while we're on the subject, let's leave my country's wrong-headed, but soft-hearted quest for being nice out of it, okay?"

She laughed. "You know the room number." It was not a question. She hung up.

He did. Jack waited at the bank of elevators, looking at the gold-leaf patterns on the walls, aware that he was being watched with disapproval by the better-dressed Waldorf guests who traveled in pairs and smelled of expensive perfume and cologne. They walked past him, brushing him back from

the elevator entrance with their furs and contempt. He entered
as an afterthought, squeezed in the front lest he leave a print
on the Siberian furs.

Nora's suite was done in French Empire and his feet sank
into the carpets. The paintings and mirrors were quietly lush
and there was a room-service tray of half-eaten fish on the
table in the drawing room. "Lots of space," he said, looking
around as if admiring a new home.

"It'll do," she said, unable to explain the real reason for the
suite. At night, lately, she woke up with Seamus in her bed. At
first, in her groggy half-sleep, he was her own fidgety and
cuddly little boy, pressing closer and closer into the crook of
her protective arm. But then, when she awoke, he was that
other Seamus, the boy she saw on the couch with a hole in his
chest, with his dead eyes open and a look on his face that
asked, "How could you let them do this to me?"

Every morning, she woke up on the Empire couch in the
drawing room. But she couldn't tell that to Jack. "Would you
like a drink?" she asked, opening the fake antique wood bar.

He shook his head. She didn't know that he'd quit drinking.
She shrugged and emptied one of the airline bottles of Scotch
into a glass and drained it. She was, he thought as he took in
the Armani gown, radiant. He was a little shocked. It seemed
indecent. Lit, he thought, by some inner, evil fire.

"The hand?" she asked, putting him on the couch and taking
the high ground—a tall-backed chair with the light in his face.
He was certain that she had a gun in the purse in her lap. The
purse was open and her hand was inside. It was, he thought,
purely theatrical. She was smoothing a letter waiting to be
mailed.

"Mending," he said, referring to the hand. "Some days it's
fine."

She nodded. "That's good," she said. "It'll come back."

"No. But more than I thought."

He was nervous. He could see how close she was to the edge
of all-out hell. When he was a cop on the street he'd dealt with

people going over the line. It was never clear-cut, never predictable. Sometimes they'd listen to reason. And sometimes, when you thought that you had taken them by the hand and were leading them out to safety, at a completely random moment, they unleashed the thunder.

"Is there some way we could stop?" he asked. "Just stop?"

She shook her head. The brittle red hair waved, as if to punctuate the finality of her decision.

"I saw Michael," he said.

"Yes," she said.

"Up to his usual tricks?"

"Well, it is our Michael."

For a moment they were silent and he took in the room-service tray. Food half-eaten. Pots of coffee. The dancer. Still fine-tuning an instrument on spiritual speculation.

"Look, I have to call the police," he said. "I don't have a choice."

She nodded. She understood.

"It would make me sad to kill you, Jack. I've always thought that you were a good man. Too good. I thank you for the hand, for trying to catch the bullet and save my son's life. It was a wonderful thing you tried to do—catching a bullet with your bare hand! But I won't be stopped now. Not after all this."

She took the pistol out of her purse and aimed it at his heart.

Jack had miscalculated. He had thought that he was safe with Nora, that he could talk her down, like a leaper on a bridge. He thought that he had her listening, paying attention, inching back from the ledge. But he was wrong. She was just waiting for the right moment.

She took a pair of handcuffs out of her purse, then walked him into the bathroom with the gun at his head. He followed her orders because he was certain that she had worked herself into a state of great determination. If he didn't obey, she would shoot him. There was that crazy glint of the religious fanatic in her eyes.

Nora locked one bracelet of the handcuff to the waterpipe

behind the commode. She attached the other to Jack's left hand. She didn't want to inflict any more pain on the hand he had used to try to save Seamus. Then, when he wasn't expecting it, she brought down the butt end of the pistol on his head, knocking him unconscious.

The plain white button worn in the lapel was a sign that the bearer had been cleared by security. Wearing his white button, Michael stood at the door to the locker room, telling the head of security who was legitimately entitled to enter the kitchen and dining area. Through a glass window, Michael could watch the activity on the dining room floor.

"How long has this guy been here, Mister Miller?" asked the security chief, pointing to a name on a large clipboard.

Michael glanced at the clipboard and saw that he was indicating Dumkowski, one of the Polish immigrants who had started two weeks ago. A willing worker, but still confused in the hubbub of the large ballroom.

"Two weeks," he said.

"Two weeks," repeated Cutler, the security head, marking a check next to the name so that Dumkowski would be given extra attention.

Then Michael saw something on the cloth of table thirty-eight, which was in his station. A red stain. He knew where to look because he had put it there.

"Julio!" he called to another waiter, one who had been cleared by security earlier. "Get a fresh cloth for table thirty-eight. Take a bin for the dirty one out there behind the column so that it can't be seen. Better leave it there."

After the bin had been placed behind the column, when Julio had tossed in the tablecloth, along with some extra napkins that Michael had also stained, Michael waited. At a moment when the backs of the security force were turned, Michael lifted the dirty cloth in the bin and planted a case filled with books of matches. He covered the case with the stained linen. The bin was alongside an American La France fire extinguisher—one of the two Michael had loaded with nerve gas.

The security checks were almost done. The banqueters were gathered, having cocktails in smaller rooms off the main room. The excitement was audible in the chatter of the staff. "Did you see what Meryl Streep was wearing?" asked Pauli Scarfone, one of the veteran waiters to his friend, Ricky, as they were rushing out some of the fruit cups for the two thousand place settings.

"Versace," replied Ricky Mendoza.

"How do you know?" Pauli shot back.

"Versace is the 'in' Hollywood designer."

"This is New York."

"Same thing. Besides, look at how tight it is. Check the cut-outs. Gianni Versace. Bet the farm."

John Dunlap came up to Michael and touched him on the shoulder. Michael jumped, but Dunlap attributed that to the higher responsibility and the tension of the evening. The mayor was due any minute. The governor was napping up-stairs. The hotel was packed with celebrities—Patrick Swayze and Demi Moore and Bruce Willis and Eddie Murphy and Spike Lee—and half-drunk, half-dressed women were floating from party to party, crooning about the spectacle and the excitement. Diplomats and politicians cut through the parties, led by their various flunkies and criers.

"You know," said Dunlap, standing near the rear door where they had a view of the traffic, "I really didn't think you could handle it."

"Not much to it," said Michael, his eyes sweeping the room for crumbs of poor symmetry or bungled assignments.

"I mean when you first came in," said Dunlap. "New Year's Eve." .

Michael looked at him and laughed. "Truth be known, neither did I."

"It's going to be fine," said Dunlap.

"I'll make you proud," Michael replied.

*   *   *

The crowds were inching into the big room, flashing their white buttons as if they were diamonds, and Nora sat in a chair outside of the ballroom, watching. She waited until the governor and the mayor and the vice president had been seated on the dais and the attention of the crowd had turned to them. Then she marched through the last guards at the doors.

The room was vast and high, rising forty feet into two balconies, spreading forth with a hundred tables. It was not possible to see from one end to the other unless you stood on a chair. The lighting was poor, but that only heightened the drama of the tables—bright and sparkling with polished silver and flickering candles. Somewhere near the front a band was playing—old melodies from old favorite movies, but it had a lively effect on the mood. Women in dresses that seemed to cling to their bosoms by nothing more than good posture grabbed their startled companions and broke into spontaneous dance. The noise level was high and the conversation rose to meet it. It sounded almost giddy.

A man held a chair for Nora, a tribute to her high color and electric attraction. It was a poor table, far in the back of the room, but she didn't mind. It gave her a long view of the arena. In the distance she spotted Michael supervising his group of important front tables. She didn't know his exact plan, but she was certain that his intention—given all the time he had devoted and all the people he had betrayed—was to make someone a target.

"Are you a performer?" asked a woman with a dress ten years too young for her body.

"No," said Nora, "I'm a film producer."

"Really?" squealed the woman happily. "My best friend was the editor on . . . Oh, what's the name of that film. George, what's the name of that film that Ruthie edited?"

"It was a documentary," said Ralph sullenly. "Ruth was the assistant to the editor."

"Did you bring my drink in, George?"

"The waiter'll be around."

"No, they won't. Do you see anybody else with a drink? They don't want drinking. Be a dear; get my gin and tonic."

George rolled his eyes and went to fetch the drink.

"My name is Cora Anne Wells," the woman said, relieved that her husband was out of the picture.

At the front of the room, Michael was snapping his fingers and sending his minions scurrying for clean silver, unwilted fruit cups, fresh rolls. A large screen rolled down from the ceiling and a predinner introductory show began, drowned out at first by the scraping chairs and high excitement.

Nora kept her purse on her lap, under her napkin. It gave her a sense of safety to feel the pistol.

He woke up with blood dripping into his eyes. He crouched there in the toilet for a few moments, trying to regain his senses. When he moved, he felt the strain of the handcuff. He was trapped, helpless to stop Nora. Then he remembered. Ever since he'd been a cop, Jack had kept a handcuff key hidden in a pocket of his wallet. He had never had to use it and no one knew about it—not even his dead wife, Natalie. He almost forgot, then remembered as he came fully awake. As he tried to turn, the gash in his head opened further and he felt the blood flowing down his head.

Damn! She'd handcuffed his good hand, which meant that he would have to use his wounded left hand to reach around and fetch the wallet. In his right-hand back pocket. When he moved, his head throbbed as if it would explode. He turned, but he couldn't reach the back pocket. His hand felt as if it would break. But he had to do it. He stretched and twisted and was certain that the bones would break again as he wiggled and reached for the wallet. He was blind from the blood in his eyes, but he kept at it. Finally, he managed to get it out, but it slipped away from his grasp. He had to feel around on the floor because he couldn't see, and then he pushed the wallet away. He reached out with his shoe and pulled it back to him, got at the key, and undid the handcuffs. He was exhausted. He put his head under the shower and let the cold water run over it.

When his head cleared he realized that he had not stopped Nora. She was on her way to do whatever she had come to do. On the floor of the bathroom was a newspaper. He had been staring at it as the water from the shower cleared his head. It was a tabloid and the headline said: TONIGHT'S THE BIG NIGHT, with a little text about the Academy Awards. That was the "big event." If she knocked him out and left him chained to the commode, it had to be something of that magnitude. He ran out of the room and managed to find the elevator. Passengers seeing his bleeding head moved away from him. The elevator stopped at the ballroom floor, and when Jack saw the security and the celebrities, he knew that he had found the bomb. If Michael had a target, it had to be in this hotel and this night.

On the ballroom floor, he attracted immediate attention. "Hold it," said the plainclothesman at the ballroom door. Two uniformed men closed in behind him.

"Get me a supervisor," Jack said. He realized that he looked bad, with his bleeding scalp and wet clothing. "I'm an ex-cop."

"You wanna take it easy." The plainclothesman was trained to pacify the loopies who tried to crash big parties. He guessed drugs because Jack didn't smell of liquor.

"You wanna get me a fucking supervisor!" shouted Jack, and one or two tables of people in the ballroom turned to see what the commotion was about. Two more uniforms closed in and grabbed Jack's arms. He knew that he had to get out of there.

"Okay! Okay!" Jack said. "I'm leaving. Just a joke."

He had an idea and raced down three flights of stairs until he found a bank of phones in the lobby.

Michael was running the waiters off the floor. "Get the soup!" he said. "The fruit cups should be gone."

In the kitchen the cooks were sweating and the waiters were panting, each trying to keep up with the other. They were calling Michael a ballbreaker. Julio, a young waiter with ambition, took as many plates as he could carry on his tray.

"Good," said Michael, nodding at him. "Nice going. You're going to have your own station."

The police units had a table set up on the first balcony and Michael made certain that they were fed first and kept busy with fresh courses. And whenever he had a chance, he dropped a napkin with books of matches rolled into it into one of three bins he had scattered around the ballroom.

Nora couldn't figure it out. She noticed that he was dropping napkins into the bins, and that had to have a meaning. But what harm could some linen do? Bombs? She wondered. It must be bombs. He would have to set them and then make his escape, so she knew that she could get to him before they went off.

She watched him dropping napkins into the bin, certain that this would be the last night of her life. It was a relief. It made her feel almost saintly.

In the news studio, Bonnie was just finishing her first report. "Lots of Canadian air coming at us," she said, smiling into the camera. "This is different from Bermuda Highs, because, believe it or not folks, Canadian air tends to be cold. Therefore, we should expect weather a little more chilly than we should from Bermuda Highs. Is that clear to everyone out there in weatherland? If not, hey, it's only weather!"

Chuck Childers, watching from a monitor in a makeshift newscenter at the Waldorf, groaned.

Back at the studio, Max Gross waved to Bonnie from off-camera. She had a few minutes before she had to go on again.

"Phone," he said. "Jack."

She took the call at a wall phone. "Hi!" she chirped.

"Listen—"

"You sound funny."

"I know. Nora bashed me over the head."

"What? I'll take her apart . . ."

"Listen, listen. This is serious. I'm at the Waldorf—"

"I know. I couldn't get the assignment."

"There's something you gotta do. Shut up and listen. There's gonna be a catastrophe here. You gotta do something to clear out this place."

"What? What are you talking about?"

"Nora's here. Michael's here. That's trouble. I don't know who they're gonna kill, but believe me, there's gonna be bodies. Are you listening? The mayor. The governor. Quayle. Well, come to think of it, maybe we shouldn't do anything."

"She hit you over the head?"

"No. No. I am not joking. Forget the Quayle joke. Bad timing. But, listen, you gotta do something. They won't listen to me. They think I'm a crank."

"I think you're a crank. What can I do?"

"I got an idea." Then he told her his scheme. He didn't think she'd do it. He wouldn't do it on the word of a freshly crowned crackpot.

But she agreed to do it. It might cost her a career, but she agreed. At the next weather break, three minutes later, when Bonnie went back on the air, she took a slip of paper off the news desk. "Oh, this just in, there's a major fire at the Waldorf-Astoria Hotel. The whole building is being evacuated." Then she looked up. "Hey, this isn't just weather!"

Police units outside the ballroom, watching the weather report in a room set up for communications, heard the news of fire, and began to evacuate the room. *"There is no need to panic,"* said a voice of authority over a loudspeaker. *"Please walk slowly to the nearest exit. Do not push and do not run. There is no need to panic."*

Nora felt her own sense of panic as word of the fire crept into the room like smoke. She got up from the table and stood there. Women with carefully painted faces now looked like clowns, with their makeup twisted and running with sweat. "My coat!" said one major star rushing to the cloakroom.

"Fuck the coat!" shouted the younger man leading her out. "That's a $60,000 coat, sonny!" cried the worried star.

Firemen in heavy coats and thick helmets arrived, and fought against the oncoming tide of spangles and heaving, overexposed bosoms, and lapelless tuxedos. Every once in a while the movement stopped as everyone recognized a familiar face—a star—and it all seemed like a movie instead of a real-life drama. And then a table was knocked over, spilling dishes and soup and bread, making the floor slippery, and reminding the momentarily star-struck spectators that the danger had been declared real.

Cora Anne Wells started to cry, so upset was she with the confusion and noise and disappointment at her spoiled night out. "Where are you going?" she cried to her husband, George.

"This way," he said, sounding efficient, heading for the exit.

"You go," Nora said, falling behind in the wake of a group of huge firemen who were heading for the kitchen—the usual scene of ballroom fires. She was knocked down once by a thick and determined man who was heading out with his arm up like a stiff-armed running back. "Watch it! Watch it!" he kept saying as he forced a passage.

The loudspeaker system kept up: *"Please make your way out slowly; there's no need for panic."*

At the kitchen door, Nora stopped to catch her breath. The firemen were inside and everyone else was heading in another direction. She looked over and saw her brother. He was dropping a flaming book of matches into one bin, then another. He stopped in front of one bin and kept lighting fresh books of matches and dropping them into the bin. Small plumes of smoke began to rise.

She followed a group of men helping a fainting woman to the door. She dropped off as they came parallel to Michael. He saw her, her expression one of confusion and hate.

He pushed her out of the way and reached for the fire extinguisher. Suddenly, she understood. His face gave him away. He had killed Seamus. Not with his gun. But with his help. The mob got him this job, and he gave them Seamus.

"You killed my son!" she said, pulling the pistol out of her purse.

He threw the fire extinguisher at her, and she fell back. From the floor, where she was kicked by the still panicky crowd, she saw him running to the north end of the ballroom.

She fought to her feet and started after him, an animal snarl coming out of her mouth. "You killed Seamus!" she repeated. At the wall, Michael broke the glass and took out the extinguisher. Before he could use it, Nora was on him, pulling his hair, kicking him in the groin. "You killed Seamus!" she screamed, and in the soup and butter and salad on the floor, she saw her son again on the couch, with the hole in his chest and his eyes staring at her in a never-ending question. She smelled the milk and blood and, most of all, the stink of death.

"You killed my baby!" And Michael couldn't fight her and hold the fire extinguisher at the same time. He dropped it to the floor. She was biting his face and kicking his stomach and he reached out and grabbed her by the throat, closed his eyes, and squeezed until she stopped saying that he had killed her baby. Her fingernails ran tracks down his face, and he kept squeezing until her eyes bulged and she turned purple.

No one noticed.

The smoke from the burning linen bin was making him blink. "Here it is!" cried Julio, the waiter, spotting the smoke in the bin of linen. He picked up the extinguisher, opened the valve and pointed the nozzle. Michael didn't try to stop him. A short burst of nerve gas ran up into his eyes. Michael wanted to scream, but nothing came out. His nervous system quickly went into convulsions. He was dead in ten seconds.

It had been a very quick evacuation. Among the score of dead were Nora, Michael, and Julio. A special terrorist unit assigned to every major public event immediately detected nerve gas and sealed off the ballroom.

Outside, Jack watched the special units race into the hotel. Then he hailed a cab and headed for the Channel 9 newscenter to pick up Bonnie, who had scooped the world on the fire at the Waldorf-Astoria.

Epilogue

In early April, after a high conference, Little Nicky Salerno—known in mob circles as "Shoot First"—took over Don Daniello Iennello's crime family. His first important ruling was to declare the business of the Irish theft over. He wanted peace on the waterfront, which was run by people with IRA sympathies, and it didn't make sense to jeopardize a hundred-million-dollar-a-year drug importing industry over a three-million-dollar bill.

Still, if they could connect the money to someone, he told his lieutenants, he wouldn't object if that someone was to take one between the eyes. As long as it didn't affect business.

Father Brian Daly, pastor of St. Michael's Roman Catholic Church in Roscommon, found that the account in his name at the Bank of Ireland contained a huge sum: well over three million dollars. The letter of explanation that came under his rectory door said he could use the money to finish rebuilding the church. It had two other stipulations. He must provide for the orphans of Galway House and see to the care of Diedre and Bridget Burns.

That night, when he returned to the church, he said a special Mass for Nora Burns.

Bonnie Hudson took a short leave of absence from the Channel 9 Newscenter. She tried writing a few freelance pieces for magazines, but found that the pastime lacked the excitement of being on television. After three months, she returned to the station, but continued to defy management and refused to use weather maps. Nevertheless, her fame grew.

Jack Mann opened his own private detective agency, continuing to survive on his precarious police pension. He saved rent by moving in with Bonnie.